I AM CONNER BRIGHT

I AM CONNER BRIGHT

FOUR ESSENTIAL CONNER BRIGHT MYSTERIES

ROBERT J. MCCARTER

LITTLE HUMMINGBIRD PUBLISHING

I Am Conner Bright
Four Essential Conner Bright Mysteries

Copyright ©2025 by Robert J. McCarter

Except as permitted under the Copyright Act of 1976, this book may not be reproduced in whole or in part in any manner.

This book is a work of fiction. Names, places, and incidents are either products of the author's imagination or used fictitiously. Any resemblance to actual events or persons, living or dead, is entirely coincidental.

Cover image © Robert J. McCarter

Version 1.0, September 2025

ISBN: 978-1-963354-22-5

Visit Robert's website at: RobertJMcCarter.com

Published by:

Little Hummingbird Publishing

P.O. Box 23518
Flagstaff, AZ 86002
www.LittleHummingbird.com

CONNER BRIGHT MYSTERIES

Each Conner Bright Mystery is stand-alone, but things do change for Conner. This is the chronological order of the stories are:

- **The Case of the Purple Unicorn**
- **Chupacabra**
- **Haunted by the Past**
- **The Devil You Know**
- **I Am Conner Bright (a collection of all four Conner Bright Mysteries)**

PREFACE

There's more about the origin of Conner Bright in the Afterword but what you are about to read is a compilation of the essential (as of now) Conner Bright mysteries.

Each one is stand-alone, but Conner does change and the sum total of these stories do create a novel-length story arc.

As a character, Conner has been around for a while. These stories take place between 2014 and 2016.

If you have read the stories individually, there is nothing new here except for this Preface and the Afterword.

PART 1
THE CASE OF THE PURPLE UNICORN

CONNER BRIGHT AND THE CASE OF
THE PURPLE UNICORN

The ringing of the phone is like a dentist's drill to my sodden consciousness. I groan, realizing I hadn't managed to get undressed when I tumbled into bed. Again. I feel for my cell phone on the nightstand, my hand connecting with a half-eaten microwave burrito before finding it.

"G'day, you got Bright," I say, remembering even in my hungover state to use my B-movie quality Australian accent.

"Got a job for you, but you've got to get here quick." The voice is feminine and a tad husky. Detective Trisha Sanchez. Why the hell is she calling me? After that jacked-up stakeout, I'm her least favorite private investigator in the Phoenix metro area.

"What kind of a job?" I say, my voice rough from too long in a noisy bar working as a bouncer and too many cheap beers afterward. I look around my shit hole of a bedroom. Dirty laundry, trash, the spring heat of the desert morning flowing in the open window. "And can they pay?"

An Australian accent is easy. Just elongate your vowels—" paay" instead of "pay"—and throw in the occasional "mate" and "g'day." In the desert southwest, that and changing my name to Conner Bright keeps my past at bay.

"They can. It's a murder, Bright, so get your ass out here now. No booze or I'll throw you in the drunk tank."

"Aces. Happy to help."

"Texting you the address now." She hangs up.

After some mouthwash for breakfast, I stop by the old cookie tin that sits on the top of my little entertainment center. It's got a shameful layer of dust on top and holds the ashes of my father inside. "Hey, Dad," I say, without a trace of an Australian accent. "I've got a case. An important one."

Sitting next to the tin is a DVD of *Crocodile Dundee*. My dad took me to that movie in 1986 when it came out. I was thirteen and loved it, but not as much as he did. When we exited, he'd said, "Now that's a man, son. That's a man."

I GET OUT OF MY 1976 EL CAMINO, MY COWBOY BOOTS crunching on the dry ground as I approach the murder scene. It's a hot day, and since the El Camino doesn't have air-conditioning, I'm already sweating. I'm at a little ranch in the desert between Phoenix and Wickenburg, Arizona. This is a big deal. There's lots of cowboys and lots of guns around here, but not that many murders in the sticks.

I get the usual assortment of looks as I duck under the yellow tape. Looks of surprise from folks that don't know me, looks of recognition or disdain from those that do. The disdain belongs to Trisha Sanchez, the detective who called me in.

And the looks from the others, it's what I expect. I'm tall and slim; at 6'5" and 170 pounds, some people call me scarecrow. I've got a bowie knife with an eleven-inch blade on my belt, a crocodile claw hanging around my neck, and a wide-brimmed bush hat on my head, all to go with my Australian accent.

"G'day, Detective," I say, tipping my hat to Sanchez as she strides away from the murder scene. She's in her late thirties, short and wiry, wearing reflective sunglasses.

"Your client's in the house," she says, grabbing my arm and pulling me away. I resist a moment, watching Helen Montana, one of the medical examiners, leaning over the prone form of a gray-haired Mexican man that has a ragged hole in his chest.

"Where we goin'?" I ask.

"To see your client, Irene. She asked for someone to help her solve this murder."

"And you called me?" Something isn't right.

She pauses, her hand still locked around my bicep, her head jabbing back to the scene. "At this point we're ruling it an accident. The victim, Edwardo Campos, has got a big hole in his chest, and we found a bull running loose with blood on his horn."

She starts to pull me forward again toward the one-story ranch house. It's small with blue vinyl siding that was popular in the seventies. The blue has started to fade, and the house looks like it has seen better days.

"Then what the hell am I doin' here?"

Sanchez smiles, showing her perfectly white teeth, looking something like a shark. "The kid says she saw it happen."

I shrug.

"She says it was a man riding a purple unicorn that killed her great-uncle."

I ALMOST DON'T GO IN. I ALMOST MARCH BACK TO MY EL Camino until Sanchez says the magic words. "She's got cash." I think of the delinquent notices stacked on my little kitchen table. I think how I'd love not to buy the cheapest damn beer in the store.

It's surprisingly neat inside the house. Not fancy, but everything's put away, the wood floors swept, the old throw rugs shook out. The living room isn't much—an old couch with a brown blanket thrown over it, a wooden rocking chair, and a shelf full of books. No TV, no stereo. It looks very much like what this house probably looked like a hundred years ago.

Sitting awkwardly in the rocking chair is a tall deputy with blond hair. He gives Sanchez a brief look of relief before scurrying out.

And then I see the girl. She's got long black hair, big brown eyes, and is maybe eight years old. I almost leave again.

"Irene," Sanchez says, "this is Conner Bright. He's the private detective I was telling you about. He's got a reputation for dealing with unusual cases."

With that Sanchez leaves. I stand there awkwardly, my hands shoved into my jeans, wishing I hadn't answered the phone this morning.

The girl's wearing a purple shirt and has a stuffed unicorn on the couch next to her. On the table in front of her is a battered hardcover of *The Last Unicorn*.

Great. Of course she saw a purple unicorn. She's obsessed with them.

"Where are you parents?" I ask.

She just shakes her head. Ah hell, she's an orphan too.

I lower myself into the rocking chair, wishing the hard seat was padded. The room smells of must and wood polish. "You got any family?"

She shakes her head again, her hands sitting placidly in her lap.

"I'm sorry about what happened to your great-uncle out there."

Her brow furrows and she stares at me a moment before saying, "Where you from?" Judging from her uncle and her appearance, I expect her to have a Mexican accent, but she doesn't. Not a trace.

"Australia," I lie. But it's a lie I tell everyone. "A little place called Scatterwood deep in the outback."

"You don't believe I saw a unicorn." She says it straight up, her voice steady, her eyes clear.

I shake my head.

"I did," she says, her voice too hard for someone so young. "And you have to prove it." She pulls out a wad of hundred-dollar bills from her pocket and slaps them on the coffee table in front of her. I notice light red stains on her hands and I imagine them pressed against her dead great-uncle's chest.

I know I should say no, but three thousand is a lot for me. A whole lot. I rub my suddenly sweating palms on my jeans. I'm dying for a drink. That would clear my head. Help me think this through.

"Well?" she asks.

I get up and start pacing. "Why don't you tell me what you saw."

The girl talks, I pace, my feet finding squeaky boards in the old floor. The money is in a jumbled pile on the coffee table in front of her. I want it even more than I want a drink.

"Been here for a few months," she says. "Came after the accident . . ." Her face darkens, and she blinks several times. "We moved around a lot, Mama, Papa, and me. We picked grapes in California, pecans in Oregon."

"Your parents were illegals?" I ask.

She nods. "But I was born here. After the accident, Uncle Ed came and got me. He was afraid they'd send me back to Mexico."

"Tell me about your great-uncle," I say.

She shrugs. "He raises cows, rides horses."

I look at the wad of hundred-dollar bills and then back to her, doubting that was all he did.

"And last night?"

Irene pauses, her hands finally leaving her lap as she wraps them around her chest and shivers. "Uncle Ed was so happy. Said things would be changing today, like a birthday party but better. Said it would be good. We were reading when the animals started making noise. He took his gun and told me to stay.

"I wasn't scared until I heard a shout. I went to the window and peeked through the curtain. That's when I saw it."

"The unicorn?" I ask, keeping my tone as even as possible.

She nods. "The moon was full so I could see good. At first I thought it was a horse with a man riding it. But then I saw the horn and the dark purple fur. Uncle Ed was real surprised. That man spurred the unicorn hard, and it ran down my uncle, its horn hitting him... right in the... He... I..." She trails off into soft sobs. I feel for the kid. She's suffered way too many losses in the past few months.

The tears don't last long. She takes a deep breath, holds it for a few beats, and slowly lets it out. She wipes the tears from her cheeks, her eyes hardening. "The man got off the unicorn and came in here."

"What did you do?"

"I hid behind the door. He walked in like he had been here before. Went right to the kitchen. I hid behind the couch and watched. I couldn't see much. There was banging, crashing, and a bunch of beeps. He marched out holding some papers."

"Did he see you? Did you get a good look at him?"

She shakes her head. "He had a bandana over his mouth. I don't think he saw me. He walked right out, got on his unicorn, and rode away."

I nod and walk into the small kitchen. One of the plain handmade wooden cabinets is open, cans spilling out onto the counter and the floor. In the cabinet is a small metal safe embedded into the wall. The door is ajar, and the safe is empty.

"Is that where you got the money?" I ask after I walk back into the living room.

Irene nods, her hands back onto her lap, her eyes way too calm.

It's a hot day and the corpse of Edwardo Campos is going to stink to high heaven soon. The smell of blood and urine and horse manure is already overpowering.

"It looks like a horn did this," Helen Montana says, pulling away the bloodied cowboy shirt that used to be a powder blue. There's been a lot of foot traffic, but I did find a few fresh hoof-prints leading to the corpse. She gets up, brushing absently at her ponytailed blonde hair. Helen is a tall, big-boned woman with blue eyes and a great smile. She's my age at around forty. There's been sparks, and we've briefly dated a few times, but never a sustained flame. Working with her is always a bit awkward.

She walks several paces back to a yellow CSI marker where I located the hoofprints right next to a shotgun. "It looks like he was hit here and thrown back."

"The bull did it?" I ask.

"I'll know more when I do the autopsy."

I nod, glancing back to the faded blue ranch house.

"Sorry, Conner," she says, and I hear that sweetness in her voice that makes work hard.

"Did they get a blood sample from the bull's horn?" I ask.

She chuckles and looks over to a corral where two deputies are trying to get a rope around the bull. He's a big Hereford and doesn't appear to be cooperating. "Maybe you should go show them how it's done."

I shake my head, feeling uncomfortable. Helen was born in upstate New York and has a thing for cowboys. Could explain her interest in a mess like me.

Sanchez walks up, her arms folded. "You taking the case?"

"Any other witnesses?" I ask, pointing at a smaller building back behind the blue house.

Sanchez shakes her head. "Campos used to have a ranch hand living there. The neighbors told us he left a few months ago before the girl got here. Said they were close, that the old man treated him like a son, but something happened."

"Did you call CPS, Child Protective Services?"

She nods. "Doesn't look like they can get out here today."

"Why the hell not?"

"Budget cuts. Short staffed. You know the drill."

"And what about Irene?"

Sanchez chuckles and smiles at me again. "You take the case, you take the girl." She walks away looking like she's having the time of her life, paying me back for that stakeout with this mess.

I GO HELP THE DEPUTIES WITH THE BULL. NOT THAT I WANT to get into the corral with a ton of pissed off beef. I need to think. And to think, I need to move. Everyone, including Detective

Sanchez, knows I need the cash. But taking a little girl's money on a wild-goose chase doesn't seem proper.

I climb over the fence and hop down onto the churned brown dirt of the corral. It stinks of horse and cow, but at least it doesn't smell of death. The jolt of the hop doesn't do my sacrum any good, and I feel each and every one of my old rodeo injuries. I rode bulls for a while, but mostly worked as a rodeo clown—keeping other riders safe was the right kind of crazy for me.

"You're just makin' the old boy mad," I shout to the two deputies. One is the lanky blond from the house. "Back away." They comply promptly.

I scrape some oats out of the bottom of the feed trough and get the specimen collection swab from the tall deputy and amble over toward the bull.

Those deputies may have been born and raised in Arizona, but they ain't no cowboys. They were afraid and trying to overpower an animal that's five times their weight. Stupid.

"Hi ya, boy," I say gently as I approach, the hand with the oats outstretched. I keep my eye on the bull and walk slowly. This is no rodeo bull used to bucking guys like me off. This fellow's older, probably kept around for stud duties. He didn't want to fight, but he didn't want to be bullied either.

People think cows are dumb, but they ain't. They seek safety and comfort just like the rest of us. The bull's big brown eyes finally leave mine and flick to the handful of oats. I'm two paces away and I stop walking, the final choice has to be his.

My left hand has the swab in it, and I hold it just back from the oats. I'd be a fool to spring it on him while he was eating. His nostrils flair and his eyes flick to the swab and back to the oats. He doesn't like the sharp alcohol scent of the swab, but he wants the oats.

I stand there like I don't care and just keep talking to him. He eventually takes two steps forward, his soft mouth in my hand as his rough tongue licks up the oats. I wipe the swab against the red stain on his horn, and when he's done eating, I back slowly away.

A crowd has gathered, and there's a smattering of applause. When I'm clear of the bull, I look back and see Helen holding Irene on the other side of the corral. Detective Sanchez is there, a question on her face.

***

"The girl is traumatized," I say to Sanchez. We're out of earshot of Helen and Irene, who are both staring at us as we walk the dirt driveway. "She needs a professional."

"The system sucks," she says, "but the girl needs something to do, and running around with you trying to find a purple unicorn might be better than her hanging out in the sheriff's office."

I'm about to say something stupid when it occurs to me that this must be Sanchez's way of looking out for the girl. But why me? "What about the robbery? There's somethin' that ain't right."

She shrugs and points towards the bull. "I've got the killer right there. As to the money, the old man just realized he bought a bunch of Home Depot stock on a whim back in the eighties. He's suddenly rich, that explains the money, and besides, the safe wasn't forced open. Until I have evidence to the contrary, I'm done."

I nod and look back at the girl. Helen has her by the hand and is walking her away from the crime scene and towards the pasture. The girl needs someone, that much is certain. But me? A mostly drunk, past-his-prime cowboy pretending to be Australian?

"Look, Bright," Sanchez says. "Just take the girl for the day.

Take any clue you can find and run it down with her. I'll call you when the social workers are ready for her."

Sanchez walks away and starts barking orders. I don't fight it. I owe her.

I KEEP IRENE IN THE HOUSE WHILE HELEN FINISHES WITH the corpse and hauls him away.

It's odd that the murderer wanted those papers, but didn't care about the money. And that damn unicorn keeps tripping me up. Maybe there was no robbery. Maybe Irene knew the combination and got into the safe herself.

I'm standing in the mess of a kitchen staring off into space when I notice Irene looking at me. Her eyes have that too-wide look of shock. That's why she's been so restrained. The poor kid is in shock. Sanchez was right, she needs something to do.

"All righty then," I say, stooping down and picking up a can. "Get over here and help me clean this up."

"Clean?" Irene says.

I nod. "There could be a clue here, so we're gonna clean up this mess and see what we can find."

WHILE IRENE IS IN THE KITCHEN, I GO SEARCHING Edwardo's bedroom. It's small and neat, with a twin bed, an old wooden chest at the end, a small closet, and a cross on the wall.

I start in the closet, going through the pale blue cowboy shirts—the man liked to dress the same every day—and patting down the two dark blue blazers. Each of them has a matchbook from the same place. The Sugar and Spice, a "gentlemen's club" in downtown Phoenix.

So the old man liked to look at young women.

"Did your Uncle Ed go out much?" I ask Irene back in the kitchen.

Irene nods. "Every Saturday night. He didn't think I knew, but he snuck out after I went to bed. Stayed out real late. He always came back smelling like smoke." She wrinkles her nose.

It's Monday morning, Edwardo was killed Sunday night. Maybe something happened at Sugar and Spice. I show Irene the matchbooks.

"What is it?" she asks.

"A clue, Irene. It's a clue."

THE SUGAR AND SPICE IS A PINKISH BUILDING WITH BRIGHT neon that sits between a bank and a fast-food joint off a busy street in central Phoenix. I shift uncomfortably in the seat of the El Camino as I drive by for the fourth time. It's Irene sitting next to me that makes me feel uncomfortable.

The fifth time I drive by, Irene sighs and says, "Just pull in."

I park behind the building.

"Are we going in?" Irene asks.

"You're kiddin', right?"

"I know what goes on in there. Men look at girls." She ends by rolling her eyes.

My reputation's bad enough without dragging an eight-year-old into a strip club right before turning her over to CPS. "Not gonna happen, love," I say as I get out the car. I walk over and open the door for her. She looks puzzled, but gets out and follows me to the McDonald's next door. As I do this, I'm convinced that I'm not the only man that's dropped off a little girl at this McDonald's before ducking into Sugar and Spice.

She doesn't complain, but she grabs my hand and holds it as

we cross the hot asphalt. Her hand feels so small in mine, and I look down at her and she's looking at me with a tiny smile on her face. That look of trust scares the hell out of me.

―――

THE INSIDE OF SUGAR AND SPICE SMELLS OF DESPERATION, with a bored blond dancing and a few rumpled men watching. I give the bartender a twenty and show him the picture of Edwardo Campos that Irene gave me. He tells me Edwardo was there the night before last, buying drinks and celebrating like he'd just won the lottery or something.

On the way out of Sugar and Spice, I'm confused. I have no motive for murder, and no idea why a robber would leave behind a wad of cash—or ride a purple unicorn, for that matter.

I'm not looking and collide with a man on his way in while I'm on the way out, the Phoenix heat swirling around us.

"Sorry, mate," I say, looking at the stranger. He's got on alligator-skin cowboy boots, a Stetson hat, sharp green eyes, and a sneer. He's almost as tall as me, but a lot beefier.

"Watch it, buddy," he grumbles, moving past quickly. I'm distracted by his boots, which would make a fine addition to my Australian cowboy look.

I get halfway to the El Camino when Irene runs up and wraps her arms around me. "That's him," she whispers between gulping breaths. "The man that came into my house. That killed Uncle Ed."

"How do you know?"

"The boots. The eyes. I'll never forget them."

―――

An El Camino is a crappy car to tail someone in. Especially mine. With its shiny blue paint job and tricked-out rims, it stands out. This car is the one thing in my life that I truly take care of. I love it. It's a car, but it's got a bed like a truck. It's rare. It used to be my dad's.

Irene is sitting right next to me, eyes wide. She smells of cheap beef, french fries, and fear. Her closeness feels strangely good.

We follow Alligator Boots in his red Ford F-150 from Sugar and Spice to a Circle K where he stops for gas. I pull into the carpet place next door. When he ducks into the Circle K, I make to get out of the car, but Irene grabs me.

"Don't go," she says. "Please."

I get lost in those big brown eyes of hers. I'm not used to someone needing me.

"I'll be right back. No worries." Those eyes don't look like they believe me.

I walk casually over to the truck and place my cell phone in the back. What I see there makes me gasp. It's a long horn with spiral ridges running its length. It's an honest-to-god unicorn horn. I'm dizzy for a moment. Did Irene really see what she thought she saw?

As I look closer, I see that the tip of the horn is rough, as if it broke off, and the other end has an odd leather harness on it.

I rush back to the car, my heart pounding hard.

It feels strange, like I'm missing something. I've left Irene with the morgue's receptionist. I had called in on a burner phone I bought at the Circle K to have Sanchez trace my cell so I could keep tabs on Alligator Boots. She told me Helen needed to see me and it was urgent.

Helen is pacing when I walk in. Her blue eyes are a bit wide and remind me of Irene's. Does Helen need me too?

The corpse of Edwardo Campos is laid out on a metal table, the wound to his chest all that much more shocking being exposed—no shirt to hide it, no blood to mask it. It's a big, red hole near his heart.

The morgue is pretty small. A couple of shining tables for the dead with bright lights mounted above. A wall of drawers for bodies to be stored in. Except for the ragged wound in Edwardo's chest, the place is spotless and smells strongly of antiseptic.

Helen's biting her lip and stands me next to the body, showing me a stainless-steel tray. In it is what looks like a piece of bone about the size of an almond. Like a piece of rib or something.

"So?" I ask, shrugging my shoulders.

"The blood you got from the bull's horn is his. But . . . I pulled *this* out of him," she says, like she's telling me the Pope is secretly a woman or something.

I give her a blank stare. I'm clueless.

She drags me over to a big, round magnifying glass and holds the tray underneath it, giving me a pointed look. I lean close and look at the little piece of bone. It's pointed and has a distinct spiral ridge. When I look back at Helen, I'm smiling. She looks worried.

"That ain't no cow horn," I say.

She shakes her head.

"Good on ya, Helen," I say, kissing her on the cheek. "You just made my case."

"What? Conner, unicorns don't exist. How can this be?"

I shrug. "Don't know. What I do know is I just saw the mate to that piece in the back of an F-150."

WE'RE BACK IN THE EL CAMINO HEADING OUT OF PHOENIX towards my place. I'm tired and hungry and don't know what else to do. Sanchez won't go after Alligator Boots. Won't tell officers to look for an F-150 with a unicorn horn in the back, says she'd be risking her reputation and won't do that for me. She wants more evidence.

Irene's smile is a mile wide. She looks so much more like a kid now. She's happy because I told her what Helen found and what I saw in the back of that F-150. Told her that I believe her. Her smile warms my wilted old heart.

It's near rush hour and the Phoenix traffic is thick as ants on honey. We're moving slowly forward in the stifling heat.

Phoenix is a flat and boring expanse except for the occasional outcrop of craggy stone. The city streets are a monotony of urban sprawl with strip malls, cookie-cutter houses, and the ubiquitous Circle Ks.

"So do you think it was a real unicorn?" Irene asks, her voice all bubbly and light.

I shrug my shoulders. Given the harness that was on the horn, I doubt that. I didn't get to telling her that part, and with her lit up like this, I just can't.

In the rearview, I catch a flash of a bright red truck weaving its way through traffic. My face falls.

"What's wrong, Conner?" Irene asks.

"Nothin', love," I lie. I point at the glove compartment. "There's a bottle of water in there. You best drink in this heat."

She nods and dutifully pulls out the water bottle and takes a drink. My eyes keep flicking to the rearview mirror looking for that red truck. Maybe it's Mr. Alligator Boots. Maybe he got wise to me following him.

At a stoplight, I pull out the burner phone and text Sanchez, *Check location of both phones.*

A minute later, as the traffic is finally starting to ease up, she texts back. *Same location.*

We didn't have the tail long. I saw him briefly right behind me and then he was gone, talking a left and speeding off.

When we're past the city and closer to my house, we pull into yet another Circle K, my stomach grumbling and my head pounding. I needed food and a drink. A stiff drink. I take Irene in. She holds my hand the whole time while I pick up a few microwave burritos and some cookies for us, and she picks out some potato chips.

I stop in front of the refrigerated section. I have to let go of Irene's hand to open the door. My hand's shaking a bit, my body screaming for alcohol. And there it is. Row after row of beer, an obscene number of choices. Dark beer, light beer, fancy beer, cheap beer, foreign beer.

Beer reminds me of Tommy Wilkins. Of the sickening sound of his scream when I ran him over. You'd think it would make me drink less, but it's done just the opposite.

I was sixteen and at a high school party near Globe, Arizona, where I grew up. Tommy and I fought over a girl whose name I can't even remember. We were both drunk, and I was trying to leave and he wouldn't get out of the way, banging on the hood of my old Toyota pickup and screaming at me while I revved the engine. My foot slipped off the clutch and . . .

It was big news in Arizona. I did my time in the juvenile system, had my records sealed, but people around here remember my name. That's why I changed it, even though it broke my dad's heart. That's the reason behind the whole fake Australian thing. That's why my life is such a—

"What?" I ask. Irene had just said something.

She smiles and points at the vitamin water. "Can I have one of those? The purple one, please."

I blink at her a few times and nod, grabbing two of the plastic bottles and handing them to her. I turn my back on the obscene array of alcohol. Maybe tonight I can sleep without the beer.

I'M NOT THINKING WELL. I DRIVE RIGHT TO MY TEN ACRES, a few miles from the Circle K, and pull in. Irene is babbling on like happy kids do, her words bright shards bouncing around my car. My fatigue and her happiness seem to lull me into a peaceful state. She goes on and on that when she grows up she's going to make a "My Little Unicorn" toy for girls, like the one already made for horses. That since unicorns are real, and once she finds one and gets her picture taken with it, everyone girl in the world will want one.

I still haven't told her about the harness.

"Maybe instead of 'My Little Unicorn,'" she says as I unlock the door to my dingy single-wide trailer, "I will name it after you." She's beaming at me now, like I'm someone important. "I'll call it 'Unicorn Bright.' That's a wonderful name."

I step into the house and am nodding when the clenched fist of Alligator Boots connects with my jaw, fiery pain radiating through the left side of my face. He was waiting behind the door.

As I go down, I curse my fatigue. He had tailed me long enough to get a look at my license plate. From there it wasn't hard to get my address or break in.

Irene screams and our food goes tumbling to the floor. On my way down I get a look at the chaotic mess of my living room. Dust covering the flat screen, piles of clothes, trash, dirty carpet.

I have a horrible realization: If I can't take care of my own living room, how am I going to take care of Irene? The thought doesn't last long. My head bounces off the carpet with a sharp crack and darkness descends.

———

I WAKE UP WITH A START, THE LIGHT OF THE FULL MOON shining above me, hard ground below me, and cool air on my skin. My head is pounding and my jaw aches. My mouth is dry and my stomach clenches. I roll over and try to vomit, but there's nothing in me.

I hear the snort of a horse and bolt upright, the motion making my stomach try to empty itself again.

"Stand up," Alligator Boots says. He's mounted on what looks like a purple unicorn, a white horn jutting from its forehead, its coat a dark purple. In the moonlight it's hard to see the harness on the horse's head, but I know it's there.

"Why might I be doing that?" I ask, trying to hide the pain and desperation in my voice.

"Because if you don't, it will go badly for the girl."

We're back behind my trailer. It used to be a horse corral, back when I could afford to keep a horse. Now it's a falling down fence and a weedy expanse of dirt. Back behind the horse and Alligator Boots, I see the trailer, my El Camino, and his F-150 with a horse trailer attached.

"What?" I ask, trying desperately to get my mind to turn over.

Alligator Boots staged Edwardo Campos's death as an attack by a unicorn. Why? So Irene, a little girl obsessed with unicorns, would see it. Would talk about it. Would be dismissed. He put Edwardo's blood on that bull's horn. He also took something from the safe, just papers and not money.

This was all about Irene. The way her great-uncle had died had been a show for her.

Alligator Boots points to his right and I see Irene. She's tied to one of my cheap plastic chairs. She's gagged and her eyes are wide, her cheeks stained with tears.

I nod, make a show of getting up, and then slump back to the ground with a grunt. "What is it you needed from that safe?" I'm leaning on my right side, where my bowie knife should be, but he's taken it.

"Stand up!" he yells.

"You're the ranch hand Mr. Campos had a recent falling out with, ain't ya? The one that was once like a son to him."

He pulls a gun from his side and points it at Irene. "Stand. Now." He's not yelling anymore and that's a bad sign.

I slowly get into a squatting position. I feel in my right boot. That knife is still there.

I remember what Sanchez had told me about Edwardo Campos's recently remembered stock. What the bartender at Sugar and Spice had said when I showed him Edwardo's picture. How Edwardo had hinted to Irene that things were about to change for her.

"He wrote you out of his will," I say as I pull the knife from my boot and hold it behind my back, shakily standing up. "That's what ya took, the will that left everything to Irene. I'm guessing he hadn't signed it yet, but was about to. He had told all his buddies at Sugar and Spice about his windfall, about how he was leaving it all to his delightful niece that loves unicorns and the color purple. Someone there told ya."

Alligator Boots doesn't speak. He spurs the horse hard, and it leaps forward. As I stand there, I have empathy for Edwardo Campos. He came out in the middle of the night under the bright moonlight expecting a coyote and saw a galloping unicorn bearing down on him. He had the shotgun in his hand, but he didn't use it. His grandniece had been babbling about unicorns, and now seeing one made him dumb for an instant, just one small instant.

Adrenaline dumps into my bloodstream, my heart pounding in my ears in time with the thundering of the hooves. But I don't move. I stand there swaying, still trying to get my bearings, hoping my body still remembers my time at the rodeo.

I wonder what Detective Sanchez will do if she finds my body just like Edwardo's, if she has a hysterical girl that talks about yet another man being run through by a purple unicorn. Once, she might brush off, twice, never. It's all over for Alligator Boots, even if I don't survive. This thought gives me comfort. Briefly.

But what of Irene? I remember how she clung to me outside Sugar and Spice, how she sat so close to me in the El Camino, how she held my hand in the Circle K. It felt strange, but good, to be depended on. My eyes flick to her. I can't hear her over the pounding hooves or through her gag, but it's clear she's screaming.

The unicorn is upon me. I smell dust, paint, and its sweat. I quickly rotate my body around, moving just to the side. I pull the knife from behind my back. I do what I need to do.

***

I WAKE UP SLOWLY AND GROAN, REALIZING I'M FULLY dressed again. I'm slumped in a half-seated position, my lower back and my neck aching, my mouth dry as the desert.

"Take it easy." I'm not sure who it is at first, a woman with a sweet voice. Helen.

And then the events of the last day tumble onto me like a monsoon cloudburst. I bolt upright and open my eyes. "Irene," I croak.

"She's fine," Helen says, putting a hand on my back, a gentle smile on her lips.

"Where is she?" Part of me feels silly. I hardly know the girl. Another part of me is desperate for her to be okay.

"CPS came while you were sleeping. She's just fine, Conner."

I nod and rub at my face, trying to wake myself up, feeling several days of stubble. I remember the charging unicorn. I remember rotating out of the way and jamming my knife through one of those alligator skin boots. I remember him screaming and falling off that spray-painted horse, struggling to get up. Me punching him in the face. Him lying still. Untying Irene. Her sobbing and clinging to me while I called Detective Sanchez.

"They took her," I mumble, mostly to myself.

Helen is looking at me, her soft blue eyes searching my face like I'm not the man she knows.

I remember what it had felt like as Irene clung to me while we waited for the sheriff's deputies to arrive. How the ambulance had come and I had refused it and Irene had refused to leave me. How they had hauled Alligator Boots away. How Helen had finally come and we had gone into the trailer. I had given Irene my bed and held her hand for hours until she fell asleep and then stumbled out to the couch. Helen had insisted on staying.

"That horn," Helen says, pulling out her phone and showing me a picture that looks like a whale with a unicorn horn sticking out of its head. "It was real. This is a narwhal, that tusk is some crazy tooth."

It all makes sense... except for how I feel.

I look up to the tin of ashes on top of my entertainment center. I lever myself up, stumble over, and say, "Hey, Dad. The girl's safe." I reach down, my head screaming at me, and pick up a stray piece of paper, a microwave burrito wrapper.

"What are you doing?" Helen asks.

"I'm cleaning up." She's staring at me, like she doesn't know me. Like we've never danced or touched or had meals together. "Will you help me?"

———

THE DOOR IS A FADED YELLOW AND THE NEIGHBORHOOD'S somewhat faded, too. It might have been cheery three decades ago, but now it's looking a little sad.

It's been ten days since I met Irene, and two days since I've had a drink. I would have come sooner, but I swore to myself I wouldn't do it unless I had been dry for at least two days. My hand is shaking as I knock.

A plump woman with a pinched face answers the door.

"I'm here to see Irene," I say. "I called earlier."

She nods, lets me in, and leaves me in the living room. There's a TV playing loudly with strange blue creatures on it dancing around. There's a couple of kids, much younger than Irene, watching it, their eyes wide.

And then she's there. This time I'm expecting it and kneel down before she gets to me. "You okay?" I whisper.

She hugs me hard. She nods and sniffs. I can feel her tears on my shoulder. I can feel my own tears on my cheek. "What took you so long?" She says it gently but it feels like a horse kicked me in the chest.

"I was . . . I . . ." I stammer. "I was trying to . . ." I can't finish. I can't tell this girl that I was trying to be worthy of her. That I have been ever since we met. That I will be as long as she'll have me.

I don't know if she understands, but she hugs me even harder and that's enough.

PART 2
CHUPACABRA

ONE

There are a lot of ways to die, some better than others. I think about this, more than I should, actually. Someone dies by your hand, or in my case, the slip of your foot, and you think about it. And I sure think about it as I stare at the corpse laid out in the desert south of Phoenix, Arizona.

He's on his back, his hands are clutched to his mouth like some teenage dweeb at a horror movie, his eyes wide and staring up at the unforgiving sun. His grey suit is cheap and dirty and his dress shoes are badly in need of a shine. There is a ragged rip in his pants over his inner right thigh and traces of blood visible on the frayed cloth.

He's got short brown hair and is maybe thirty years old. Whatever happened here, this is not a good way to die. Baking in the Arizona sun in the middle of nowhere. And the cheap suit and those shoes? God, I hope I die in my cowboy boots.

I swallow hard and try to focus. I've got the beginnings of what is going to be an epic hangover and got a whopping three hours of sleep and haven't eaten in twelve hours. It feels like there are needles behind my eyes threatening to poke through and my tongue feels like sandpaper.

There is never a good day to go see a corpse, but this is the worst day for me. An anniversary of sorts, and this guy reminds me of my best friend in high school, Tommy, who died twenty-five years ago. Today. By that aforementioned slip of my foot.

Detective Trisha Sanchez is standing about six feet away staring at me. She's got her reflective sunglasses on, her limbs held slightly bent with coiled energy like she's about ready to pounce. I wouldn't be here if she hadn't called me at 7:00 a.m. over and over until I actually picked up, telling me she had a case for me and that I had to get to the police station by nine or no more consulting work with the Maricopa County Sheriff's Department.

Helen Montana, the blond-haired medical examiner and my on-again off-again girlfriend, is next to me staring at the corpse too. Her blue eyes look haunted and she's got her arms wrapped around her chest.

Something about this just isn't right.

I mean, besides my hangover and the corpse reminding me of Tommy and this being the worst day of the year for me.

The man has a sunburn but there is something else going on with his skin. It's wrinkled in a strange way like he's a third of the way to becoming a mummy. The position of his hands isn't natural, they should have fallen away when he passed out and long before he died.

And the smell... well, you get that with most any stiff. It's that deep, dark, cloying scent of blood and flesh just starting to rot.

There are three other sheriff's deputies here, searching the desert for evidence, but it is strangely quiet. I can hear the hum of the I-10, which runs from Phoenix to Tucson, in the distance, but that's the loudest sound.

"Sanchez," I say, nodding toward the detective, my voice coming out a bit of a croak. "Mind tellin' me what I'm doing here, mate?"

It is about ten o'clock in the morning and much too early for me to be up and for my brain to be functional at all, or for all the beer and whiskey I drank in the wee hours to be completely out of my system. But I've got my bowie knife strapped to my belt, my alligator-skin boots on, a bush hat on my head covering my unwashed sandy brown hair, and my B-movie quality Australian accent up and running.

Yup, I look something like a really tall Crocodile Dundee and sound like it, even though I'm an Arizona boy. I've got a past that I do all of this to try to keep at bay, especially today of all days, and I've got to tell you that staring at the corpse and pondering the ways we die isn't helping at all. It's only years of talking this way that keeps the accent going.

Sanchez smiles her patent-pending predatorial smile that shows off her white teeth and always reminds me of a shark. Way back when, we had a good working relationship before my drinking screwed up that stakeout I was helping out on. She nods at the corpse. "Ain't this weird enough for you?"

"Plenty weird, I'll give ya that, but..." I look back at the stiff, a shudder running through my body. "Why do you need my help? This looks like straight-up, old-fashioned detective work, not somethin' ya need a private eye for."

I didn't want the case. I do catch the weird cases, for sure, but I don't really like the gross ones, especially not today. I want to go buy more beer and keep drinking and get past this rather grim anniversary of mine with as few memories as possible.

Seeing this guy's hands over his mouth, his unseeing eyes open to the sun, just makes it worse. The poor guy looks like his end was terrifying.

Forget drinking, I'd settle for going to be a bouncer at the bar

I work at or do one of the occasional handyman gigs I do, just trying to earn enough money to scrape by. I want to do anything but figure out why and how this poor guy died and who did it.

"End of quarter," Sanchez says with her shark smile. She has on a crisp blue pantsuit with her long black hair pulled back in a ponytail so tight that you would think it would give her a headache. "My case load is a mile high and I've got the funds to pay you. I don't use them, I lose them." She shrugs her shoulders like that explains it, like she isn't tossing this one to me knowing I need the money, knowing that I still owe her from my screwup, and knowing I can't say no.

She is torturing me, is what she is doing. She's a detective, and a good one at that, and although we've never talked directly about it, she knows all about my past, about the name I left behind. And I wouldn't be surprised if she knows the grim anniversary I am trying to hide from today.

And it's clear that she is enjoying every minute of this.

"Listen up," she says, raising her voice, the deputies roaming the desert stopping and looking at her. "Bright is taking lead on this. All data goes through him. Now I know he's no Einstein, but he's got a nose for this bizarre shit. Pretend he is me." There is some chuckling at that. I'm 6'5" and only 170 pounds and I tower over the petite woman.

"I'm serious," she says, as if that needed to be emphasized. The woman is always serious. "Copy me on everything, but Conner Bright here is leading the investigation. Everyone got it?"

None of the other deputies say "yes" or "uh huh", they all say, "Yes, ma'am."

Sanchez stalks over to me, her wiry form looking more coiled with energy than usual. Something is going on with her. She wants me on this case for reasons other than torturing me.

"Don't fuck this up," she says, a bright smile on her face. "And you run every move by me and you don't do anything dangerous without me." She pauses, looking me up and down, her eyes lingering on the bowie knife and the crocodile claw that hangs from around my neck, two buttons on my khaki short-sleeved shirt undone so it is clearly visible.

"You can count on me," I say as cheerfully as possible.

She purses her lips and shakes her head. "Don't fuck this up," she says again and then turns and leaves, and I'm left there with the corpse, my sometimes girlfriend medical examiner, and three deputies.

And they're all looking at me.

TWO

I AM A LICENSED PRIVATE INVESTIGATOR, WHICH MEANS, for one thing, that I don't have any felony convictions.

That death that occurred by my foot happened when I was drunk and sixteen. I ran over my best friend. We were fighting over a girl and he was standing in front of my old pickup and I was being an ass and revving the engine. My foot slipped off the clutch. He died. It was big news for Arizona.

I did my time in the juvenile system and my record was sealed, so no felony conviction.

I studied criminal justice at the community college after riding bulls in the rodeo and running from them as a rodeo clown beat me up enough so I thought I should find something else to do.

I worked under another private investigator, my mentor Sal Wilson, for the requisite three years.

I've worked a lot of cases. Plenty of the stupid "get picture of my spouse cheating" or "who keeps spray-painting graffiti on my garage door" cases, but plenty weird ones too.

There was the old man skewered by what appeared to be a

purple unicorn, or the apparent alien abduction, and there have even been a couple of murder cases.

All of this is to say that I have training and experience, but I am, in no way, prepared for what Detective Sanchez just dumped in my lap. And her doing this is in some ways the bigger mystery. Something is up with her. Especially if she did this on a murder case and she did this with me.

Helen Montana clears her throat and I realize that everyone is staring at me while I'm staring at Sanchez's car as it kicks up dust on the dirt road out of here.

Helen is a big-boned woman with lovely blue eyes, a fabulous smile, and is right around forty, about the same age as me.

She also has an unfortunate thing for cowboys. I don't just wear alligator-skin cowboy boots and an Australian bush hat, I've earned the cowboy moniker riding horses, getting bucked off bulls, and getting chased as a rodeo clown. And she thinks I'm really from Australia, which just adds to the mystique.

I look around and smile. There are three deputies dressed in brown pants and tan short-sleeved shirts staring at me. A young woman with black hair by the name of Johnson. A young man with blond hair, Deputy Taylor. And a middle-aged man with a bulging belly, Deputy Clemons. The older guy has on a cowboy hat, but Taylor has on one of those Mountie hats with a gold emblem and cord around it that just makes me think of Dudley Do-Right.

"Right," I say. "Let's keep sharp, mates. We've got three priorities right now. Find out who he is, how he died, and how he got here."

I turn to Helen and she is giving me an encouraging smile. "Helen and I are going to examine the body, the rest of you keep looking for evidence. Mark any tracks you find, any garbage, anything at all. I want to see it. And take pictures."

It is late spring, the day is already hot, but not oppressively so, the thermostat under three digits, but still I am sweating like it is the height of summer.

I look down at the body, seemingly frozen in a moment of terror, and then realize I don't hear anything except for the highway. No one is moving. No one is speaking.

"What?" I ask, looking around, trying to imitate Sanchez's commanding gaze. "You all got any questions or can we get to work now?"

One of the deputies, Taylor, the one with the Dudley Do-Right hat, clears his throat. He's young, still in his twenties with blond hair and a weak-looking chin. He points at the corpse and says one word. "Chupacabra."

I feel a tingle at the back of my neck. Okay, this is a hell of lot weirder than I first thought. The chupacabra is one of those legendary creatures like bigfoot or the Loch Ness monster. This one supposedly goes around sucking the blood out of its victims and is said to be some kind of hairy lizard with big fangs.

Well, this explains why Sanchez called me in, but not why she put me in charge. I don't buy that line about the end of quarter and the budget. Not a bit.

Deputy Clemons is staring at the victim, his middle-aged wrinkles forming a sour look on his round face. The other one, Deputy Johnson, is staring too, her brown eyes opened wide and biting her lip.

"Relax, mates," I say. "You got me on the case now and this kind of thing is my speciality. I've heard that the chupacabra hops like a kangaroo and I used to wrestle with the 'roos in the outback just for fun. No worries. You got that?"

There is some reluctant nodding and I look at the young blond one that brought it up. "Find me some tracks, mate. Chupacabra, human, tire tracks, I don't care." They still aren't moving so I again pretend that I am Sanchez. "Now!" I yell with a clap of my hands.

That gets them moving and I look at Helen whose eyes are wide. "Do you think that..." she began, her tone barely above a whisper.

"Oh, Helen," I said, shaking my head. "Things are rarely what they seem." I don't add "take me for example" because I am genuinely fond of her. Even though I think she deserves better than a broken-down, beat-up, barely functional detective like me, I need her.

We squat down to examine the corpse and I feel my forty-one years in the creak of my knees and the pain in my back. Getting bucked off bulls will do that to you.

I pull out a handkerchief and cover my nose, the scent getting much worse as we get down there. Helen doesn't seem to mind, an occupational hazard, I guess. She's got on blue latex gloves and hands me a pair and I dutifully put them on.

She gently touches the skin of his cheek. It's wrinkled like he's a slice of apple that's been in the dehydrator for half a day, the flesh not bouncing back correctly. While there are signs of sunburn on his nose and cheeks, he's very pale. Too pale. She puts gentle pressure on one of the hands covering his mouth, but it doesn't budge, like it's glued there or something.

"How long he been out here?" I ask.

She puts a little more pressure on his hand. "Rigor mortis peaks at about twelve hours and lasts about forty-eight hours. So we're somewhere in that window. I won't be able to tell more from here."

She cautiously opens the rip at the man's inner right thigh and I choke back a cough. There in the too-pale flesh are two puncture wounds about two inches apart right over the femoral artery. There is dried blood staining his thigh, but not much.

It kind of looks like a large fanged creature got a hold of him here and sucked his blood out. Kind of explains the terrified pose of his hands.

"Chupacabra," Helen whispers, her voice nearly breaking.

THREE

I hush Helen, and we work quickly without a word, looking for and not finding any ID. I watch over the stiff as the deputies comb the area and Helen gets a body bag and a stretcher from her meat wagon.

As we are zipping up the body bag, she gives me this wide-eyed look, her blue eyes seeming to be haunted.

"This ain't that," I hiss.

"How can you be sure?" she whispers.

We carry the corpse on a stretcher to her vehicle. She helped out with the purple unicorn case so I'd hope she'd learned to be more rational after that.

But superstition... it gets to us all. I don't think us humans are actually wired to be rational, it's something we have to fight for.

But then again, she keeps coming back around to me despite the mess that I am. As much as I think she should find someone better, I am grateful for her company when we can find the time, so who am I to complain?

After the corpse is stowed, I walk her around to the driver's side door and she gets in and rolls down the window. "You tell Sanchez, all right, but otherwise keep this quiet."

Her brow furrows in a way that I find adorable and I have a hard time keeping my mind on what I'm actually supposed to be doing.

"But Conner, what if it was really a..." She gives me a pointed look, but away from the body I catch a whiff of her perfume which has a subtle cinnamon note and I'm even more distracted. We've been off again for the last few months. It was a bad spring for me, and I have rules about the people I really care about. If I need to drink myself to sleep, I stay away.

I take a deep breath and a step back. "Look, Helen. Man or beast, I promise you I'll find out what did this. But keep this quiet, all right?"

She nods and I stand there for a few moments watching her van kick up dust on the barely-there dirt road we took to get here.

What if it was an animal? I shake my head. If it was an animal, then we have a lot less to worry about than if it was a human making it look like an animal did it.

Humans are far more dangerous than animals.

FOUR

A day in the Arizona sun searching the desert for clues is not a bad day in my book. Hot, yes, but the spring weather kept it below 100. Boring, yes, but for me billable hours are something I really prize. And while the first hour was pretty awful, my head pounding form the hangover, the heat and some water actually helped. Cowboy boots are crap for walking around all day in, but I'm happy to have my mind occupied.

A crime scene like this is hard to keep secure, so I decide we will find what we can, take a ton of pictures, bag anything we find, and get out of there.

It is my case, right? Sanchez gave it to me and I'm going to run it my way.

The three deputies with me don't seem to appreciate it much. They complain about the heat and I seem to spend more time getting them water and listening to complaints than actually looking.

Turns out my good day is a terrible day for them.

And I don't care.

The corpse was found by high school students driving out

here to drink. In fact, the area is littered with beer cans, broken bottles, and a smattering of shotgun shells. The road out here is a rutted unmaintained road that is easy to miss if you don't know it's there.

The corpse was laid out on the hard ground, half on some dried grass right near the skeleton of a dead bunch of prickly pear cactus, the spines still sticking out of the fibrous remains.

There are scuffs around the body, but nothing we can make out. The soil is hard there and doesn't hold a print.

Taylor, the blond-haired Dudley Do-Right, calls me over right around noon. We've been slowly widening our search out from where the body was found, walking slowly and carefully. We've found the aforementioned garbage, rabbit tracks, and a few coyote tracks, but nothing significant yet.

The boy's voice doesn't sound right when he calls out my name, and the other two deputies stop dead in their tracks and stare. I call to them, "Keep at it, mates," and stroll off to the young deputy. I try not to hold that weak chin and stupid hat against him, but something about it and his baby face makes me want to give him a wedgie and throw him in the girl's bathroom like we were in high school.

And yes, I was one of those kids. I wore a cowboy hat and regular cowboy boots, no alligator skin back then, and usually had some chew tucked between my lip and gum. I was full of myself.

Life hadn't bucked me off enough yet to soften me, but one slip of the foot, one tragic death, and everything changes on you.

I shove down my impulse to bully him and say, "Whatcha got, mate?"

He points down to some sandy soil, his hand shaking. There is a line of footprints heading away from where we found the corpse towards some low rugged hills. Most of them are indistinct, but one print is clear. It's about as big as a child's hand with five distinct digits, all of them ending sharply.

He opens his mouth to speak and I hold up my hand. "Don't say it, mate. Just don't bloody say it. Get some photos. Mark the spot and let's track it back."

His eyes get wide and he says it anyway. "Chupacabra."

This is Arizona. This is the desert. There are big lizards here. Plenty of them. But not that big.

"It's probably a Komodo dragon," I say. It's the only lizard I can think of big enough for these tracks, although off the top of my head, I have no idea if they are native to Arizona. But that doesn't matter, anything is better than this chupacabra madness.

Now the other two deputies are staring. Well, they are going to be distracted by this so I might as well embrace it. "Johnson, Clemons," I yell. "Mark where you are at, mates, and carefully walk over here. Taylor here has found what look like some Komodo dragon footprints."

They don't buy it. They think it's a Chupacabra, but you don't want to mess with a Komodo. A male can weigh up to two hundred pounds and their bite is venomous. I don't think they are vampiric, so I don't think a Komodo explains the killing, but it's something we have to look into.

I look at the tracks again and there is a swishing pattern caused by the lizard's tail that wiped out a lot of the tracks.

This is not going to be easy.

"Listen up," I say when they are all here and I've pointed out the tracks and the signs of the tail. "Two questions. Do these tracks lead back to the vic? And, is the Komodo still in the area?"

At least two of them say "Chupacabra" under their breath.

"Now which one of you wants to head out into the bush with me to find the bugger?"

The terrified looks on their faces just about makes my day,

but it's Johnson, the female deputy, all five foot two of her, that speaks up. "I'll go," she says and then bites her lip.

"Good on ya." I turn to the less brave men. "Go slow, boys. Mark what ya find. We're gonna get some gear and head out, but I want to hear from ya on the radio every fifteen minutes."

They are a bit too wide-eyed for my taste. I'm sure these are fine sheriff's deputies, that they know their way around the city, but they don't have a clue about the desert.

FIVE

I'm not a trained tracker, but I still have good eyes and I'm not stupid.

Well, let me clarify that a bit. I am certainly stupid, about many things, like not dragging my ass to Alcoholics Anonymous or at least a therapist years ago, but when it comes to the outdoors, well, I've spent most of my life in the desert and it's in my bones.

And I think I have avoided AA because even though it says "anonymous" there right in the title, my "slip of the foot" was big news in the state, so how am I supposed to be honest with people about why I drink?

I know. That excuse held water when I was in my twenties, maybe even all the way to thirty, but I'm over a decade past that and it's been decades since my real name was in the news, so even I know that excuse is crap.

"What's with ya and the chupacabra?" I ask Deputy Johnson when we are out of earshot of the others. It is slow going, the soil mostly hard packed or covered in dried grass and not showing many prints.

Deputy Johnson is pretty, but with an intense look to her face as if she is always looking out for the next bad thing to happen. She has dark skin and almond-colored eyes, her jet-black hair cropped very short.

"You hear things," she says with a shrug.

"In Phoenix?" I ask.

She shrugs again. "Locker room talk, I guess. Folks started talking about it a few weeks ago. Some homeless guy was found with puncture wounds in his leg and his blood drained."

I stop and Johnson continues on a few steps before she realizes I have stopped. When she turns, I role up my right sleeve and expose my bicep. There is a semicircular scar that is a series of puncture wounds on both sides. "See that?" I say, my tone a little strident. "That there is what a bite wound looks like. Not two holes, but a bunch of 'em."

"What... what did that?" Johnson asks.

It was a dog and I was drunk and where I shouldn't be and deserved it, but I say, "A dingo fancied me for dinner one night in the outback."

Her eyes widen. "What did you do?"

People want to believe things. I wear the silly getup that I do, maintain my terrible accent, and tell some stories, and everyone totally believes I'm from Australia, not an Arizona boy who couldn't leave but just couldn't face his past.

I want to teach her a lesson and here I am deepening her belief in a lie. My lie.

I point back the way we came. "That poor guy wasn't bitten by any animal, not unless there are fifty-foot-long snakes roaming around. That homeless man wasn't either." I point to my bicep. "Think about the biology, mate. A mouth full of teeth doesn't leave a mark like that, it leaves a mark like this." I point at two bigger dimples in my skin. "Right there is where the canines landed, they sunk in deep, but the other teeth got me too."

"But..." she begins.

"Are you telling me this chupacabra is running around the desert with only two bloody teeth in its mouth?" My tone is loud, too loud, and I feel my heart pounding in my head and my cheeks flush red.

I could blame the lingering hangover for my mood, but it's the day. A day of truth for me. Not a day when I can let such silliness be.

She looks sheepish and then purses her lips. "Then why are we tracking what you think is a Komodo dragon even though they are only native to Indonesia?"

She's either got a good memory or did a quick search on her phone when I pulled the Komodo dragon idea out of my butt. I smile, it's a tight-lipped, strained thing. This chupacabra thing has gotten under my skin and I need to let it go. "Because, even though the odds are against it, I might be wrong. Maybe someone imported one of the monsters and it got away." I pause, watching her eyes widen as she glances around the desert as if expecting my fifty-foot snake or something equally terrifying to appear.

"Come on, Johnson, buck up. Odd are that whatever made these tracks is just a big, dumb lizard and just passed through and has nothing to do with it."

I take some long strides and pick back up the trail.

"Yeah?" she asks when she catches up.

"Oh, yeah. With the dead homeless guy with the same holes in his legs, odds are we are looking at a serial killer."

SIX

JOHNSON AND I DON'T GET VERY FAR. WE COME TO SOME softer grass-free soil, the prints as clear as can be, and then... nothing. They disappear.

A slight breeze has kicked up, bringing with it the dry dusty scent of the desert and I welcome its cooling effects on my sweaty body. We're closer to the hill now. It's covered with prickly pear cactus, some rabbitbrush, the tops a dull yellow, and dried grasses, the brief rains of spring long gone.

We stand there staring. One moment the tracks are clear, the child-sized clawed feet, the swishing tail wiping much of it away and then... nothing, just smooth sandy soil covered in pebbles.

The young woman opens her mouth. "Don't say it," I say, holding my hand up.

"But..."

"Are you telling me that the chupacabra just bloody flew away?" I ask.

The sandy soil looks windblown like a gust came through and wiped out the tracks, just not all of them. We are in a bit of a clearing not too far from the dirt road, our path has been roughly parallel to it.

We go in the direction it was traveling, we circle around, but no more tracks.

Damnit. I did this, in some ways, to try to get these deputies' heads on straight, but this is just going to make it worse. The chupacabra is no longer just an animal, it is a mythological creature.

Johnson's radio crackles to life with a burst of static "Bright, this is Clemons. Come in."

I nod to Johnson and she clicks the radio on. "This is Johnson. What's up?"

"We found something," Clemons says. "You guys need to get back here."

SEVEN

CLEMONS LOOKS WORRIED, HIS HANDS BALLED INTO FISTS and his arms clutched stiffly to his side. He's older than me, the grey of his hair far along. At his age he should have moved up the ranks which makes me wonder about him. Why, at his age, is he still wearing the uniform out in the field? Why isn't he a detective or why isn't he working a desk job and not out in the sun today?

Johnson and I went to the road and walked quickly back so as not to add any more of our tracks to the scene.

Taylor is next to Clemons, his weak chin looking even weaker than usual. Now him, it makes perfect sense why he's out here. His youth and inexperience. He keeps pacing slowly, short little steps, and he keeps staring at the ground.

When Johnson and I get close, Taylor points and says what I am beginning to think is his favorite word, "Chupacabra."

There on the ground is a large grey claw, a couple of inches long. It's a wicked-looking thing, prehistoric and dangerous. It's not as long as the crocodile claw hanging from a cord around my neck, but it is impressive.

I ignore the single word statement and their worried looks. "What happened with the tracks?" I ask.

Clemons nods back to where we found the corpse. We're pretty close to the road here. "We lost the tracks back there on the other side of where the victim was and picked them back up over here, and then they just..." he shrugged.

"Let me guess, mate," I say. "In soft sandy soil they just appeared like out of nowhere, like the bloody big lizard thing can fly like Mary Poppins or somethin'."

Okay, so I am grumpy. It's the day. It's the hangover. This is my show here and I'm squandering Sanchez's trust in me battling against their superstition by being facetious.

But that's the thing about superstition--logic often doesn't work.

Taylor nods, his brown eyes wide.

"So we've got tracks vaguely leading to the body and then vaguely leading away, but none at the body?" I ask.

Clemons nods. I swear they are imagining a big furry lizard that now has wings that flew in, left us a few tracks, flew to the victim, clamped two large fangs down, sucked his blood out, flew a little more, walked to leave us some more tracks and then flew off again.

Yeah, I get to be grumpy with this kind of insanity. I now have to wonder if Sanchez hand-picked this team for me as a more advanced form of torture. I, frankly, wouldn't put it past her. I can imagine her having a larger crew show up for this and then seeing the thigh wound before anyone else did, dismissing the ones that hadn't already been infected with this chupacabra thing, and then calling me in and throwing it in my lap.

Yeah, so who's being superstitious now?

I squat down despite my protesting knees and look at the claw. There is a spot of blood on the end, which isn't consistent with the narrative of this murder. The lizard would have been here first before it got to the victim.

"Who was on site here first?" I ask, not looking up.

"I was," Johnson says.

"How many sets of tracks were near the body?"

"Two," she said. "They came from the road, stopped short of the body, and then went back to the road. It was the high school kids. They spotted the body from the road."

"And the victim's footprints?" I ask as I stand up and look around. This crime scene was prepared. I am sure of it.

She shakes her head. "We never found them."

"And were any other footprints found?" I ask.

Her eyes widen and I am hopeful that the "logic" beneath her superstition is about to break. "The soil is hard there, but no, we never found any tracks for the victim or anyone else."

I smile at her and nod. "And last I checked, mate, people don't fly."

EIGHT

I send Taylor and Clemons back to get on the computer in their car. There was some kind of big lizard here, maybe a Komodo, and while that in and of itself isn't out of the realm of possibility, the coincidence and strange pattern of tracks strains credulity. I am having them search their database for anything regarding Komodo dragons or related lizards.

"If... why...?" Johnson sputters.

We're back to where the victim was found.

"Why would someone stage a murder this elaborate?" I ask.

She nods.

I shrug. "Want to hear my own superstition conspiracy theory?"

She nods rapidly.

"I think the vic back there died of natural causes. I think Sanchez has a friend with a Komodo dragon and brought it out here on a bloody leash and laid down some tracks. I think she put the vic in a cheap suit, poked a couple of holes in his thigh with an ice pick, and bribed the kids to call it in."

Her eyes are so wide I have a hard time not laughing. "But... the... the tracks disappearing...?"

I shrug. "Quick work down with a leaf blower. That's how all the tracks around here were wiped out."

Her jaw hangs open and she swallows hard. "But... why... why would Sanchez do that?"

"Oh come on, Johnson. Surely you've heard the tale of the stakeout I screwed up, the months of work I cost Sanchez."

Her eyes get even wider. "And this is... this is revenge?"

I purse my lips and make my face as serious as I can. "Oh, this is revenge, mate. Sanchez putting me in charge here is revenge. But the rest? That's a heap a lies. I made that up. Sanchez wouldn't do that, not even to me."

"What... why... why would you tell me a story like that?" Despite her dark skin, her cheeks flush a bit red.

"Because, mate. I need someone out here with me with their head on. I'm pretty sure the leaf blower thing is true and I bloody know this crime scene was prepared. You need to understand that just because I can come up with a few pieces that sound like they work, it doesn't mean I know what the hell I'm talking about."

She nods eagerly. "So... no chupacabra?"

I just shake my head.

She's staring off and into the distance, her brown eyes roaming the craggy cactus-covered hills. She's thinking. It's getting hotter, the buzz of the highway a distant drone. I give her time to think as I let my eyes softly focus and roam across the scene.

We're missing something here and I can feel it. And yes, this feeling could be as based in fact as Taylor's belief in the chupacabra, but I've come to trust my gut... when I'm sober that is. When I'm drinking, my gut is a damn fool.

I take a deep breath of the dry air, smelling the dust and a hint of something musky, the scent of the corpse still lingering.

Someone drove the corpse out here. Someone staged the murder. Maybe the same someone that killed the homeless man. But why dump the body here near the highway?

They drove the body here. They walked it over the desert. They brought a Komodo dragon with it and handled a dangerous creature just to create the chupacabra illusion. They left a claw.

Despite the heat, I feel a chill run through me. Whatever it is I am missing, I can't get it.

"What now?" Johnson asks when I look at her.

"Now we leave the chupacabra twins out here to secure the scene and we go see what Helen has found."

NINE

I don't like the morgue. It creeps me out. It's this little way station for the dead and I always imagine the wall of stainless-steel drawers with a body in each one of them.

And on bad days, I imagine that Tommy is in one of those drawers and I'm still sixteen and my newly dead best friend's body is broken from me running him over with my truck.

On really bad days, I imagine his body is in every drawer and I have this sick desire to open one and look at what I did. Even after all these years, even after all I've tried to do to amend for that horrible mistake, I don't think I've been punished enough.

And today... well, with this being the twenty-fifth anniversary of that slip of my foot and Tommy's death, I can practically hear him banging on the inside of all those stainless-steel drawers. Wanting to get out. Wanting to show me what I did to him.

And that is what I saw on my first visit to a morgue when I was sixteen. I saw the broken body of my best friend, saw what our alcohol- and jealous-fueled argument had created, what the slip of my foot had done.

I think my father thought it would be good for me, that it

would scare me straight, that it would make me never drink again. It clearly didn't work. As I stand there in the doorway, I want nothing more than enough drinks to make the echo of that day disappear.

And yes, I do get the irony of me dating a medical examiner and ending up in morgues even more often than I would as a private investigator. No one has ever said that I make things easy for myself.

I blink and stare in at the Maricopa County Morgue, trying to get my brain in gear.

There are two stainless-steel tables in the middle of the room with bright lights mounted above. Helen is in scrubs now with safety glasses and a mask over her face.

The room smells strongly of rubbing alcohol and other kinds of antiseptics and the room is cool enough that I feel a chill after so many hours in the hot desert.

I sent Johnson to go update Sanchez and I stand just outside the door watching. Our victim is laid out on one of those gleaming tables, still dressed. She's dissected open the thigh wound and is gently probing it with a long pair of tweezers. She hasn't noticed me yet. She's lost in her work.

I have to imagine for her it's not a person anymore. It's flesh and blood, it's muscle and bone, but it's not an individual, it's a collection of biological parts.

I mean, if it is a person, how the hell do you do that?

She's mumbling under her breath, talking to herself, and as much as I dislike the morgue, I like to watch her work. I like the precise economy of her movements and the obvious intelligence and training that drives them.

She's a doctor, for god's sake, and she sometimes hangs out with me. The functional alcoholic hiding from his past. The loser who just happens to be the right age, the right look, and the right amount of cowboy.

It's moments like these that I am sure I should break up with her for real, release her to find someone better, but she's one of the two lights in my life that keep the darkness at bay and I just can't do it. I know it's selfish and I feel guilty about it, but I can't.

When she looks up and notices me standing there, there's a brief furrowing of her forehead and her eyes narrow in frustration at an impending interruption, but I can see the moment when she knows it's me. Her forehead smooths out and even through her mask I can see her smile.

I feel something in my chest that I would never label with a word that starts with "l," but I am glad for the feeling and I welcome it--and believe me, this is no small thing.

"Conner," she says. "I'm glad you are here."

I stare at her lovely blue eyes and can't hear Tommy banging at drawers anymore, can't see his broken body anymore. I take a stride forward and I can't keep the smile off my face. "And I'm glad to see you, love."

She blinks and her cheeks flush just a touch. Right then and there I vow to get my act together, to become a good enough man for her, to finally let go of my past.

But it's a moment I've had so many times with her and I've failed so many times. The weight of all that comes crashing down on the light and happy moment, but I keep the smile on my face because Helen deserves it.

"Find anything interesting there?" I ask.

"Oh, yeah," she begins. "This is... I don't even know what to think about this."

She nods for me to come closer and under the bright lights she parts the flesh of the victim where she has carefully dissected around the wound. "See there," she points, and I nod. I've been through this with her before. Yeah. I see flesh in several shades of pink, I see the skin and I can even identify a bit of the muscle and maybe an artery, but it's just biology to me. I can't distinguish that much.

She points out the path of the puncture wound from the skin through to what appears to be an artery. "Whatever did this," she says, "punctured cleanly and right to the artery. Not through the artery, mind you, but right into it. It was precisely done."

She looks up at me, her blue eyes wide behind the plastic of her protective glasses.

"And this is how his blood was drained?" I ask. I really didn't need to. The narrative of the crime scene was a consistent one except for the bloodied claw being in the wrong place.

She nods.

"And no other marks on the skin besides the two punctures?" I ask.

She shakes her head.

"So not like a real bite," I say, nodding towards my bicep which she knows all about.

She shrugs her shoulders and I just smile at her. I'm not going to fight the superstitious urge with her like I did with Johnson. I'm going to solve the case and just show her.

I pull out the evidence bag with the claw. "We found this out there. Looks like a Komodo dragon claw with a bit of blood on the tip. Can you check it?"

She nods. "His blood work is at the lab. I should have something soon. But there's something else." She shows me his hands, the bed of the fingernail is darker than it should be, almost purple. "This could be signs of cyanosis. There are other things that point toward hypoxia, which is not consistent with the bite wound and hypovolemic shock. Time of death was about thirty-six hours ago, but he was out there in the sun for a while, so the evidence is not as clear as it could be."

She nods and looks at me expectantly.

"In English please," I say.

She smiles and narrows her eyes which deepens her crow's feet in a distracting way. "He was deprived of oxygen before he died."

Now that's something. "So that wouldn't normally happen from blood loss?"

She shakes her head. "Not like I'm seeing, but I've still got a ways to go."

I want to stay. I want to see the smile underneath her surgical mask again and see her eyes squish up. I want to get her out of the morgue and smell that cinnamon note in her perfume. I also want to get away from the stainless-steel drawers and the imagined ghost of my best friend that I killed. And I want to do my job.

"Thanks, love," I say and get one last smile. "Call me on my mobile if you find anything else."

TEN

Detective Trisha Sanchez is behind her desk, the navy-blue suit jacket draped over her chair, the white sleeves of her blouse rolled up. She's leafing through an old case folder. I know it's old because she's leafing through paper not poking at the computer that dominates the beat-up metal desk.

There's a framed picture on the desk, it's facing away from me but I've seen it before. It's a picture of Sanchez and her daughter when the girl was four. They are at Disneyland, huge matching smiles on both of their faces.

This is a part of her that I've never seen--she seems to always have the predatorial smile queued up for me. But it makes me wonder about her and her life away from this place, away from all the crime.

The fluorescent bulbs in her small office are putting off a high-pitched squeal that just puts me on edge. I've mentioned it to Sanchez before and she can't hear it. I am paranoid enough to think that she hasn't changed them just to annoy me.

Now, that particular thought doesn't stray into the realm of superstition. I have plenty of evidence that the woman takes deep delight in annoying me.

I stand there in the doorway and wait quietly. She knows I'm here, she probably heard me walking down the hallway, my boots making a sharper sound against the linoleum than what most the folks around here wear.

She's making me wait, which I have no issue with. This is billable time.

She finally looks up and nods at the chair across the desk from her. Without the reflective sunglasses, I can see her brown eyes. They are fierce, as you would expect, but sad too. She looks to be a bit shy of forty, but not one grey hair in her black ponytail. I have to imagine that she pulls them out ruthlessly whenever they appear.

"You've taken an interest in Deputy Johnson," she says. It's not an accusation, like I did something wrong, but it wasn't how I expected to start this conversation.

I shrug. "Just trying to shake the superstition loose. They've all got chupacabra on the brain."

Sanchez's brow furrows and she looks down. "I know she told you about the homeless guy, but there was another victim six months before that, and the first one three months earlier."

That makes four victims. I just blink. I open my mouth to ask her what the hell I'm doing on this case, but she silences me with the pursing of her lips and a widening of her eyes. She gets up and closes the door to her office and sits back down with a sigh.

"Are you drinking?" she asks, her voice almost gentle.

I nod. "Only after work. Sleepin' aid, ya know."

Her brow furrows and a frown pulls down her round face as she studies my face and I just want to run away. A raging bull I'm happy to face, but the disapproving look of Trisha Sanchez? No thank you.

She holds my eyes for what feels like hours, but it was maybe thirty seconds, and then she slumps back in her chair. "Keep it to a minimum, okay?" she says quietly. "I need you on this one."

My jaw drops open because I am considering for the first time that this is not about torturing me, about making me pay for my mistake, but about helping her catch a killer. And she doesn't ask me to just stop drinking as if it's just a matter of will power like so many people think it is.

"Are we talkin' about a serial killer here?" I ask.

She nods, but barely. Her message is clear. The department isn't labeling it as such, but that is exactly what it is.

"That crime scene is way beyond strange," I say. "Tracks erased. What looks to be a Komodo dragon brought in for effect, even a claw dropped off. But the claw with the drop of blood wasn't even in the right spot, it was before the tracks hit the body. This whole thing is starting to give me the willies. Why would they do that?"

A sour expression takes over her face and then she swallows. "News of this will leak, any time now. The tracks. The claw. Chupacabra will be in the headlines. Again." She glances past me out the glass front of her office. "And the news shouldn't be leaked."

Suddenly it's clear why I am here. She wants someone outside the department to help her. She doesn't trust them and she's desperate enough to rely on me and hope I don't drink too much and ruin it.

I also suspect that my chupacabra-obsessed crew was chosen intentionally. Maybe she figures they aren't the ones leaking the news.

"What have you gotten me into, Sanchez?" I ask.

She smiles, and it's some small comfort that the predatorial nature of it is still intact. "Just keep your drinking under control and everything will be fine."

Right. As if it could possibly be that simple.

ELEVEN

"The only Komodo dragon they could find in the area is at the Phoenix Zoo," Johnson says. We are out in the parking lot, she found me there pacing after my talk with Sanchez. At least I wasn't completely off the mark with the Komodo idea, but that doesn't matter.

Serial killer. Someone leaking case details. Bizarre staged crime scenes created for the news. That all deserves some pacing.

Not to mention this day. It deserves some good pacing all on its own and some enthusiastic drinking.

I stop and just give her a pointed look. I don't have a shark-like smile, but I've been told my gaze combined with my gangly height can be pretty intense.

"I already called the zoo," she says quickly. "The Komodo is just fine. Did you know that there are only a few thousand of them left in the wild and those are in Indonesia?"

I didn't know that. I resume pacing. "Maybe it wasn't a Komodo. It could have been a bizarrely large Gila monster, those are out there for sure. Maybe the prints were all faked."

"And the claw?" she asks.

I shrug. "Bought it on eBay."

She pulls out her phone and taps on it quickly. "Nothing like that," she says, holding up the phone, but I just ignore it.

I shrug again. "Doesn't matter, mate. Whoever did this found a claw, a big one. Might not even be Komodo."

I really want to leave, get in my vintage blue 1976 El Camino and drive away. Go get some beer and let it slowly wash this day away. We don't have the victim's identity. We don't have any leads. And we have the kind of case I would rather stay away from, and this is the day every year I don't want to remember.

I keep pacing behind the sheriff's cars, breathing in the dry air, hearing the sound of vehicles on the road, not really thinking about the case but thinking about a case of beer.

And this is my problem. When the going gets tough, Conner Bright goes drinking. But that's not good enough for Sanchez or Helen or for Irene. Even today.

Irene is the little girl I helped with the purple unicorn case. I saved her from the man that killed her great-uncle, her last living family member. She's nine years old and staying with a foster family now. Even more than I want to stay sober for Helen, I want to stay sober for Irene. I don't go see her unless I've been dry for two days. It's been weeks since I saw her.

When I'm like this I try to see her round face and shining brown eyes. I try to feel her little arms around me hugging me. I try to hear her laughter at my funny accent and my strange stories telling her about Scatterwood, deep in the Australian outback, and all the strange characters that live there.

Sure, I made up Scatterwood and everyone who lives there, but after what that kid's been through, anything that makes her laugh is good by me.

Irene needs me and I'm not a man that is used to being

needed. Helen wants to need me but knows it's not safe. And Sanchez needs me now too.

It's this, much more than the details of the case, that drives my restless pacing. I am not the kind of man you should rely on. Could explain why my most steady work is that of a bouncer at a big country and western bar. Could explain why Helen and I have been seeing each other less and less over the past year.

"What now?" Johnson asks when my pacing and the silence has gone on for far too long.

I feel sweat dripping down my back and I can see it beaded on the dark skin of the young woman's face. I stop and stare at her, trying to get my mind out of its rut. I can think of only one productive action, so I pull my keys out of my jean's pocket and hand them to Johnson. No keys means no beer which means maybe I can get through this without disappointing anyone. "Keep these, eh."

"What... why?" she stammers.

"Just do it," I mumble and go back to pacing.

TWELVE

THE COOL OF THE MORGUE IS A SHOCK TO MY OVERHEATED body. I was out there pacing for over an hour, sending Johnson back in before she wilted too much.

I would still be out there but for Helen's call. She's got an excited look on her face. "Tetrodotoxin," she says triumphantly, as if that explains everything or anything.

The victim's body is still on one of the stainless-steel tables, his chest cracked open revealing a mostly empty torso, Helen having made progress on the autopsy. I don't want to see it and I don't want to get any closer to the dark stench, so I'm standing by the door again.

"What is that?" Johnson asks.

"It's a neurotoxin," Helen begins walking over to the corpse and standing next to it, a proud smile on her face.

She likes to solve mysteries just like me. That could be something beyond me being a cowboy that keeps her coming back. The smile on her face is so incongruous next to the hollowed-out remains of the victim, but I still can't help smiling myself.

"It's a potent one at that," she continues. "Take enough of it and it will paralyze your diaphragm and you will die of asphyxia-tion. And you'll know it's coming too. Paresthesia--that numb pins and needles feeling--of the lips and tongue and then the extremities. The sweats. Trouble breathing. There is no antidote."

I take a step in, closer to the stench of the corpse. I can't help it, it's like the mystery is calling me. "Hypoxia, right?" I say.

She nods and picks up the man's hand, her fingers going to the dark purple at his nail beds. "Hypoxia. It wasn't hypovolemic shock that got him." She blinks, looking at Johnson's blank expression. "Blood loss. I'm saying he died because he stopped breathing not because of blood loss."

"That came after," I say with a smile.

She nods. "After."

"No chupacabra...?" Johnson says tentatively.

Helen shakes her head. "No. I don't know what bit him, or even if these are bite marks, not yet. I can tell you that the blood on the claw you found was his."

I watch Johnson as the wheels turn in her head. She's certainly smart enough and I want her to figure out what the next question is.

Sanchez was right, I have taken an interest in her. She can be more than a deputy. Her smooth brow furrows and her brown eyes dart from the corpse to Helen and back. "Where does this tetro... tetrodi... tetro-stuff come from?"

"Tetrodotoxin," Helen says. "The name is a derivative of the name of a fish, Tetraodontiformes."

"Poisonous fish?" Johnson asks.

Helen nods. "The one you've probably heard of is the pufferfish."

I smile. A lead, finally a lead. "Right," I say. "Pufferfish is considered a delicacy, a dangerous one at that. It's served at high-end Japanese restaurants." I cross my arms and look at Johnson pointedly.

She's biting her lip, the wheels still clearly turning and then her brown eyes meet mine. "I'll go find out where it's served in the area." She's got a huge smile on her face as she runs off.

"And tell Sanchez," I yell after her.

I'm left there with Helen and a partially disassembled body, the triumphant smile still on her face. I want to kiss her, even with the corpse right there. That would get me to stop thinking of drinking, to stop thinking about Tommy.

But I just stand there, like I'm still in high school and not over forty. "Any luck IDing him?" I ask.

The smile fades from her face and I miss it. She shakes her head. "The prints didn't match anything in our databases, and from what I've heard there are no missing persons reports that match his description."

I turn to go and she says, "Conner, are... are you all right?"

This is not the first time Helen has asked me that question and I'm sure it won't be the last. This is the question people close to me often ask.

"All the pacing," she adds, as if she needed to explain herself.

Seconds tick by and I know I should turn around. I know that standing here like this is making it clear that I am not all right. I conjure a lame excuse for my behavior and a happy tone and almost speak it, but I want to be good enough for Helen and that means not hiding from the truth.

"I just really want a drink," I say quietly. "Especially today."

She's silent and I think maybe I didn't speak it loud enough for her to hear.

"Why don't I take you to a meeting," she says gently. She's taken a couple of steps towards me and I can feel her warmth behind me driving back the cool of the morgue.

I tried AA. Years ago, I tried. All the smoking and coffee

drinking and holier than thou stuff made it hard for me. The giving it over to a "higher power" made it nearly impossible.

I don't believe in god, just looking around this world provides ample evidence that there is no god, not one worth a damn. What higher power am I supposed to turn it over to?

"You're a good woman, Helen," I say and walk away without looking back. "You deserve better than me."

THIRTEEN

So there are ten places in the Phoenix Metro area that serve fugu, the sushi made out of pufferfish. There are more places than that to go buy a live pufferfish.

It turns out that tetrodotoxin is not hard to come by, so while knowing how our victim died is important, it's not really any kind of lead. At all.

I'm back in the parking lot pacing, trying not to think about beer or Helen or AA. And most of all I'm trying not to think about the victim and how he makes me think of my best friend Tommy and how his mangled body looked after I ran him over.

Johnson is there leaning against a sheriff's car watching me pace, her head going back and forth like she's watching a slow-motion tennis match, my boots beating out a metronomic rhythm.

The sun is heading towards the horizon, and while it's gotten a bit hotter, the sun being lower actually makes it more bearable. Still, I'm sweating and I've done enough of that today so that I can smell myself, and that's never a good sign. If you can smell yourself, that means everyone else can smell you too.

My feet hurt and I'm pretty sure I've grown a few blisters out here today. But none of that matters. If I'm pacing, I'm not drinking. Johnson has my keys so I can't jump in the El Camino and go get any booze. I need to be here.

And yes, I realize that I look like a crazy man out here. But that is better than drinking. Anything is better than drinking.

"So what's next?" I ask Johnson after she gives me her report.

I can feel her stare--she's giving me another one of those pursed-lip looks. She wants me to tell her, this is my investigation after all.

"I don't know," she says.

"Think," I bark back.

My boots beat out their rhythm and the cars flow by on the street and a siren warbles in the distance. I don't know how long it takes her to reply. I don't care.

After a time, she sighs and says, "Tetro... tetrdi... tetrodo-whatever is easily obtained. His death could have been accidental, maybe this isn't even murder."

I stop pacing and stare at her. She looks so damn young. Frankly, everyone under thirty looks like a baby to me anymore. I have no idea what her life has been like, but I wasn't expecting her to come up with something I hadn't thought of. "Explain, will ya?"

She shrugs, her hand brushing at her short black hair. "I don't know? The dummy found a YouTube on how to prepare a pufferfish." She notices my glare and nods. "Yes, there are plenty of those."

"Go on."

"So he follows the YouTube, he screws it up, he dies and then..."

I can see the wheels are turning behind her brown eyes so I start pacing again, but slowly this time.

"He wasn't alone," she continues. "He invited his friends

over, put his best suit on. Except no one will try it with him, so he does it alone and..."

"And his lips get numb," I offer. "Tingling. And then he starts to sweat and get dizzy."

"His friends freak out," Johnson says, "and... and..."

"...and they don't call 911?" I finish for her. I stop right in front of her, my hands shoved into my jean's pockets.

Her face pinches in disappointment.

I continue, "And then they drain his blood and haul him out to the desert and stage a chupacabra attack."

Her checks flush a bit despite her brown skin.

"That was a good train of thought, though," I say. "Good on ya. Let's keep at it."

I resume pacing and we resume spit-balling accidental death ideas. We come up with a ton, but the only thing concrete we decide on is to go back out to the scene in the morning. While I've got some faith in Johnson, Clemons and Taylor did nothing to impress me and they might have missed something.

The sun has set and I'm still in the parking lot. Johnson went inside an hour ago saying she wanted to check the missing persons reports again, said she was going to search social media for hints of our accidental death theories.

All of them crashed and burned, though. If he was alone, how did he end up in the desert chupacabrad? And if he wasn't alone, why didn't someone call 911?

We also spun theories of a loan shark force feeding him fugu because he didn't pay up and other colorful fantasies.

The fact is it was all in vain. We didn't have enough information to do anything else.

So I kept pacing. And when I got tired of pacing, I sat. And when I got tired of sitting, I paced.

"I'm calling it a day," Johnson says, striding out towards me. She's got on jeans and T-shirt for a band I've never heard of. She looks even younger than she did earlier. So young I'd card her at the bar I work at.

"It's been interesting," she says and holds out my keys.

I eye them like they are even more poisonous than the pufferfish. "Keep 'em."

Her smooth brow furrows. "How are you going to get home?"

I shrug. Such logic doesn't matter right now. My desire to drink is a need, and if I give myself any chance at all I'll be buying a bunch of beer and drinking until I pass out.

Johnson shakes her head. "Sanchez said you might do this. She said, and I quote, 'Tell the stupid dingo to grow up and take responsibility for his damn life.'"

Now it's my turn for my cheeks to flush red. Johnson looks a little surprised that she actually said it, and she put some energy into it too. I guess she's had just about enough of me today. But the shame quickly turns into anger. If all it took was a little willpower to not drink, there wouldn't be any drunks in this world. Why is that so hard for people to understand?

I stop my pacing and stand in front of her, my arms crossed, my jaw set. And yes, I'm acting a bit like a child. I don't care.

Johnson sighs and shakes her head, shoving my keys into her pocket. "Where do you live? I'll drive you home."

FIFTEEN

The car's air-conditioning is blasting and I've got the window rolled down letting in the hot air, the two swirling and mixing around me, parts of me hot and parts of me cold.

It's a strange sensation. I learned this trick from my uncle. He really loved the wind on his face but he didn't want to be too hot. And yes, it's a waste of energy and not at all the right thing to do, but I love it.

Like my father, my uncle is gone and this brings back pleasant memories. I need all the pleasant memories I can get.

"So what's your name?" I ask as she gets us on the I-10. Someone offering to drive you home in Phoenix is no small thing. The metro area is big, the city sprawled out over the desert floor, and it can take a long time to get from one end of town to the other. She's being kind and I feel bad that I don't know her first name.

"Eliza," she says, glancing at me as she drives, a puzzled look on her young face. She doesn't understand me. I don't blame her. I'm not sure I understand myself.

"I appreciate this," I say.

"Take an Uber next time, okay?"

She thinks I'm being difficult, unreasonable. She doesn't have the first clue as to what life can do to you.

I mean, that is a bold assumption. She's a woman of color trying to make her living as a cop. That young face has got to hide some interesting history. She's got to have a few scars by now. The kind that don't quite heal and change how you walk through this world.

"Why'd ya wanna be a cop?" I ask.

She flashes me a look, another pursed-mouth narrowed-eyed look, but this time it feels a little dangerous.

I should let it go, but I need a little danger. "I'd really like to know."

"Why?" she spits out.

I shrug. I can't tell her the reason. I can't say, "Because you telling me things you don't want to tell me would be a fine distraction for the state I'm in." So instead I say, "We're working together and all I know is your first name and you've got a good head on your shoulders."

That compliment does what it's intended to do, and her shoulders drop just a touch. "Why did you want to be a private detective?"

I chuckle, a dry little thing. "I got too old for the rodeo, you know," I say. "And I met a private detective by the name of Sal. He was look'n for a stolen horse. I helped him out. He took a shine to me. Taught me what he knew. Helped me get my license."

She nods and licks her lips. "My dad never saw a cop show he didn't like. They were always on when I was a kid." She flashes me a goofy smile, and I don't buy it. Well, I'm sure the sweet "Daddy loves cop shows" bit is true, but it's not enough. There's something else there. Probably something more about her father.

"So you wanna be one of the good cops, eh?" I ask.

"Yes," she says, her face getting serious. "I... I <u>am</u> a good cop."

"I know you are," I say with a smile. "So be a good cop, eh, and pull into that Circle-K. I need me some burritos."

The pursed-lipped, narrowed-eye look is back and I suppress a laugh, but she pulls off the road, drives past the gas pumps, parks in front of the convenience store, and just stares at me.

"You goin' in with me?" I ask.

She shakes her head.

"Then you'll be the one to explain to Sanchez why I bought beer instead of burritos and drank all night."

She's out of that car so quick that I can't help laughing. But the sad part is I really did need her to go in with me.

Why does a drunk drink? Well, that's like asking why the sun comes up every morning in the east. But on a normal day, not drinking is better than even odds for me. My willpower is often enough. Since Helen and Irene both give me a reason to fight, it's gotten a little better.

But today is a bad day. The bad day, really. It's the anniversary of Tommy's death. Twenty-five years since my foot slipped off the clutch and my Toyota leapt forward and I heard his scream and the crunch of the breaking bones.

Twenty-five years.

I have a tradition this time of year and that is being blind drunk from the day before to the day after today. But Sanchez called me, dragged me out to the desert despite my protests only to confront me with a corpse that looked way too much like Tommy.

So yeah, I needed to give Johnson my keys. I needed her to drive me home. And I very much needed her to chaperone me in the Circle-K, making sure I stayed away from the beer section with its lurid array of alcoholic temptations.

SIXTEEN

I own ten acres on the edge of the city, land the metropolis hasn't quite swallowed yet, although the city is getting close. Eliza Johnson drops me off in front of my old, dingy, single-wide trailer and her car kicks up gravel as she speeds away.

I don't blame her. She had to drive a lot farther than she expected, and this hasn't been an easy day for me and she took the brunt of it. On the bright side, I've got six microwave burritos instead of a case of beer, so that's something.

And I know there is no booze in the house, because I drank everything I had last night. And the closest place that sells liquor is a mile and a half away and my feet are pretty destroyed from all the pacing.

My headache is epic and I am starving, but this is a good outcome for today. The best I've had on Tommy's death day. I am actually sober. I've never been sober on his death day. I even crack a smile. I'm sure it looks twisted and scary, but it's looking like I'm going to get through the day without drinking.

Well, I was drinking until 2:00 a.m. this morning, but you get what I mean.

I look at the remains of my horse corral, the old wooden fence falling down and the weeds that have taken over the dirt that was once churned by the hooves of my horse.

Those were better days. I've had some good runs, times when the drinking hadn't taken over completely, but it has been a while. I can't afford to keep a horse and it wouldn't be fair to even try right now.

My ideal life would be to keep living in the crappy trailer, but have a nice barn and a healthy horse. To bring Irene out here and teach her how to ride. To be in a real relationship with Helen. To eat something better than microwave burritos, maybe even learn how to actually cook. To be able to have one or two beers and then stop.

With that thought, my stomach growls and I go to unlock the door to my trailer, but it's not locked.

"Shit, you dummy," I say under my breath. I must have been so out of it this morning, with Sanchez calling me until I woke up, dragging me out to the desert, that I must have forgot.

I walk in and see the chaos that is my living room. Food containers and wrappers on the floor. Crushed beer cans strewn about. An empty pint bottle of whiskey--I usually stay away from the hard stuff. A blanket on the couch. I had enough foresight to know I wouldn't make it to bed last night.

The unkempt chaos is so much that I don't notice the man sitting there. Not at first. He's so still.

My heart leaps when I see him. His bland greying hair, his protruding belly. It's Deputy Clemons, out of his uniform and dressed in poorly fitting jeans and a grey button-down shirt.

I swallow the fear and the surprise. A man doesn't break into your home unless he means you harm, but I'm not going to show my fear. "Wanna burrito, mate?" I ask, nodding towards the little kitchen on the far end of the trailer.

He smiles, showing teeth that are just a little bit crooked. It's not the predatorial shark-like smile of Trisha Sanchez, but something a lot more twisted. It's a contemptuous, arrogant smile. While Sanchez's smile says she's happy to make me pay for my mistakes, Clemons's smile says he knows he's better than me.

His arm is draped over my dull brown couch that is fraying at the seams. He lifts his hand and gestures with a small, black Smith & Wesson 9mm pistol. "Have a seat. Glad to hear you're hungry, but no thank you."

"All righty," I say, stepping in front of the dusty flat screen towards the kitchen. "But I'm famished, mate."

"No, no," he says, tisking at me like I'm a boy and I've been bad. He points the gun at my chest. "Drop the damn burritos and slowly take that big ole knife out and toss it that way."

Behind me, on the entertainment center, is the cookie tin that holds my father's ashes. It's squarish and tall and is red with an evergreen tree on it. Next to it is a picture of me dressed in my rodeo clown gear running like hell from a bull. My father took the picture. He had cancer at the time, but it was a good day for both of us.

These are the two things in this crappy trailer that I care about the most. What remains of my father, and the image he captured on a day when he was really proud of me. Me distracting that bull saved an injured cowboy's life.

I talk to the tin, like my father's still here. I don't use an Australian accent. I use my real voice. I want to tell him I haven't had a drink, that it's the anniversary of the accident and the sun has gone down with me sober.

But I just glance, to make sure both things are still there, and then I slowly remove the bowie knife and toss it towards the kitchen. It bounces on the dirty shag with a clunk-clunk.

"Have a seat," Clemons says. There's an old plastic chair right inside the door. A relic of the seventies, a faded orange.

I sit down and the adrenaline in my system gets my mind working, and before I think it through, I say, "You dragged that body out into the desert, didn't ya, mate? You're behind the chupacabra killin's."

He sneers, the gun still pointed at my chest. "So you're not as dumb as you look."

Now he's just insulting me for fun. I've solved a lot of cases and I may be a drunk, but I'm clearly not dumb.

"I had no idea, ya know," I say.

"You were getting there," he says. "Johnson has been keeping us in the loop. Told us you two were going to go back out to the scene first thing." He ended in a weak shrug.

So there was something out there. Something he had kept me from seeing, and he was used to detectives like Sanchez who were too busy to do things twice.

And then I felt my face flush as I realized that Johnson was in on it, part of it. She had been babysitting me all day. The shame was worse because I had taken an interest in her. For a moment I felt like my mentor Sal, like maybe I had found someone worth teaching.

I slump in the chair, my head banging against the wall. "So do it then, eh. I know you are here to kill me."

Clemons gives me that sick arrogant smile again and I want nothing more than to erase it with my fists. He nods at the coffee table, and on top of the trash and about six books I started reading but never finished is a small cellophane square. In it is something that looks pale and moist. "You said you were hungry."

The adrenaline must be really doing its job because I know what it is. "Fugu, eh?" I say.

"It's a delicacy, carefully prepared." He smirks, and since I'm sure I'm going to die, I do the odds of my fist breaking his jaw before I bleed out from the bullet wound when I lunge for him.

I'm not afraid to die. I used to run from raging bulls to make a few bucks. I've outlived my best friend by twenty-five years and it's been a long time since I felt I was worthy of my life. My cowboy boots are on. I'm sober. Why the hell not?

I mean, the odds aren't great, but at least I'll go down fighting.

"No way, mate," I say, hoping he'll relax just a bit and improve my odds. "I'm not eatin' no pufferfish, you'll just have to shoot me."

He nods. "Thought you'd say that. So I've got a little insurance." He unlocks his phone with his fingerprint and sets it down on the table.

He's distracted. This is my moment, but then I see the picture. It's a nice two-story house with a rock and cactus front yard, like you see in the desert a lot, and a prominent saguaro out front.

Irene's house.

"I swear to god," I growl, "you hurt her and I will tear ya limb from limb."

He's not threatened, his condescending smile only getting wider. "Taylor's there right now. You eat up or things get real bad for your little _niña_."

He says "niña" with such contempt that I want to ring his neck just for that. My head is spinning. Clemons is here and is going to make me eat bad fugu and die of asphyxiation. Taylor is in on it too and ready to harm Irene if I don't cooperate. Johnson was telling them everything I did today, making sure I didn't get too close.

How the hell did I end up at that crime scene with the three dirty cops that were behind it? Had Sanchez suspected them and that was the real reason she had left them with me? That didn't make any sense. She didn't want me dead. Maybe they just volunteered so they could cover up evidence.

"And just to sweeten the deal, <u>mate</u>," he says, pulling a pint of vodka from beside him on the couch and setting it on the table.

I hate vodka, but god do I want to guzzle the whole thing right now. There's a reason I almost never drink the hard stuff.

I shake my head and look back at Clemons. "That's just a picture of a house. Prove it." I'm just buying time. Thinking, trying to find a way out of it besides the suicidal lunge.

He leans over and flicks to the next picture, which shows Irene and her foster parents going in the front door. And the next one is a selfie of Taylor in front of the house, a stupid grin on his weak-chinned face. Clemons leans back. "Satisfied?"

I shake my head. "You coulda taken those last week."

He's not amused, the smile evaporating into a sneer. "Don't make me call him."

"Why don't ya."

His face reddens a touch. He must have an easier time with the other people he's bullied before. He levels his gun at my chest, snatches the phone, dials it, and puts it on speakerphone.

I have a knife in my boot, just a penknife, and I consider pulling it while he's distracted. But that won't work. He may not look like he's fast, but he knows how to use that gun.

"Taylor here," the voice from the phone says. A way too cheerful voice.

"How's the stakeout going?" Clemons asks.

"Such a nice family," Taylor says, still cheerful. "They're done with dinner and working on a jigsaw puzzle in the living room. Such an adorable little girl. It'd be a shame if something terrible happened to them."

My heart sinks. Irene had recently gotten into jigsaw

puzzles. I brought her one of Mount Rushmore the last time I saw her.

"Hey, Taylor," I say, trying to make my tone as cheerful as his.

"Hey! What's up, outback man?"

"You hurt one hair on that girl's head and I'll break every bone in your goddamn body. Got that, mate?"

Taylor chuckles, his tone not changing one bit. "Got it. Now eat your dinner and drink up like a good boy so I can go home."

Clemons smiles at me, and as much as I want to beat it off his face, there is nothing left for me to do. I won't risk Irene. I won't. Not for anything.

She was my client for the purple unicorn case, a nasty bit of business. I only spent a few days taking care of her, finding out who had killed her great uncle, almost getting killed myself, but I'd do anything for that girl. Including eating bad pufferfish and dying a horrible death.

Clemons tosses me the fugu and then the vodka. I slowly unwrap the sushi. It's warm and clammy to the touch. I hate sushi. Eating raw fish has never made any sense to me. A burger or a steak? Sure. But raw fish is just disgusting.

"Sure you can't just shoot me?" I ask, a piece of the pufferfish flesh delicately held between my fingers.

He shakes his head. "Bottom's up, Bright."

SEVENTEEN

I'M NOT A MAN THAT EVER THOUGHT MUCH ABOUT HIS legacy. I mean, not in the way that normal people do, wanting the world to remember you in a pleasant way. I obviously thought about it when I changed my name to Conner Bright legally. When I put my past behind me. That drunken mistake was not the legacy I wanted.

Since then, it's not something I've thought about at all. I've been too busy surviving and too busy drinking to wonder what the world will think of me. I might get as far as, "Well, he drank too much, and was a weirdo, but he cracked a few tough cases at least."

After I swallow the first piece of fugu whole, barely keeping the slimy thing down, I start to think about it.

I'm not interested in the "what the world thinks" kind of legacy anymore. I'm interested in a more personal legacy. I'm interested in being a better man for Irene and Helen. I'm interested in making their lives better.

And, yes, this is a moment of crystal-clear clarity brought on by my impending horrible death. I get that. But it keeps me thinking. It keeps me looking for an opportunity.

Like how I'm eating the fugu. I'm swallowing little pieces whole because I can't stand raw fish, but mostly because I want to slow down the digestion of the poison and give myself time.

I have no idea if that is real, if it will help, but I am hopeful. And hope is the most important thing to a man who knows he's about to die.

There is a bottle of water on the entertainment stand next to me and I wash the sushi down that way.

"Yummy?" Clemons asks, that smug smile on his face.

"Oh, you know, mate. I've never had better fugu than this."

He points his gun at the pint bottle of Vodka. It's the cheap stuff, the kind I would buy if I ever bought vodka. "Now drink up."

He wants my blood alcohol level up, which makes me wonder whether I'm going to get the full chupacabra treatment. It might be better for them if I'm found having eaten some tainted fugu and trying it because I'm a drunk idiot who is known as something of a thrill seeker.

I ignore the bottle and look at my surroundings. I see my trailer more clearly. It's a mess from my attempted bender with beer cans and food wrappers. But beyond that it's untidy and unorderly. My DVDs in a heap, my books strewn about, some open. My rodeo trophies scattered and dusty. And the room smells, a moist moldery smell of long-ago spilled beer and a carpet that hasn't been vacuumed in way too long.

My bed is unmade back in the bedroom, my clothes in three piles: clean, dirty, and dirtier. And I don't even want to talk about the bathroom.

The swamp cooler on top of the trailer is chugging along, keeping up with the spring heat, but it will be no match for summer.

"Another then, if it's so good," Clemons says, gesturing with his gun. "And wash it down with the vodka or I call Taylor."

Looking at my living circumstances with my impending death clarity, I don't mind that I don't have much, but I do mind that I haven't taken care of it properly. I haven't taken care of anything properly. Not where I live. Not my relationships. Not myself.

I've not done well these last few years, and I resolve that if I survive this, I am going to do better.

And since I'm so clear, I realize that I've faced death before. I've resolved to do better before. But I ended up back here. Will I do any better this time if I survive?

"Stop stalling," Clemons says.

I give in with a nod and grab the bottle and crack it open, a sigh escaping me despite myself when the strong tang of alcohol fills my nose. I delicately pick another strip of the flesh from the little bundle and put it in my mouth and wash it down with vodka.

I cough, but just a little. The hard stuff isn't my usual thing, but I'm a drunk. I'm something of a professional at this.

Now I actually like the fugu, the whole thing burning its way down my throat, warming my stomach, making me relax, just a bit, for the first time in a couple of days. I take another swig for good measure.

"Mind tellin' me your evil scheme before I die?" I ask, taking another swig from the bottle. I figure he is just arrogant enough to go for it, even though my odds are long on doing anything about it.

He shrugs lazily. "Sometimes people need people to die."

"Oh, I get that, mate. But why this? Why not just shoot 'em or somethin'?" I point to the remaining fugu sitting on my knee with a disgusted look. Who knows, maybe the stuff has a wonderfully delicate flavor, but I wouldn't know. I'm not chewing. It's the slimy texture I can't get over.

His forehead furrows and it's a reasonably good show given that he's middle aged and hasn't taken particularly good care of himself. "That was young Taylor's idea. Stir up superstitions and distract everyone."

"All righty, so the tetrodotoxin from the pufferfish is the venom," I say, mostly just trying to delay now. I'm trying to figure out how to hide some of the fugu and not eat it. "What about the fangs?"

He shrugs. "A couple of alligator fangs mounted on a wooden mouth. Easy peasy."

"So you have a pet Komodo dragon, too?" I ask, remembering the weird tracks.

Clemons shakes his head. "The kid has got an imagination, I'll tell you that much. He rigged up some shoes with fake claws and dragged a fake tale behind him." He gave a satisfied little chuckle. "Brilliant, really. Sure had you going."

I'm about to ask about the claw we found on the crime scene, and then to find out more about who their clients are, who would employee these bizarre hitmen, but I gasp and touch my lips. They are tingling like your hand does when you cut off blood flow and it goes to sleep. And I haven't had nearly enough to drink yet for that to be it.

Shit. I was hoping for more time. I was hoping to be able to do something.

I gently touch my lips and then my cheek.

"It won't be long now," Clemons says, his tone hushed, almost reverent. This is the part he likes, watching his victims die. It's clearly not just about the money for him. "Tell me how you are feeling, Conner."

I ignore him and suck down some more vodka and suddenly I

understand the victim with his hands covering his mouth, his eyes wide. The tetrodotoxin had paralyzed his diaphragm, he couldn't breathe, he clutched at his mouth with his last bit of energy, unable to gasp for the breath he needed, his eyes wide open in terror.

Clemons and Taylor had liked that part, thought it would add to the fun of it. Had waited for rigor mortis to set in before moving his body. Maybe even done something to keep those hands in place.

They were the ones leaking details to the media, further confusing everyone about these murders. Creative murder for fun and profit by Deputies Clemons and Taylor.

"And who was that guy out in the desert, eh?" I ask, ignoring his question. I'm not going to help him get off watching me die.

Clemons shrugs casually, as if I asked him who his plumber was and he hadn't bothered to remember anything about him. "Just a guy who owed way too much money to another guy. Now our client can claim if you don't pay up, his pet chupacabra will come and get you." He laughs, but not hard enough for him to take his eyes off me. His tone gets serious and he gestures with his gun. "Eat some more. Drink some more. Now."

I do as he says. Hope has faded and the darkness is descending on me. No, I'm not actually dying yet, I'm speaking about my emotions. There is no way out of this that doesn't put Irene at risk, and the poison is already getting to me, the tingling numbness spreading, my tongue starting to feel thick.

My death for Irene's life may be a trade I'm willing to make, but I just wish I had more time. To make things better. To leave a personal legacy. To see Irene again. To kiss Helen again. To be subject to more of Sanchez's gleeful torture and her predatorial smile. To talk to my father's ashes and watch *Crocodile Dundee* yet again.

But there is no time. My last conversation will be with a

sadistic serial killer. My last sight will be my slobbish trailer. And I will end this most terrible of days with vodka in my belly.

I wash the third piece down and slump over in my chair. I am defeated. I am dying. I am done.

And then I hear the sound of tires crunching on my driveway outside. I'm on ten acres--you don't hear a car unless it's coming here.

Clemons stands. "Who the hell is that?"

I reach into my boot and grab my knife, remaining slumped over, but shifting my weight forward a bit.

The tetrodotoxin is doing its work, I feel the tingling numbness in my finger and this rising panic. It's too late for me, I know that, but if I can get to Clemons, get his phone, text Taylor and tell him it's done before I die, then that is the right kind of death for me. One where my boots are on and the bad guy gets what's coming to him.

"What are you talkin' about, mate?" I say.

The sound is gone now but I here footsteps approaching. "Are you deaf? Someone is here." There is an edge to his voice. He didn't think anyone ever came to visit poor old Conner Bright out in the boondocks. And he's right, no one ever comes to visit me besides Helen, occasionally.

And then my heart is racing. What if it is Helen? Given my display today, the endless pacing, she sure has reason to check on me. Or maybe it's Sanchez come to make sure I'm not drinking myself into a stupor.

This changes everything. Whoever is walking up the steps to my place is in danger now. It's not just Irene. I have to do something.

The door is yanked open and I feel the hot desert air rushing in. I don't wait. I leap.

"I'm so stupid to come back..." a voice begins. It's a woman, a young woman. I'm not looking, but I know it is Eliza Johnson, she's the one that's come to check on me.

I can see Clemons, the gun is pointed at the door. He is braced to fire, his knees and elbows bent.

"...but Sanchez will kill me if you aren't sober in the morning," Johnson continues.

I leap with all the strength I have. The pent-up worry for Irene. The frustration at having nothing to do. The knowledge that I am dying. That anger at it all. I am an animal backed into a corner with nothing to lose and Clemons is my enemy.

The penknife is in my fist, but I don't have time to do anything with it. I don't even think about it. In an instant I am on Clemons and the gun fires.

I feel fire blossoming along my right side, bright pain, but it just fuels me. I smell the acrid smoke of the gun and the iron scent of blood, but none of that matters.

I crash into Clemons and he hits the wall of my trailer hard enough so the whole structure shakes. And then my fist finds his face and a sharp crack rings out as I break his jaw.

I hit him again for good measure, and because I am too much animal to do anything else. And then I hit him one more time for making me drink, and then I come back to myself.

Clemons is unconscious, draped awkwardly on my couch, his face bloody. It looks like I broke his nose too and I am glad. The penknife in my right hand made it much stronger. My knuckles are scraped and bleeding, but that is the least of my worries.

Johnson is in the doorway, her eyes wide as she takes in the scene. She kneels down, pulls a small pistol strapped to her ankle and draws on me.

"What the hell is going on here?" she yells.

I'm breathing hard, harder than I should be. I just can't seem to get enough oxygen and I'm suddenly sweating like I'm running a marathon or something.

"Clemons and Taylor are behind the chupacabra murders," I gasp, holding my hands up. "Clemons made me eat tainted fugu at gunpoint." I point to the slimy remains on the dingy carpet. "Taylor is at Irene's house threatening to hurt her if I didn't eat it. And..." I look down to my side to the fiery pain I felt. Blood is flowing freely. "Clemons shot me."

I sink to my knees. I just can't breathe right. "And... I'm dyin'."

My mind has gone sluggish now that the moment is all over and Clemons is down. Johnson came back, but she was telling them what we were doing all day. But that doesn't mean she was in on it, she was just treating them like we were all part of the same team. Something I should have been doing.

She holds the gun on me for a moment, her eyes darting around the trailer.

"Clemons's phone has pictures. Taylor at Irene's house. We need to text him. Call him off. We need to..." The room starts to spin and I feel lightheaded. "Please. Irene."

"Back up," Johnson says, her gun pointed at my chest. I lean on the coffee table and try to lever myself up, but I end up shoving some books off and slumping back down. I get a look at my side. I am losing quite a bit of blood and I'm further ruining my already terrible carpet.

Maybe I'll bleed out before the tetrodotoxin paralyzes my diaphragm. That might be a better way to go. But then I think of Helen and how she would call it hypovolemic shock and how I don't want her to see my dead body. How I don't want it to be on one of her stainless-steel tables.

But I shake that off and crawl away a few feet. "Please, Johnson. Please save Irene."

It occurs to me that she just met me today. She has no idea

who Irene is and I haven't exactly been the kind of guy you want to do favors for.

But Johnson grabs the phone and curses. It's locked. I slide back farther, facing her, watching her. She grabs Clemons's index finger and presses it to the fingerprint reader on the back of the phone. She flips through it with a practiced ease I could never manage. Her fingers fly and it looks like she is texting.

"Please," I say, finding it hard to find enough breath to speak. I've scooted my way to the wall of the living room and am slumped against it. "Irene is just a kid. She..."

Johnson is not paying attention to me, her fingers still flying.

She pulls out her own phone from her back pocket and jabs on it and holds it to her ear while watching the other phone. "Yes, this is Deputy Eliza Johnson of the Maricopa County Sheriff's Department. We've got deputies down, send two ambulances. There's been a shooting and a tetrodotoxin poisoning."

She continues, but I smile, she got the name of the damn poison right, but I know it's too late for me. I'm losing blood. I'm so dizzy. I can't really breathe. I can't focus.

And then she is on the phone again. "...he says her name is Irene. Do you know who that is?" She pauses. "Yes. I believe him. Taylor was there threatening her to force him to eat the puffer-fish. Yes, ma'am, I'll..."

Things are fading in and out and I can hear my heart beating in my head. It's loud, so very loud, and my face is so damn numb.

I focus on the old cookie tin containing my father's ashes. It is one of the more cheerful things in the room, looking vaguely Christmasy, even though it contains the carbon remains of the man that sired me and raised me. "I think we got it, Dad," I mutter.

And then Johnson is there with me and I can feel her pressing something to my side and it hurts. "Hold on," she says, and the emotion in her voice makes me come back to myself and

I focus on her young face and her big brown eyes. "I texted Taylor, bought us some time. Sanchez is going to take care of Taylor and the ambulance is coming. Just hold on, Conner."

I smile, or at least I try. I can't tell if it is working or not. "Not a damn chupacabra. Right?"

"Right," she says with a laugh that doesn't hide her worry.

My boots are on, Clemons is unconscious, and Irene is safe. This is the right way for a cowboy like me to die. I keep the smile on my face until I pass out.

EIGHTEEN

I wake up to eyes. One pair of blue eyes and three pairs of brown eyes.

I wake up to females. Three women and one girl.

I wake up to family, and that is the part that is most remarkable. That I'm alive, believe me, that is a surprise, but the people there are all people I care about and they clearly care about me, and that is the bigger surprise.

Helen's blue eyes, full of tears, are the first I see as my eyes flutter open.

Trisha Sanchez, her fierce brown eyes soft for once and her smile looking like one of joy--although I frankly find that hard to believe.

Eliza Johnson, her big brown eyes looking relieved but also something else. Maybe there is a new friendship in the making there. Maybe there is something this aging cowboy can teach this intelligent young woman.

And Irene, her brown eyes showing the kind of joy only a nine-year-old child can show.

Helen is holding my hand. Irene is trying to give me a hug

despite the fact that I am hooked up to beeping machines and have an IV in my arm. I am clearly in the hospital. Sanchez and Johnson are both smiling.

There are words to say, many things to discuss. There are things I need to do so that the next time I face death, I don't feel like I've made such a terrible mess of it all. But I let that all go. I just take a breath, which comes easily although my side hurts like hell. I take a moment and take it all in, looking at their beautiful smiles and their lovely eyes.

"Are you okay, Conner?" Helen asks, squeezing my hand and breaking the spell. I don't mind, it was just a moment and moments don't last very long. I can feel her hand just fine, no numbness at all.

"How?" I croak, my throat so sore, clearly I had been intubated. "No antidote."

"They intubated you and that kept you alive while the toxin cleared your system," Helen says. Her eyes are red-rimmed, she's been crying a lot and I feel terrible about it. "And then they took the bullet out of your side and repaired your large intestine. You are lucky to be alive, thank god you didn't eat more of the pufferfish."

I nod, getting lost in Helen's eyes for just a moment. Written there is worry and fear of losing me and I have no idea what I did to deserve that or to deserve her here by my side. But I am grateful and I resolve to do better.

I turn and look at Sanchez and narrow my eyes.

She nods, knowing what I want to ask. "Taylor lost his keys at the murder site. They had used the kid's truck to haul the body out. That's what they were worried you would find when you went back out there. He had a spare hidden on the truck, so they weren't stranded with their murder victim, but the Einstein has his initials on the keyring."

"Clemons?" I croak.

"He'll survive," she says, her predatorial grin back. "And then he'll go to prison. Arrogant bastard didn't hide his tracks very well. We've got his employers dead to rights. We've got the money. You did good, Bright."

Praise from Detective Trisha Sanchez, Helen by my side, my Irene safe and happy, and a new friend to boot. Now if only I had my cowboy boots on, I would be perfectly happy to die.

I smile and savor the moment.

MY STOMACH IS RIOTING AND HELEN IS HOLDING MY sweaty hand and I can hardly breath. We're in her Prius parked in front of a rather plain Lutheran Church on a Wednesday afternoon.

I'm not poisoned. I'm not facing down a killer. It's hard to breathe because what I am about to do is a whole lot harder.

"You got this, Conner," Helen says, a smile on her face.

I try to smile back, but it comes out all twisted and I'm surprised she doesn't scream and run away. But if Helen Montana was going to run away from me, she would have done that long ago.

It's been two weeks since my showdown with Clemons and I picked up a brand-new reason to hate sushi. It's been a week since I got out of the hospital, and Helen and I have been spending a lot of time together, and it's been sweet.

And miracle of miracles I haven't had a drink. Not one. There have been some moments, believe me, but I was able to get through them. Barely. But now... I know I need something more to do this long-term.

"You can do this, Conner," she says, her blue eyes wide. God, I could just get lost in those eyes.

I nod, but I don't believe it.

She leans in and kisses me softly. This isn't a passionate kiss, but it is an intimate one. Her full lips are soft and firm and I get a good nose full of her musky cinnamony scent. She is trying to fill me up with her belief in me, the thing that I so lack.

After twenty-five years of losing the battle with the bottle, I have good reason.

"You better go," she says when she pulls back, licking her lips.

I nod and take a deep breath of her scent hoping it will give me the courage I need to walk into that church. I open the door and unfold myself out of the small car and take a step toward the church.

Helen rolls down the window. "You got this," she says.

And then I realize I still have the bowie knife strapped to my right side. It's got an eleven-inch blade. Not good for a church.

"Right," I say to myself and pull it out and reach in and place it on the passenger-side floor. And then I take off my bush hat and take off the crocodile claw from around my neck.

Helen gives me a look, but I don't explain. I can't, not yet. But maybe one of these days I can tell her the truth.

I almost feel naked without those things, but this is how I need to be. At least I still have my cowboy boots on.

My hands shoved into my jean pockets, I walk into the church, turn right down a long hallway, and enter one of those plain general-purpose rooms every church has. This one has a pot of coffee brewing, cheap metal folding chairs pulled into a circle, and a collection of about sixteen people.

They are young and old. Male and female. Rich and poor. We are a rich cross section of this society, there is nothing that, by looking at us, would join us all together.

The meeting starts and everyone speaks their piece and I just get more and more nervous. When it is my turn, my throat is dryer than the desert and I'm sweating hard.

I'd rather ride a bull or run from one.

I'd almost rather eat more fugu.

I would most certainly rather be tortured by Detective Sanchez.

I clear my throat and try to find my voice. Not my B-movie quality Australian accent, my real voice. The one I've hardly used in the last twenty years.

"Hi, everyone. I... my... my name is... Evan. And I'm.... I'm an alcoholic. It's been two weeks since I've had a drink and a least ten years since I've been to a meeting."

"Hi, Evan," they all say.

PART 3
HAUNTED BY THE PAST

HAUNTED BY THE PAST

THE GUY LETTING ME INTO THE NOW DEFUNCT Metrocenter Mall in Phoenix, Arizona, looked me up and down. All six-foot-five and 170 pounds of me. It's not that I look like a scarecrow that makes people gawk, it's the unmistakable Crocodile Dundee outfit complete with alligator-skin boots, a wide-brimmed bush hat, a crocodile claw hanging from my neck, and an eleven-inch bowie knife on my belt.

I won't call it a costume because this is my everyday wardrobe. And I want people to gawk—it keeps them from remembering my history which was big news in Arizona twenty-five years ago. Alcohol. Teenage jealousy and rage. Death. That will get people talking for a good long time.

"G'day, mate," I said with as much energy as my sleep-deprived brain could manage, complete with my well-practiced B-movie-quality Australian accent. "My name is Conner Bright and I believe I am expected." I stuck out my hand but he just stared at that too.

This guy wasn't much to look at. Mid-fifties with a face that reminded me of a weasel, his short brown hair most of the way to grey. Faded jeans, and an oversized Clint Black concert T-shirt that wasn't big enough to hide his bulging belly, glasses, and a sloppy goatee. A forgettable face except for his oversized nose and prominent mole which was hard not to look at. His breath smelled like stale cigarettes and his eyes kept flicking around like he didn't know what to look at.

"I'm the private investigator," I offered, trying to get his brain in gear. It took five minutes of pounding to get him to answer the door and, frankly, the empty parking lot of this 1.4 million-square-foot mall on Christmas Eve was kinda freaking me out. Where were all the guys doing their last-minute shopping? Where were the teenagers gossiping? "Detective Tricia Sanchez sent me over. Hear you folks got a bit of an odd situation here."

His eyes widened and he gave a lazy nod looking kind of like a bobblehead that had been barely touched. I had no idea what the case was at this recently closed mall. Sanchez was still pissed at me and didn't tell me, but I wanted to get this over with.

I fingered the three-month AA recovery chip in my jeans pocket to settle my nerves. It was the reason I was so tired. I was either a drunk or an insomniac and on days like this I wondered which was better.

"We got ghosts," he said, his voice hushed like someone might hear us at the entrance to this abandoned husk that was once a monument to American consumerism.

I swallowed a string of swear words. Sanchez always gave me the weird cases and I could almost hear her gleeful cackle. Purple unicorns. Alien abductions. Chupacabra attacks. So far it had only been creative criminals, and I expected this one to be the same, but Jesus-H, couldn't I just get a nice "I think my husband is cheating on me" case? A nice boring stakeout where I could charge more per hour than I get working as a bouncer?

But this one was different. They had called the cops, talked to Sanchez, but they had asked for me by name.

"Then I'm your man," I said as cheerfully as I could manage. "Let's get started, eh?"

To a kid like me that grew up in the small town of Globe, Arizona, coming to Metrocenter was pretty much like going to Disneyland. There was so much to see and so much to do and so many other kids your age running around. Even if you didn't have more than a buck in your pocket it could be fun.

At twelve, I kissed a girl for the first time in front of the Orange Julius. Her name was Amy. She had curly red hair and wore overalls. I met her in B. Dalton and impressed her with my knowledge of Piers Anthony's Xanth books series. We giggled at some of the more adult items in Spencer's Gifts. And we kissed in the food court, her mouth all cold and orangey.

I had memories from Metrocenter, important memories, so when I saw the empty husk of it, our footfalls echoing loudly, you will understand that I felt a little freaked out, maybe even freaked out enough to believe it was haunted. There was just something wrong with it being so empty and so very quiet.

I looked around as I followed the odd man with the mole on his nose and felt my happy memories of this place eroding by what I saw. A manikin arm lying here, a head over there; the dark shadows of signs taken down above some of the barred shops; an antique chaise lounge under the expansive skylights that ran the length of the main concourses all by itself; a lonely pile of dirt where a potted plant must have stood; shopping carts all over the place full of odds and ends getting ready for auction; parts of cabinets just lying on the floor; turned over signs; and escalators that would never run again.

The magic was gone and my stomach tightened on the long walk under those skylights and then down some narrow hallways in the bowels of the structure into a cramped office with a metal cabinet, two beat-to-hell office chairs, a broad metal desk, and lots of LCD screens with black and white views of this empty place.

I never got the man's name who let me in, but the guy in the office was different. He had a big steel-grey mustache, a firm handshake, and a round face that squeezed his green eyes into slits when he smiled. He even had on a clean button-down shirt and looked like he shaved regularly.

"Glad you could make it, Mr. Bright," he said.

"Happy to help if I can," I said. My guide was already gone, scurrying away like some scared mouse. "But call me Conner, please."

"Conner it is," he said. "I'm Mitch, Mitch Jones, and I'm overseeing operations here." He paused and looked me over and chuckled, his eyes lingering on the bowie knife. "I will say that your reputation precedes you but... you are even more than I expected. And I mean that in a good way."

I didn't know how to take that. My Conner Bright persona was not meant to be impressive, just so overwhelming that my past stayed hidden. But I didn't want to explore it either. I wanted to get out of here. "I hear you've got a little ghost problem," I said.

His smile evaporated and he bit his lower lip. "That we do. There's a lot of work to be done here. Auction what we can. Get rid of what we can't. Keep the lookie-loos out. But I can't keep people." He paused, looking around. The door to the office was open but there was no one else back here. "At least not the kind of people you want to keep."

He was referring to my guide.

"These aren't ghosts, mate," I said. "I can assure you of that. Just someone tryin' to slow ya down, stop this process for some reason."

He blinked and looked away. He thought there were ghosts too. He sat down at the desk, tapped at the keyboard, and pointed at one of the screens. It was timestamped "DEC 21 02:02" and showed a long view of the mall from a camera on the ceiling. A man was running and looking behind him. "I didn't mean to hurt her," he yelled. "I didn't mean to. I swear. I swear!"

The footage was grainy black and white but clearly shot in low light with an infrared camera, the man glowing on the screen like some kind of ghost. His running was erratic and he kept looking behind him. He soon tripped over a sign and went sliding down the tiled floor and bumped into a column and didn't move.

Mitch paused the video and swung around to face me, his cheap office chair creaking as he leaned back. "This kind of thing happened to two other people and now I can't get anyone to stay the night."

"What was he hearing?" I asked.

"He told me he heard his dead mother," he said, rubbing at his mustache, "but he wouldn't tell me what she said."

"I'll need his name and address, then," I said. "And that of the other two that had themselves an 'experience.'"

He nodded but didn't move to write anything down. "So... you don't believe in ghosts," he said, his voice hushed again.

"No, sir," I said. "I do not."

"Then you won't mind being the security guard here tonight," he said, his green eyes locked with mine. "And maybe if you happen to have an 'experience,' *you* can get to the bottom of it."

I didn't bother to tell him it was Christmas Eve, that I had somewhere to be tomorrow and I really, really needed some sleep, and that without a stupid amount of beer I only sleep every third night and this was the night. I didn't tell him there was a reason I had made it past three months and earned that AA chip, and that her name was Irene and she was nine years old, and I had saved her from what appeared to be a rampaging purple unicorn, and that little girl's trust had turned my life around, and I wanted to be there for her on Christmas, sober and awake.

That was none of his business and the two hundred dollars in cash he offered right then and there, enough to keep my utilities going for another month and fill my gas tank and get Irene a nice present, was all I needed to take the job.

But I didn't want it. That mall felt haunted. And, sure, there was probably no literal ghosts, just some enterprising criminals, but a lot of us are haunted by our past. Some more than most. And this derelict mall was a literal part of my past.

It felt like the setup of some lighting-laden, B-horror movie where the protagonist enters the obviously dangerous cobweb-filled mansion on the hill on the flimsiest of pretexts.

But I was going to enter that "haunted" mall and my pretext didn't feel flimsy at all.

I only had a couple of hours before the night shift started, and instead of spending most of that time driving home and back, I went to the Walmart Supercenter just south of the mall, bought a cheap thermos, filled it with cheaper coffee, and found Irene a nice stuffed unicorn and a unicorn jigsaw puzzle. She's still unicorn crazed even after the madness we went through. I then drove back to the mall, parked in the middle of the empty parking lot, lay down on the bench seat of my vintage 1976 El Camino, and tried to sleep.

Tried being the operative word. I didn't sleep at all, just hoped for a quiet night so I could go be with Irene.

My boots clicked against the tiled floor of the empty Metrocenter Mall and the keys to the place jangled at my side. It was past midnight and officially Christmas and it felt like I had been at this for days already.

The moon was up, casting a ghostly light through the arched skylight that ran the length of all the main concourse. Each was two stories tall with the upper floor extending out a bit but leaving a wide airy pathway down the middle. There were bridges on the second floor here and there and dead escalators every fifty yards or so.

The mall opened in 1973 and it showed in the style of the place. The ceiling was gently arched and a lot of the surfaces were slightly rounded, most noticeably the cantilevered edges of the second floor.

My flashlight beat the darkness back some, but it seemed like not enough in the big space, every sound I made echoing in strange ways.

Mitch Jones had given me the tour at the beginning of my shift, showed me how to log my passes through the mall on the computer, given me a taser, and told me to call 911 if something happened.

When I asked him about that, he had said, "It's Christmas Eve, Conner. I'm going to be with my family." I decided then and there that I didn't like the guy. Did he assume I didn't have a family to spend time with or did he just not care?

He gave me a bottle of Jim Beam to sweeten the deal. It was the cheap stuff with a beat-to-shit red and green bow stuck to the top. I didn't bother to tell him I was an alcoholic in recovery. Hell, it had been a major accomplishment to admit that in a room full of alcoholics, and I hadn't built up to telling a stranger yet. After he left, I stowed the booze away in the metal cabinet in the cramped office so I wouldn't have to look at it all night.

This looked like a simple case to me. Maybe not easy, but simple. Someone was "haunting" the mall to slow operations down. An investigation would have two prongs, interview those that had an "experience"—one or more of them was likely involved—and follow the money, someone was benefiting from this delay.

But if being a security guard on Christmas Eve was what it took to audition for the work, so be it. This was a big case and could turn things around for me.

This was my fourth pass through, one an hour, and I had my route laid out and went the same way every time. My main job was to check all the doors and make sure they were still locked. Every door. That meant walking through the debris filled bowels of the big department stores as well as the little shops. Every single one of them that had an external door.

At its height, the mall had 175 shops, not all of them were on the ground floor with an external door, but plenty were. Most were chained and padlocked from the outside and were easier to check, but it was still a lot of doors.

My secondary job was to have an "experience," which was just a timid euphemism for being haunted. Which I wasn't worried about because I was already plenty haunted and going past the empty cavities that used to contain Spencer's Gifts and B. Dalton Booksellers, walking past the counter that was once Orange Julius, wondering whatever happened to Amy was haunting enough.

It was on that fourth pass that something happened. Well... I think something happened. I had just exited, and locked behind me, the cavernous remains of Dillard's, glad to leave behind the pile of manikin parts piled just inside the doorway when I noticed something different.

Dillard's sat at a right turn in the concourse where it went south and west. To the west I noticed a shopping cart on its side. This wasn't unusual at all—there were shopping carts all over the place, most filled with all kinds of junk. This one was on its side with a manikin torso hanging out that was wrapped in a grimy tinsel garland.

I remembered seeing it. There had been a Santa hat perched where the head should be and I thought it someone's bizarre nod to the season.

But it was turned over now and I was sure it wasn't before. I approached slowly, my footfalls echoing loudly and swept my flashlight across it. I stood quietly and listened. I saw nothing. I heard nothing.

I didn't touch it, but went back to the security office and found the right camera and wound the footage back at high speed. I saw myself walk backwards to it, a ghostly form to the infrared camera, staring at it, and then walking backwards and through the doors into Dillard's.

I had been in the department store for about five minutes, and about two minutes further back, the cart just turned over on its side. All by itself.

I leaned close to the monitor, the office chair creaking eerily, and used the arrow keys to back it up one frame at a time. I was no expert on grainy infrared video, but I could see no sign of anything touching that cart.

I checked the other security feeds. There were blind spots, plenty of them, but no one could get there without them showing up on a camera.

But I didn't find anything. Nothing at all.

I suddenly became very aware of the bottle of Jim Beam in the cabinet behind me.

IF I THOUGHT THIS ABANDONED MALL WAS CREEPY BEFORE, it was a hell of a lot more now. I didn't stare at the security feeds until it was time to go walk through again. I walked back and found that shopping cart. I searched all around it, first at a distance and then close, looking for something... anything to explain it. Obvious footprints in the dust, a bit of fishing line used to jerk it over from behind a pillar, something jury-rigged to knock it over.

It had been three days since I had a decent night's sleep—which for me is passing out for four hours—and I was a bit hyped up on coffee and creeped out by the vast space I found myself alone in, so maybe you will forgive me if I tell you that I did wonder whether it might have been a ghost... or something else out of the ordinary.

People believe in a lot of weird shit. AA relies on turning things over to a "higher power," and believe me that can get plenty weird, really quick. I don't go in for conspiracy theories and I'm not easily spooked, but I also firmly believe that I don't know everything, that we humans sure don't know everything.

Something happened here and I didn't know what. So I was determined to investigate it and not rule out anything. Not even ghosts.

THE SHOPPING CART TURNING OVER LIKE THAT, THE LACK of evidence, the impossibility of it was like a thorn under the saddle blanket of my psyche, causing it to get restless and try to buck me off.

And getting bucked off by your psyche to an alcoholic meant drinking. And drinking meant I couldn't see Irene—my agreement with her foster mother is that I am at least two days sober before coming over. The last drink I had had was at gunpoint on the Chupacabra case and I wanted it to be my very last drink. Something kinda romantic about that, right?

So when I got back to the security office and saw that bottle of Jim Beam with the worn ribbon sitting on the desk right where Mitch had left it bathed in the grey glow of all those monitors, my psyche started bucking harder and prickly sweat broke out all over my body.

I opened the metal cabinet and my new thermos was sitting right where the Jim Beam had been. I rubbed at my face and wished I was a whole lot better rested.

I'm not the kind of cowboy where you would put quotes around the word when describing me. My cowboy boots are earned. I grew up in rural Arizona and started riding not long after I could walk. I worked as a rodeo clown for a few years when I was flirting with more direct ways of getting myself killed than alcohol (mostly the protect the rider, bullfighter variety, not the entertaining, barrelman variety, to get technical). I even rode bulls in the rodeo for a bit but wasn't very good at it.

So I know what it feels like to be on a bucking animal that doesn't want you there, and I know what it feels like when your grip is slipping and you are about to be thrown off.

So I left that office and ran back out into the mall.

MAYBE IT WAS TOO MUCH CAFFEINE AND NOT ENOUGH sleep. That is the thin thread I held on to try not to get bucked off as I ran out into the mall. My mouth was dry and my heart was banging in my head faster than my boots were slapping against the tile as I ran down the concourse.

But I didn't go far. Part of me knew I wasn't right, that the bucking psyche was just one part of me, the fear coursing through my body had a logical explanation.

I came to a stop and stood there bent over, panting, sweating, realizing how thirsty I was. I swung the flashlight around and felt another wave coming. I was right where the B. Dalton was, not for a long time, the whole chain went down years ago, but it used to be here. You see, I left an important part out of that story, the adorable first kiss story.

I wasn't in the bookstore alone when I spotted the cute girl with curly red hair and overalls on. I was with my best friend Tommy Wilkins. He's the one that dared me to talk to her. He's the reason that first kiss happened in the first place.

And I killed Tommy. That was the big news that gripped Arizona that I mentioned: Alcohol. Teenage jealousy. Rage. Death. It was a few years after Amy and the mall and we were sixteen and out in the desert near Globe at a party. We were very drunk and fighting. About a different girl. I was trying to leave in my old Toyota pickup. He was in front of the truck banging on the hood screaming at me. I was revving the engine screaming back.

My foot slipped off the clutch and the truck lurched forward and I ran over Tommy. My best friend Tommy.

He didn't die right away, but he died. And part of me did too.

That part of my past came back to haunt me again in full force and my psyche started bucking. This time much harder. I had to get out. I had to get away. But I didn't move, the rational part of my mind trying to gain control.

But then I heard it. The revving of an engine. The sound of

someone slamming on the hood of a car. It was distant and echoed through the empty mall, or was it just echoing in my mind? I couldn't tell.

And then I heard a voice, a ghostly voice, distant and reedy, full of pain. "Evan..." it said, calling me by my given name. "Evan... you killed me. Why did you kill me?"

I ran. There was nothing else I could do.

⸻

I WOULD LIKE TO SAY THAT THE ACCIDENT IN THE DESERT explained everything that was wrong with me. Why I used to let angry Brahma bulls chase me while an audience roared and hoped they'd get to see a man gored. Why I sank so far into the bottle. Why I have trouble holding down normal jobs and staying in a relationship. Why I changed my name to Conner Bright and started wearing a crocodile claw around my neck and strapped an eleven-inch bowie knife to my belt.

Well... the last part is most certainly true, but it feels cowardly to blame it all on that slip of my foot. Alcoholism is a disease, right? And killing your best friend is going to mess you up, a lot, but isn't twenty-five years enough of blaming that for everything?

Tommy is the reason I have such a difficult relationship with sleep. I can sleep when I'm good and drunk or beyond exhausted, but rarely any time else.

Tommy wouldn't want me to be like this. We fought, yes, we were like brothers, but we loved each other too, just like brothers.

But that's not what filled my head as I ran as fast as I could down the concourse away from the long ago home of B. Dalton. The revving of the engine and taunting of Tommy's voice was all I could hear.

I wasn't even in a rational enough state to wonder if it was a ghost or not. I was officially haunted. I was running from my past.

I ran to the south, turned the corner to the east and was approaching the spot where that troublesome shopping cart was. I was vaguely aware of the fact, but I still heard the rev-rev of the engine. I still heard someone banging on the hood of the truck. I still heard Tommy saying, "Why did you kill me, Evan?"

And then I was flying through the air, it felt like something had grabbed my foot. Like a skeletal hand. Like Tommy back from the grave.

My flashlight was facing forward and I could see that I was flying towards that shopping cart but something had changed about it. The web of metal had been cut and bent up, sharp prongs pointing at me.

It was just a flash in my mind but my survival instincts took over. I have the aches and pains from my time as a real cowboy and a rodeo clown, but I still have a modicum of the reflexes too. I twisted in the air, my side crashing into the cart just past the bent prongs. The cart slid under my weight and the breath was knocked out of me as I rolled off the cart.

I hit the tile hard on the flat of my back and couldn't breathe at all. My head banged into the tile and blossomed in pain. I heard the cart sliding across the floor and crashing into the doors of the shuttered Dillard's.

I was pretty sure I had cracked a rib or two, that I might have a concussion, and I hurt everywhere. But I wasn't bleeding and I was very much awake.

I was also very, very angry.

I KEPT BEING A RODEO CLOWN LONGER THAN MADE SENSE.

Through broken bones and a torn rotator cuff and several concussions.

I used to stuff straw into my waist, neck, and wrists and the announcers would call me scarecrow. This is before the clown makeup costuming went out of style.

I did it because the only thing that felt better than getting so drunk that I couldn't think was surviving a close brush with death.

I did it until the private investigator thing just kind of fell into my lap.

On the cold tile floor of that big empty mall, I just breathed in the stale, dirty scent of the floor and didn't move. I pretended I had myself safe in a steel barrel at the rodeo and the bull was just a few feet away, its horns ready to ram into me if I left.

And while it's true I didn't think us humans knew even a tenth as much about the real world as we think we do, I knew this wasn't a ghost doing this.

"Odd thing is," Sanchez had said when she called, "they asked for you by name."

"I will say that your reputation precedes you but... you are even more than I expected," Mitch Jones had said when he met me.

Surviving had given me clarity and focus and had stopped my psyche from bucking. This case was a whole lot simpler than I thought. It was a setup.

"Evan..." the voice said, seemingly from all around me. "Are you okay, Evan? You're not bleeding, are you?"

If this was an inside job, there was nothing about the security feeds I could trust. If this was an inside job, then the goal of it was for me to end up bleeding and dead on top of that shopping cart after the whole haunted mall thing had been established.

The police would look at the security feeds, which would be

doctored so that cart never fell over by itself and had always been that way, and call it an accident.

"Evan... are you dead yet?"

There would be a few lurid stories that dragged up my past and highlighted my ignoble end, but that would be it.

That's why I didn't move. Because this was all about me. And I wasn't dead yet.

WHEN I WAS A RODEO CLOWN, I SPENT A LOT OF TIME WITH the athletes. We camped together, we followed the circuit together, we drank together.

This meant that I knew who had drunk too much the night before and had a good chance of underperforming. Or who had just lost their girl and wouldn't be focusing. I knew who was flush with cash and who barely had enough to eat. And I knew who had a fire burning in their hearts and something to prove.

I'm sure it will come as no surprise to you that there were bookies skulking about, laying odds and taking bets. I didn't make a lot of money betting on the rodeos I worked, but enough for it to count. Enough for me to be in the flow of it. Enough for me to know when something was off and people started losing more than they should have, people that really needed some cash.

At the height of my game as a rodeo clown / bullfighter, I worked the National Finals Rodeo in Las Vegas in December. NFR is considered the Super Bowl of rodeo and it was an honor to be there. The whole thing is Christmas themed with Santa hats abounding during the event even on some of the riders. I was only slightly irked that it had taken some injuries to pull me up to the big leagues.

This was Vegas, so the usual bookies weren't needed, but

when I saw one skulking around, when the odds-on favorite for the bronc riding lost out in the finals and I lost a ton of money, I knew something was up.

So I worked it. I got a couple of riders drunk. I got the info and confronted the bookie with a tape recorder going. I turned it over to the police and saw the guy arrested and handcuffed on Christmas Day.

He was this short little weaselly guy with shifty grey eyes and a sloppy goatee named Fred Arlington.

Yeah. Just like the guy who let me into the mall, but without the big nose and the gross mole.

And I had to hand it to him. He did the same thing I do with my Australian outfit. Distract people with something outrageous so they don't look too hard at what I don't want them to see.

"Oh, no, Evan," the voice from all around me said and now I could recognize it as Fred's. "You are still breathing. What a pity. I was hoping this was going to be easy."

Arlington went to jail but that was a long time ago. And with as much effort as he had put me into getting me here to try to kill me, there was no way that the shopping cart stunt was the only trick up his sleeve.

Fred Arlington was laughing at me. Not through the speakers which I now knew were hidden in the random shopping carts, but close. I could hear his footfalls, I could see the beam of his flashlight on the floor all around me.

"A fake nose and seventeen years and you don't even recognize your old buddy Fred," he said mildly and then his voice raised into a yell. "Do you?"

I slipped the taser out of my pocket and held it behind me as I slowly pushed myself up, letting a painful groan escape. The mall spun around me briefly and I had at least a couple of ribs broken and my left shoulder where I landed on the shopping cart was pretty numb.

"Sorry, mate," I said, shielding my eyes from the bright light and still using my accent. "Have we met?"

"Drop the act, Evan. It's unbecoming." He lowered the flashlight so it was shining between us and I could see him. The nose prosthetic with the fake mole was gone, but he still had the Clint Black concert T-shirt on stretched over his big belly, but now the T made a whole lot more sense. Clint Black had a concert that year associated with the rodeo. Fred had left me multiple clues and I had missed them in my sleep-deprived state.

"Waddaya want, Freddy?" I asked, keeping the accent, knowing that he hated being called Freddy.

He scratched at his chin and looked me up and down. "Been watching you," he said, his face pulling into a sour pout. "Hoping you were out there breaking the law and I could return the favor. But no. You're even working for the cops."

I didn't have patience for this. When the room stopped spinning, when he took another step and was close enough, I pulled the taser from behind my back and fired.

The prongs stuck in his Clint Black concert T and... nothing. He just pulled them out and laughed.

"Oh... you thought the taser worked," he said, his voice loud and echoing in the empty space. "That is so adorable." When he stopped laughing, he pulled a snub-nosed .45 revolver from his back pocket and pointed it at me. "But don't worry there, Evan. This gun works just fine."

As Fred marched me up the dead escalator at gunpoint, my survival clarity almost fled. I was limping and in a lot of pain. The room kept spinning around me. And Tommy's screams started echoing through my head without any help from Fred.

Since starting the whole PI thing, I had tried to help people. Tried to make up for that one moment all those years ago. Fred knew about the moment because I didn't change my name until after I caught him. By then I was tired of the looks and the whispers and no one was going to hire me if they remembered those months when Arizona's media was obsessed with the tragedy. So, after his arrest I changed my name and got my private investigator's license.

But thoughts of the past weren't helpful, so I focused on the pain. It hurt to breathe and my left shoulder wasn't numb anymore but alive with sharp, prickly pain. Bulls had done worse to me, much worse, and I had gotten up out of the manure-scented loam of the rodeo arena and either faced the bull or run for cover.

Except I was a lot older now.

But I also knew that Fred didn't really want to shoot me. That would mean a murder investigation. I may not be Detective Sanchez's favorite person, but we've been through enough that she would make sure the truth was uncovered.

That thought died as soon as I had it. This was an inside job. There were no witnesses to my interview. They could claim that I didn't get the job and was furious about it. That I came back drunk and crazed, pulled my bowie knife, and he had to shoot me in self-defense.

It would take altering security footage, which was already part of the plan, and getting some alcohol down me while I was alive, but it was doable.

The bottle of Jim Beam made a whole lot more sense now. They were hoping I would fall off the wagon and drink on my own.

I felt dizzy and stopped my slow limp about halfway up the escalator. "So what's your plan here, mate?" I asked.

I twisted around and tried to look at him. As I did, I reached into my back pocket and was glad to find that my cell phone hadn't been damaged in the fall. I didn't take it out, I found the volume up button and did a long press and the phone vibrated briefly. I had an app on it to map the buttons and do custom actions. My phone was now recording audio. At least this would give Sanchez a chance of finding the truth if he shot me.

Fred snorted. "You're going to jump," he said. "Suicide, plain and simple. I'm hoping it's a slow death, but I'll take fast too. It's your Christmas present to me to make up for the one you gave me all those years ago."

He was down the escalator a few stairs and was out of my reach.

"Sorry there, Freddy," I said. "I think I'd prefer a bullet, thank ya very much."

He just smiled and shook his head. "Maybe you didn't hear me before," he said. "I've been watching you. I know what you care about... or rather, *who* you care about. That blonde medical examiner—what's her name?—Helen. And that adorable little Mexican girl, Irene."

I just stared at him. I didn't say a word. I felt a rage brewing in me that would put an angry Brahma bull to shame.

"So you're sayin' that if I don't jump, you're gonna hurt them?" I said, trying to keep the anger out of my voice.

"After we get up there, I'm going to hide," he said, gesturing with his little gun. "And you're gonna run like a ghost is after you and then you're going to jump. You put on a nice show for the cameras or I'll put a bullet in their heads."

Fred was a stupid sociopath giving me a choice like that. He couldn't imagine how that would make me feel or maybe he just didn't care and trusted that gun and my need to protect Irene and Helen too much.

"How much does your buddy Mitch Jones know about this?" I asked, trying to sound casual.

He shrugged. "He doesn't want to know too much."

"You musta paid him a lot," I said.

He shook his head and grinned. "Nah. Remembered you telling stories about this place, how you used to love coming here as a kid. So I got a job. Saw that Mitch's been skimming proceeds. Got a nice bit of evidence against him and we had a little talk."

"You're a bastard, you know that, Fred Arlington," I said. All of this was just for the recording, just for evidence.

"Takes one to know one, Evan," he said.

"Don't call me that," I hissed, letting some of the anger steam out. "My name is Conner Bright."

When he shook his head and rolled his eyes, getting ready to lecture me on my past, I moved.

My body hurts from my rodeo days, every day, but it remembers. I used to dodge angry 2,000-pound bulls and I learned a few things. The kind of things you can only learn by facing serious threat to limb and life over and over. I learned when it was time to move. I learned how to ignore my pain. And I learned how to entertain while I was at it.

I let my feet slip from under me and landed heavily on the escalator step using my right hand to cushion the fall just a bit. I let out a sharp cry of pain that was not faked in the least, and slid down a step.

Fred was laughing at me, but he was within reach now. I kicked him in the chest. Hard. With my alligator-skin boot. He went flying and tumbled down the escalator. When he got to the bottom, he didn't move.

Detective Trisha Sanchez was not at all happy about me waking her up early on Christmas morning or having to come out to the dead Metrocenter Mall, but it was a big collar and she was ambitious, so she did it.

I'd call it a wash in terms of our relationship, but getting Sanchez involved got me out of there quicker than I would have otherwise. She took my statement. Listened to the recording on my phone. Watched the security footage of the confrontation. Had the paramedics check me out. And let me go after a loudly protesting Fred Arlington was hauled away with a broken arm and a pretty bad concussion. He deserved more.

I drove home and got to see the sun rise over the desert, yellow and orange driving back the indigo of night. It felt symbolic somehow, like this night looking at my past had changed something for the better.

I took a shower. Taped my ribs up. Ate some food. And made it to Irene's house in time for the unwrapping of presents.

Irene was dressed in purple pajamas with a unicorn print—of course—and hit me like a freight train the moment I got in the door.

It hurt like hell, broken ribs and all, but she smelled clean and soapy and I had a big smile on my face as I held her tight.

"You made it, Conner!" she said.

"For you, my Irene girl," I said. "I would do anythin'."

Her foster mother was standing in the neat, festively decorated living room in a blue robe, her black hair pulled back into a ponytail, and her round face looking tired. I could hear the other kids shouting farther in the house. Her arms were crossed and she was staring at me.

I freed one arm from Irene, pulled the three-month chip from my pocket, and tossed it to her.

She caught it deftly, her eyebrows raising when she saw what it was. This was a good place for Irene. One of the ways I knew that was all the strict rules her foster mother had placed around my visits. The girl needed me, but she needed me sober.

"For Irene," I said quietly as I still hugged the girl.

She nodded and said, "Merry Christmas, Conner."

And it was. The best Christmas I had had in years. Lack of sleep, bruises, broken ribs, and all.

And when I went home, I slept. Really slept. It seems that night in the empty mall facing my past had helped.

PART 4
THE DEVIL YOU KNOW

ONE

People don't get it.

A drink offered casually can be like pointing a gun at an alcoholic. It's that dangerous.

But, then again, probably best that most people don't get that. I wouldn't want the people I care about to have to feel like life is such a minefield, such a dangerous place, where something as socially acceptable as imbibing an alcoholic drink can take your life straight to hell.

But at least the woman casually offering me liquid danger was something to look at... and happened to be dressed like the devil herself.

I'm six-five, and I was a good eight inches taller than her, even with her heels, but there was a presence to her. She had long blond hair, green eyes, looking like she was in her mid-twenties, with curves in all the right places and at the right proportions.

She had a smattering of freckles across her cheeks and her captivating eyes were decorated with substantial eyebrows, we are talking Brooke Shields level eyebrows, not the delicate things that would usually go with someone as beautiful as she was. All that unusual contrast did, though, was make her more intriguing.

Her form-fitting dress, which left just enough to the imagination, was a deep red, maroon even, and perfectly matched the color of her lipstick. Two horns of the same color peaked out of her blond hair. The accent to her perfectly applied makeup was glittering gold eye shadow.

"Can I get you a drink, Mr. Bright?" she asked as she looked me up and down, a smile on her red lips that was more than a little flirtatious.

I flashed her my best smile, first impressions and all, and said, "My ol' man once told me that if the devil herself offered me a drink that I should do two things," I said with my B-movie quality Australian accent that always seemed to go over just fine in the deserts of Arizona.

I'm not sure if my accent was that accurate, but I had been using it so long that I didn't have to think about it anymore. The accent and my Crocodile Dundee outfit were my very loud shield design to drown out my grim past.

"And what was that, Mr. Bright?" the devil herself asked with a smile on her red lips.

"First, that I should accept it with a smile on my face and drink it as fast as I could, because you should never turn your back on hospitality when offered. And second, that after I finished the drink, I should run as fast as I could for as long as I could."

She laughed and it was a sound to behold. It wasn't a carefully crafted laugh but a real belly laugh, the kind that only a person that is comfortable in their own skin can let loose, and it went perfectly with those eyebrows.

And while I was the one trying to make a good first impression on her, she was making quite the first impression on me.

"Good advice," she said, her smile a thousand-watts bright. "So, what can I get you, Mr. Bright?"

"Club soda, please," I said. "And call me Conner."

I guess I can't blame her for offering me a drink. We were in a little bar in Tempe, one that is, undoubtedly, filled with college students at night. It's long and narrow with high ceilings, exposed ductwork, and red brick showing on the exterior wall.

The place is full of Sun Devils merchandise and memorabilia. The Sun Devils are the football team for Arizona State University, better known around here as ASU. The place was also done up in the Sun Devils colors, maroon and gold.

All of this befit a bar called "The Devil You Know" and explained her devilish outfit.

And, of course, the place smelled like a bar, all sour and stale, a smell so common to me I suspect that's what I smelled like after so many years of exposure. It was like smelling my own stink and I didn't like it.

She waved me into the bar. It was early—too goddamn early to be awake if you ask me—and she had just unlocked the door for me. I took my Australian bush hat off as I walked in.

The blond somehow managed to ambulate on her impossibly tall and, I suspect, impossibly expensive heels behind the bar and made me a tall club soda with a twist of lime.

I am one hundred percent against women wearing such torture devices, but in this case I can't say that I minded the view. At all. And I am as sure as I can be that that was the point.

As she walked, her maroon tail, which completed the ensemble, moved rhythmically and drew attention to her lovely hips.

It was a show, to be sure, but who the hell dresses up like this at 9:00 a.m.?

"Are you Ann McGee?" I asked as I walked up to the long bar which was made of dark wood and lined the exposed brick wall, my alligator skin boots sounding loud in the empty space.

My ambulation was not nearly as smooth or as graceful as hers. I used to be a rodeo clown when I was younger and that kind of life leaves a mark. Many marks, actually. My demons were louder then and I would rather have faced a raging bull than my past. Let me tell you, a ton of furious Brahman bull charging at you will make you forget your past... for a little while, at least.

"I am she," she said. "Please excuse the costume. I am trying to figure out whether I can live with it or not." She twirled behind the bar and added, "What do you think? If female bartenders and waitresses are dressed this way, will it help bring in the customers?"

"They'll be linin' up around the block, love," I said, regretting the last word.

Her smile brightened so much that she was, honestly, hard to look at. She wasn't girl-next-door beautiful, she was girl starring in a big budget rom-com beautiful. Her smile was a little more flirtation than I, or the hour, deserved. But, again, I can't say I minded it and that's what worried me about this whole thing.

I cleared my throat, trying to get my hormones under control and said, "Detective Sanchez, she said you had some kinda strange problem I might be able to help ya out with."

The fact was that she had said little more than that. Detective Trisha Sanchez of the Maricopa County Sheriff's Major Crimes Division was dead set on torturing me with the most bizarre cases until she felt like I had paid for the mistake I made back when she would still hire me for normal work here and there.

As to when I will have paid back for being drunk and screwing that stakeout up, flushing months of work down the toilet, has become quite clear. Never. Or the day I die. Whichever comes first.

You might say that now that I am a private investigator

instead of a rodeo clown, that Detective Sanchez is the Brahman that charges me and brings me into the moment.

Ms. McGee poured herself a shot of whiskey, top shelf, the sharp, glorious smell of it making me want to dive into a pool of it and never come back.

As she held the shot glass full of amber temptation, I really looked at her face. She had delicate crow's feet fanning out from those green eyes and her makeup made her look younger than she was. She was really mid-thirties, maybe a little older, and she wasn't sleeping well.

I took a sip of the club soda to distract myself while she shot the whiskey back with practiced ease.

"Ghosts," she said. "I think this place is haunted, Mr. Bright. Detective Sanchez assures me that you can help."

TWO

I won't say there are no such thing as ghosts.

The world is a strange place and anyone who thinks they have it all figured out is either full of it, very badly deluded, or both.

What I will say is that I've never seen convincing evidence of ghosts and most of the time it's just simple misattribution. Your brain is designed to produce answers, because we feel better when we have answers, even if it's the wrong damn one.

So I was standing in a bar, The Devil You Know, in Tempe Arizona at the ungodly hour of 9:00 a.m., having gone to bed at 3:00 a.m. after my shift as a bouncer at the country and western bar I worked at. My stomach was full of coffee that had turned heavy and bitter and nothing else, and the last time I took on a haunting case I almost died.

Sure, Ann McGee was gorgeous and flirty, and her red dress that matched her expertly applied lipstick was absolutely drool worthy, but it was just not worth it.

"Sorry, Ms. McGee," I say with my best smile and a nod. "I

don't do hauntin's. I'm just a PI from Scatterwood, Australia. Ghosts are not my area of expertise."

I turned around before the frown could fully form on her lovely face and walked back towards the door.

"Please, Mr. Bright," Ann said, her voice thick enough to stop me in my tracks, but I didn't turn around. "This place is all I have. My father left it to me. I've..." She took a deep breath and let out a long sigh. "I've put everything I have into this bar and I'm going to lose it if I don't figure this out. Please, Mr. Bright. I need your help. I have nowhere else to turn."

This was a scene ripped right out of a Mickey Spillane novel. A beautiful damsel in distress and only I can help her. To top it off, I had lost my father early and I had empathy for someone wanting to preserve their father's legacy.

I would have kept going except for this. My father's ashes were in a cookie tin next to my well-watched DVD of *Crocodile Dundee* and I talked to him every day. My father was a good man and lung cancer took him too damn early. I miss him every day.

I reached into my pocket and fingered my six-month Alcoholics Anonymous chip. I was sober and dedicated to staying sober, making this a very, very bad idea.

"Please," she said, her voice raw with emotion. "At least let me tell you about what's happening."

I needed to leave. I should have left. I knew this wasn't going to be good for me, but in spite of all of that I said, "I'll listen to ya, but not here. Anyone make decent eggs close by?"

THREE

As much as I hate the stale smell of beer and sourer smells that permeate a bar is as much as I like the smell of frying bacon.

I know bacon isn't that good for you, but there is something about the smell of it, something that almost wakes me up as much as coffee and makes my stomach grumble in happy anticipation.

When I asked Ann McGee about a place that had decent eggs, I meant a restaurant, but we were in her one-bedroom apartment on 5th Street a couple of blocks away from her bar and she was in the kitchen frying up bacon while I sipped coffee and wondered how the day had gone so sideways so early.

I shouldn't be here.

I shouldn't take this case.

Sure, Detective Sanchez would give me hell, add more to the debt I owed her, but the warning signs were abundant and unmistakable, but I couldn't turn away. There was just something about her.

And no, I'm not talking about her little red dress and high, high heels.

I was in her living room sitting on a sleek, modern, and not very comfortable couch looking at an ASU Sun Devils jersey framed on the white wall opposite me. The back said McGee and had the number 21.

Despite my cover story, I am an Arizona native. I know that for the Sun Devils, number 21 belonged to Jack McGee and was retired with him. He was a star quarterback for the Sun Devils a few decades ago, led them during one of their best seasons, had the NFL drooling over him, before he was sacked and, literally, broke his back.

But Jack McGee was not to be stopped. He beat the odds, learned to walk again, became an announcer for the Sun Devils, and opened a Sun Devil themed bar. The one I had just been in but hadn't been quite awake enough to realize. Ann McGee was Jack McGee's daughter.

"Sunny side up or scrambled," Ann called from the kitchen.

"I'm easy," I said, immediately regretting my choice of words again, my cheeks flushing red. To cover, I added, "Whatever you like, is fine with me."

How long had it been since someone last cooked for me?

How long since I had been in a beautiful woman's apartment?

I really should leave, but I knew the rest of Jack McGee's story, or at least as much as anyone knows.

He was shot to death in the alley behind his bar about eight years ago, his murderer never found.

With the cancer, I got to say goodbye to my dad. Ann McGee had woken up one day to news that her father, someone beloved in this town, was dead. There was no saying goodbye. So I sat there, sipped my coffee, and didn't do what I knew I should.

My former girlfriend, a wonderful woman named Helen Montana that works as a coroner for Maricopa County, likes to drink. Like most people. And I have no problem with that. If you can manage the addictive substance that is alcohol, more power to you.

I can't.

I am sober and working hard to stay sober.

There's a little girl named Irene that I met on the purple unicorn case—I told you, Sanchez is always giving me the weirdest cases—and I stay sober for her.

Let me take that back. I'm far enough into the program now to know that I have to do it for myself. And the reward is if I'm sober, if I stay sober, Irene's foster mother lets me spend time with the girl.

Irene is a bright, beautiful kid who lost everything. It does my withered old heart good to see her smile.

Back to Helen and alcohol. I'm too early in the program to be with someone that drinks. And I'm far too early in the program to be with someone that owns a bar. And if you ask anyone in AA, I'm far too early in the program to be with anyone at all.

I know, I know. Ann McGee was being flirty with me because she was probably a little flirty with everyone that walks into that bar. I work in a bar. I know how this goes. It's just part of the business.

But tell that to my hormones that are all ginned up by loneliness and being decidedly single and extra loud because I'm extra sober. It's one of those weird quirks of being human. You can be lying to yourself, know full well that you are lying to yourself, and still believe it. It really is a wonder we have survived this long as a race.

"Those are some grade-A eggs. Thanks," I said with a

grateful nod. We were in the living room and hadn't talked much while we ate scrambled eggs, bacon, and liberally buttered toast.

It wasn't exactly a gourmet meal, but being cooked for was a treat.

Ann smiled shyly, which was surprising, and nodded. When we arrived she had shucked her heels, took her horns off, and put on a green silk robe over that slinky red dress, although it did little to blunt her beauty.

She opened her mouth to speak but I jumped in before she did and said, "Before we start, let me state that whatever is happenin' to you, whatever strange things are happenin' at your bar, it's not ghosts and this is not my kinda of case. My suggestion is to follow the money. Look at who would gain the most if your bar were to close."

As I spoke, the shy smile faded and her face hardened into what looked to me like the face of a business woman that had seen some hard times and was stopping her anger from getting the best of her.

My mouth was still moving even though I told it to stop, that this was the wrong direction, that I should be kinder to my host. "I heard of your father, there," I said, nodding up at the framed jersey. "He seemed like he was aces. Let me say that I am sorry for your loss."

Her face softened briefly when I spoke of her father but as she took a deep breath, her face hardened again. "Are you done?" she asked.

I nodded and felt my cheeks flush hot.

She sighed. "Believe me, Mr. Bright, I am aware that ghosts are a stretch here, but I have followed the money. My landlord loves having me there. Downtown Tempe has a plethora of bars, mine being there or not makes little difference to any of the other bars. I pay my bills. I keep my licenses in order. I pay my employees as much as I can.

"I am no damsel in distress in need of a man to rescue me. I am merely a business woman at her wits end asking for help."

"Apologies," I said. "If you can indulge me for a moment, I'd like to explain my sadly ungraceful reaction."

She gave me a small nod, her face still hard.

"Last winter," I said, "I worked a case at the old Metrocenter Mall. The place was, reportedly, haunted, but of course it wasn't. It was an enemy from my past that set a trap for me. I was supposed to die that night. This is why I'm just a bit off my game. Please forgive me, Ms. McGee. I would like to hear what is happening to you and then we can both decide if I can be of any use in this case."

FOUR

Follow the money is good advice when trying to understand why things are happening. So is "follow the power" and "follow the grudge."

My lines of work, both of them, have left me cynical. I'm an alcoholic in recovery that works as a bouncer in a bar and as a private investigator. I spend most of my waking hours seeing folks who are not at their best.

I spent the next hour talking to Ann McGee in the living room of her apartment trying to follow the money, power, and/or grudges and came up with nothing.

Zip and doodah. Zilch. Nada.

I reached for my coffee mug—Ann had kept it nicely filled— but hesitated. The jitters had arrived and more caffeine was not going to help. My tongue had the bitter taste of coffee and just wanted more. The space still smelled like it, making me want it even more.

Caffeine is not alcohol, but it is an addictive substance and I needed to be careful with it.

"Tell me about the hauntin' again," I said, easing back on the not-so-comfortable couch.

She shrugged and let out a weary sigh. "Started last month. Things kept moving. The jug of orange juice wasn't where I just left it. I would be in the office and the folder I had just got out would be back in the cabinet." She rubbed at her face like that would do something to drive back the fatigue she obviously felt. "Figured it was just me. Just too tired. But then the voice started."

In truth, I was pretty sure the first part of this was just her. Overwork can easily make things like that happen. "When did the voice start?" I asked. She had been through all of this but I wanted to hear it again, see if anything in her story changed.

"Three weeks ago on a Saturday night," she said. "And it's not me. I haven't heard it. It's customers. Sometimes they are in the bathroom, sometimes they are in the bar, but they all hear the same thing."

"And what is that?" I asked.

She sighed again and shook her head like she had trouble believing it. "The voice says, 'I am the devil you know and you will die tonight.'"

"And you haven't heard it?" I asked. This was an important question and worth asking again.

"No," she said, her voice a little too loud. "And I know what you are thinking. That no one heard it and someone put them up to it. But the first guy to tell me this, Vince Rogers, died that night. Not even two hours later."

"In front of the bar," I said, prompting her to continue.

She nodded and said, "A car hit him." She swallowed hard. "I saw it happen."

I wasn't about to tell her that someone paying Vince Rogers to tell Ann McGee he heard voices was not mutually exclusive with his death being an accident—or not an accident. Ann, it seemed, had tumbled into superstition, and in my experience it takes a lot more than someone telling you that you are being superstitious to pull you out. In fact, that usually just entrenches them further.

Belief is a tricky thing, a sharp two-edged sword. Belief can help you get up every morning and face your day and it can just as easily destroy you or turn you into a monster.

Ann sniffed and pursed her red lips. "I wasn't the only one he told he heard the voice. I wasn't the only one that saw him die. Word has spread and my bar is a ghost town most nights."

This was a difficult position, to be sure, and explained the devil costume she was modeling when I arrived. I wasn't sure what I could do. What if I was able to prove that the "haunting" had a perfectly mundane explanation—would that even help?

"To summarize," I said. "Five people have told you they heard this. Vince Rogers, Stephanie Fry, a friend of yours, and three other people you don't know the names of and haven't seen since."

"That's about it," she said. "Can you help, Mr. Bright?"

"It's Conner, Ms. McGee," I said, glancing up at the jersey of her tragically killed father.

The details of this "haunting" and my ideas of what might really be happening were roiling around my mind now, the mystery begging me to solve it, but I knew I should walk away.

"Conner," she said, and I liked the way my name sounded. "Can you help me?"

Maybe it was a beautiful woman asking for my help. Maybe it was the shared loss of a father. Maybe it was a bit of boredom and a need to live on the edge—I used to be a rodeo clown after all. Whatever it was, I found myself speaking before I could really think it through and said, "I can try."

FIVE

A MYSTERY IS NOTHING MORE THAN AN ASSEMBLAGE OF facts and guesses that don't make sense. There is, to put it another way, no clear cause and effect.

The effect here was a terrifying voice only a few people heard scaring customers off from one of downtown Tempe's many bars. And, perhaps, contributing to someone's death.

The cause? That was my first piece to investigate. The first thing I needed was Ann to believe that what was happening to her was something other than ghosts. It didn't matter too much if I was right, I just needed a workable theory that made sense.

My problem with this particular investigation is that I'm, more or less, a cowboy. I grew up in Globe, Arizona riding horses. I rode bulls before I ran away from them as a rodeo clown. I know how to use a computer and a smartphone, but it's just not my expertise.

But I got a guy.

Well, she's a woman, but saying "but I got a woman" just doesn't feel right.

It was about 10:30 and I was cruising north on the 101 in my mint 1976 El Camino, you know that cross between a car and a pickup truck created by Chevrolet in the sixties and seventies.

The car was my father's, he restored it originally, with some of my help. He loved this car so much and I have inherited that love. It may not have air-conditioning, which is nuts given where I live, but February temperatures in the Valley of the Sun are livable. I had the windows down, breathing deeply of the exhaust filled air cruising along with the thick traffic heading north.

No fancy tech in this car. Just a steering wheel, a gas pedal, and a brake pedal. All that is needed and nothing more.

I was trying to let the road, the hum of the tires, and the wind take away the caffeine jitters and let me focus a bit.

There were multiple possibilities I had to hold in my mind at once:

One: Ann McGee had clever people trying to drive her out of business using some rather unusual techniques.

Two: This had nothing to do with Ann McGee. Vince Rogers, who died in front of The Devil You Know, may have been the target all along.

Three: There are no strange voices at all. Ann is lying to me for reasons I can't fathom.

Four: Something entirely different is going on.

This is the problem with my line of work. The necessary and inevitable cynicism is caustic, and while it can protect you, it can isolate you and make you see things that are not there.

This wasn't me keeping an "open mind." This was about ten exits down the proverbial highway after that. I had no idea what was going on here and it was important that it stayed that way. I needed to be open to anything so I could, hopefully, see what was really going on.

My attraction to my client was the X factor here. Just

because I was aware of it, didn't mean it wasn't affecting my behavior.

I exited the 101 and took Grand Avenue west into the heart of Sun City. For those of you not familiar, Sun City was built as the first active retirement community in the United States.

That's right. Not only is my tech expert a woman, but she is collecting social security and likes to play golf.

SIX

Emma Shapiro is a wiry and fit seventy with a deep tan, short grey hair, and eyes so blue it was not surprising at all that she was married four times and now that she was single had many suitors.

She was not dressed in the cliched tracksuit, but wore deep green pedal pushers and a light grey sweater. We were in her backyard as she kneeled and tended to a robust tomato plant in a raised bed.

No pool for Emma, she was an avid gardener and thought that the endless pools around here were "a goddamn waste."

Emma also used to be the chief technology officer of a software development company. She was there when personal computers first appeared and rode the wave her entire career.

I had called ahead and let myself into the backyard as instructed.

"If it isn't my hero, Conner Bright," she said with a smile that I'm sure contributed to the depth of her dating pool. She didn't pretend to be young, she had let her hair go grey and she had plenty of wrinkles, but the light within her could not be diminished by something as common and everyday as age.

The "my hero" bit was because of a problem with a particularly insistent suitor she had a few years ago, back when I caught a lot of "normal" cases. And because she knew it embarrassed me.

"G'day, Emma," I said, tipping my hat to her. While Emma was well tanned, her complexion was a little sallow, which caused me some concern.

"Get to weeding," she said, pointing at a knee pad next to her and cutting off that train of thought.

I do not have a green thumb. I do not like to weed. But when in Emma's domain one does what Emma wants. Especially when you need something from her. I think she had been a leader for so long that she didn't know how else to be in the world.

I carefully kneeled, my knees cracking loudly, and started weeding. It was winter in the Valley of the Sun, in the low seventies and the smell of the loamy earth was, to my surprise, quite relaxing.

I found myself no longer in a hurry, like the fertile earth here had absorbed some of my impatience, had slowed me down and put things in perspective.

Emma's garden was neat and orderly, not one weed was allowed. I didn't know her well enough to know if the rest of her life was that way but there was something appealing about it.

"So, what's this tech mystery you need help with?" she asked after about five minutes of weeding. We were done with the tomatoes and down the raised bed a bit working on some bell peppers.

I smiled because I realized that Emma knew me. She knew that I'd be in a hurry, want my information quick, and be on my way, but she had engineered this time outside, this weeding to mellow me out.

"Right," I said. "Is there a way to create—and excuse me, but I don't know the right word for it—localized sound?"

"Localized?" she asked, her busy hands stopping their task as her mind engaged. "That can mean different things."

"Gotcha," I said. "Let me put it this way. Could someone beam sound at me so you couldn't hear it with us being this close together."

"Ahhh..." she said, her blues seeming to get even brighter. "Not my area, but I seem to recall someone was trying to weaponize high-decibel sound using two different incomplete sources that let them pick a precise target where the sound waves of those sources met."

The look of confusion on my face wasn't because I was surprised Emma came up with something so fast, but because I didn't understand, at all. I had no idea what the hell she was talking about.

She gave me a small smile, nodded, and started using the dark earth under the bell peppers as a drawing surface. "So, two speakers, for lack of a better term, both producing sound waves you can't hear."

She dug little holes for the two speakers. "Here's your target," she said, pointing at a remaining weed. "The speakers transmit sound you can't hear but when the waves join here, the sound becomes audible."

She snatched the weed leaving a triangle in the dirt.

"Crikey! That's brilliant, Emma," I said with a smile.

"Are you looking to do this?" she asked, her voice wary.

"No, love," I said. "I think someone else is doing this to my client."

"Because..." she said with a smile that showed real hunger. Emma has one of those minds that always needs to be busy and the price of her help was stories. She doesn't need the money; she needs the mental stimulation.

"Are you on the case?" I asked, implying that I was hiring her, that I would pay her a token amount to seal the deal, and anything I said was confidential.

"Hell, yes," she said. "This one sounds like fun."

SEVEN

With Emma happily doing research, my next stop was a visit to Ann McGee's friend, Stephanie Fry. The one that had claimed to hear the voice.

After what I had just learned, it was much more likely that she did hear the voice, but I had to keep my mind open. What I had was a possible explanation for the voice; it did not mean that it was the correct explanation.

Back on the 101, I took the El Camino south and east back to Tempe to a little yoga studio on the edge of town.

It's one of those fancy "hot" yoga places which I related to about as much as a cat relates to baths. Yoga, I kind of get. You get older, you need to stretch. Sure. But doing it while the thermostat is turned way up when many days of the year you can just walk out into the desert heat... I just don't get it.

Stephanie Fry was in her mid-thirties, petite with her long brown hair pulled into a tight ponytail, her lean body encased in blue tights, and her skin slick with sweat.

The wood-floored room was hot, but the El Camino doesn't

have air-conditioning and I was a desert rat anyway, so I managed.

Class had just ended and a sea of sweaty bodies were flowing around me.

Stephanie took a long pull on a fancy stainless steel water bottle and eyed me. "Who are you supposed to be?" she asked.

"G'day," I said, extending my hand. "Name's Conner Bright. I'm working for your friend Ann McGee. I believe she texted you about me."

"Ah," she said, not taking my offered hand. "The Aussie detective."

"Righto. That's me," I said.

"And you want to talk about..." she looked around the emptying room like she wanted to make sure we weren't overheard.

"I do," I said. "Do you have a few minutes?"

She nodded and sighed. While she was clearly in great shape, there seemed to be a tiredness to her. Maybe that's what comes from doing yoga and sweating all day. Maybe it was some-thing else.

"Not much to say," she said. "It was a voice. A scary as hell voice. It said terrible things and no one else heard it."

"At Ms. McGee's bar?" I asked.

She nodded her head.

"When?" I asked.

"Almost three weeks ago," she said. "It was a Saturday night, cheat day, I was there with some friends sitting at a table. I had had a few when I heard it and no one else at the table did."

"And what did the voice say? What did it sound like?" I asked.

She shivered despite the hot room. "Do you really need me to repeat it?" she asked.

"I'm afraid so," I said.

She bit her lip, took a deep breath, and sighed. "The voice sounded... strange. It was loud but not loud, if you know what I mean. A man's voice, rough like they were old and smoked their whole life, kind of distorted, a little, umm... otherworldly."

She took another drink and looked away.

"And what did it say?" I asked.

"Seriously?" she asked.

It was clear that she was lost in superstition too, and I can't say that I blamed her. This was either a pretty serious trauma or she was a pretty good actress.

She sighed, did a half eye roll and said, "It said, 'I am the devil you know and you will die tonight.' I will never forget that sentence, not as long as I live."

"How many times did ya hear it?" I asked.

She looked at me like I just asked her how often she vacationed in hell. "Once," she said. "I didn't stick around and I haven't been back."

"Do you—" I began, but she cut me off.

"I'm not going back," she said, holding her hand up. "Ever. Now please leave. I need to center myself before my next class."

EIGHT

I am a recovering alcoholic and I work in bars.

This, really, tells you about all you need to know about me.

Well, not all, but it tells you something. At first glance, it makes it clear that I don't make it easy on myself. Look closer and you might suspect that I believe I deserve the punishment—just add on the past I'm hiding from and you can pretty much count on that.

If you dig deeper, if you saw where I lived, you might realize that there is more to it. That I need the money and I'll do whatever it takes—within reason, of course—to earn it.

When I was a professional drunk and then an off-hours-only drunk, it was easier to show up to a bar and work. To exist in the heady, hazy air full of the sharp smell of alcohol and the sharper smell of sweaty bodies. Back then, I knew that once I was off work, once my responsibilities were over, I could hole up and drink myself to sleep.

Now? I have to exist in the midst of the temptation knowing that I do not get to succumb.

Meetings help, although many at AA have told me I should,

under no circumstances, set foot in a bar, much less work in one until I am at least a year sober.

My blue six-month sobriety chip, which was always in my pocket, helped. I treated the damn thing like a talisman, like if the urge got too strong all I had to do was touch it and I'd be okay.

The human psyche is a strange place, believe you me. Because, sometimes it worked, and most of the time it helped.

I was holding that chip tight when I walked in The Devil You Know that evening. Feeling the texture, rubbing at the 6 in the middle. Feeling the words engraved along the edge, "To thine own self be true."

I was on a case. I was here for a reason. Ann had agreed that I should work the door, keep an eye on things, be there if the voice showed back up.

"Thank you for coming," Ann McGee said in her maroon devil outfit. She was behind the bar with a brunette named Juniper who was dressed the same way. There were only a few people in the bar and it was quiet, too quiet, and I could hear her clearly.

"Not a problem," I lied as I tipped my hat to her. I was still holding my six-month chip, reminding myself that recovery wasn't always one day at a time, but often one breath at a time. "Happy to help."

Ann pointed at a stool positioned next to the door and I perched myself on it. I had a boring night ahead of me carding folks and putting wristbands on them.

This was my idea. I'd get to meet everyone coming in. Ann was still worried that not enough people would show up, and judging by Stephanie Fry's reaction to "the voice," she had good reason to worry.

I settled in for a long night of resisting temptation and

hoping that the devil voice made an appearance and provided me with some kind of clue.

I GOT LOOKS AT THE ENTRANCE TO THE DEVIL YOU KNOW, I'll tell you that. It wasn't just the Crocodile Dundee regalia, complete with a wide-brimmed Australian bush hat, alligator skin boots, and an 11-inch bowie knife sheathed on my hip. It was me.

At six-five and 170 pounds, my sometimes nickname of "Scarecrow" fits. And being over forty in this sea of youth made me stand out even more.

Take this young woman, gothed out in black everything, tights, skirt, lacy top, boots, and even nail polish and lipstick. She was with two other similarly dressed people. While the rumors of the voice was scaring away some clientele, it was attracting others.

"You're different," she said, her dark eyes looking me up and down.

"Identification, please," I said with a smile. I was used to people looking at me. This one was too young to remember when I was big national news, but drawing attention to myself and hiding in plain sight had served me well.

"Is that real?" she asked, pointing at the big bowie knife sheathed at my side.

"You can't come in without an ID," I said, ignoring her question.

"And that?" she asked, pointing at the crocodile claw hanging from a leather strap around my neck.

"ID," I said.

She took a step back and really looked me up and down. "I

don't get it," she said. "What is all of this?" She gestured at me lazily with one hand.

People my age never ask that question. They watched the Crocodile Dundee movies. They got it in an instant. There was a cliched image of an Australian that I fit right into. Not so much with this generation.

I smiled, unfolded myself from the stool, and stood up. I was a good foot taller than her.

What the young think of me matters not one little bit. I'm not here to live up to their expectations. As long as I don't drink tonight, this will be a victory. If I get any kind of a clue in the case, it will be a celebration. But I did have a job to do and I damn well was going to do it.

"Young lady," I said. "I need to see your identification or you can't enter the premises."

She looked at the bar, there were maybe a dozen people in there when it would hold ten times that on a good night. Her eyes lingered for a moment, probably on Ann in her devil outfit, and then she looked at me.

She swallowed hard and said, "Has it...? Did it...?" Her friends were speaking to themselves behind her, also eying the bar suspiciously.

And now it all made sense. The girl, despite the black everything, was scared. She wanted to hear the voice and she was terrified of hearing the voice.

"Nah," I said, "I don't believe it has. Lookin' forward to hearin' it myself."

She looked at me, blinked twice, gave me the smallest of nods, and handed me her driver's license.

I looked at it closely. It looked real but could have been a fake. It read, "Amber Black," which just seemed way the hell too convenient.

"What's your major?" I asked.

"Journalism," she said, and then with a twist of her full lips asked, "What's yours?"

"Findin' fake IDs," I said. "What year?"

"Junior," she said, standing up straighter.

Maybe.

"What's your hardest class?" I asked.

"Oh for God's sake," she said, pulling her phone out of a black clutch purse, typing at it madly for a few moments and showing me a photo of her with some guys that looked like the type that had trouble finding dates. The photo listed her as the editor of *The State Press*, an "independent, student-operated news publication of Arizona State University."

I let her in with a big smile on my face.

ANN McGEE LOOKED TIRED, EVEN THROUGH THE LAYERS OF makeup, even with her devil ensemble distracting the eye, she looked tired.

It was 3:00 a.m., the bar was empty but for the two of us, and it hadn't been a very good night. Sure, some people had shown up. The ignorant and the curious, like the goth girl journalism major, Amber Black, and her friends, but not enough to support a place like this. Rent in the Mill Avenue District of Tempe had to be sky high.

This part of Tempe is very Mayberry with a touch of Disneyland with red brick buildings, old-fashioned street lamps, and wide streets with plenty of parking that just screamed at folks to get out and spend their money.

"We'll get it," I said with an encouraging nod.

She was behind the bar still, her shoulders slumped as she stared at the worn wood. "What?" she asked, shaking her head but not looking up.

I walked over to the bar and said gently, "We'll get it, Ann."

She looked up at me, her green eyes distant, a frown pulling at her face. "We'll get it," she said, but there was no energy behind it, she was just repeating what I said like I was a customer and she was repeating back my drink order.

Clearly she was a strong woman who carried a lot on her shoulders, but seeing her like this, seeing her vulnerable, just made me want to grab her. Grab a drink and then grab her and have a few minutes where the world and its problems just didn't exist, a few moments where there is just raw passion and flesh.

I thought that she must have felt it too, but then told myself that I was just being an old fool.

"Do you want to…" she said, her voice just above a whisper as she leaned forward just a little.

Her eyes met mine, and if she wasn't feeling the same thing I was, then she deserved an Oscar.

Something I learned in recovery is to say no early and often. You can't take your desire for a drink up to the tipping point where it requires a huge act of will. The human will is an amazing thing, but it is a limited thing, and if you take it to the brink you might not have enough will left to turn back.

I took an awkward step back, and said, "I got some things to run down in the mornin'. Meet you here at two to go over what my tech person found?"

She nodded, her head moving slowly like it was a great effort. She wanted escape. She needed escape. And I was a nearby avenue of escape. This wasn't about me. And, honestly, if I had said yes, it wouldn't have been about her.

"Yes," she finally said. "Two. Thank you, Conner. I'm…" She took a deep breath and sniffed before continuing. "I'm so glad not to be alone in this anymore."

"We'll get it," I said before I turned and left. This took what little will I had left and all I wanted as I walked out was a lot of beer and a lot of her.

NINE

I spent what was left of my night in my El Camino in a Wal-Mart parking lot.

I present to you the glamorous life of a private investigator in the sprawling metropolis that is Phoenix, Arizona.

I live on the outskirts of this metropolis in a single-wide on ten acres with a sadly empty horse corral. It would have taken me half an hour to get there and with traffic forty-five minutes to get back. I didn't have the time and my will was depleted enough that seeing the empty corral would have not been good for me. At all.

Thus a Wal-Mart parking lot halfway to Emma's house where, for some reason, you never get rousted.

At her place, Emma welcomed me in the morning at 10:00 a.m. with a cup of coffee, a homemade carrot-bran muffin, and a listening ear.

I mean, it was part of my deal with Emma. She wanted the story, the gory details, the step by step of it all. I was her living true crime podcast and she was my single audience member.

The inside of her faux adobe house was museum-neat but

somehow it still felt livable with comfortable furniture and colorful throw rugs over the tile floor. She favored southwest flourishes, like the handmade Navajo blankets hanging on the wall, a few kachina dolls, and a stunning oil painting of the Grand Canyon with a storm coming.

Emma had a nice house that was clearly well appointed, but it wasn't the kind of mansion you would expect given her time in tech. It was one of the things I liked about her—she had money but I had never seen her throwing it around.

She didn't ask any questions at my rather rumpled appearance, although I did notice her taking some deep breaths through the nose as I came in, making sure my rough and not-so-ready look wasn't about alcohol.

She graciously let me use her bathroom without comment, and then while I caffeinated up and munched on the muffin she made, I told her about the rest of my day, not that it was much.

"So, waddya find out about the voice?" I asked once I was starting to feel human.

"You like her," Emma said with a devious smile. She was dressed in a different pair of pedal pushers today and a fancy blue T-shirt from a marathon she had run a few years back before I met her, after she had beat ovarian cancer.

I pulled out my blue six-month chip. "I gotta while before I can like anyone."

"But you like her," she said.

I sighed and nodded. "Beautiful, strong as hell, a real laugh. What's not to like?"

She paused and really looked at me, her blue eyes getting positively penetrating. "But this is some kind of AA rule?"

"Rule might be a bit strong," I said. "In early recovery ya need to focus on yourself. Get comfortable with livin' in your own skin. Learn how to cope. Crap like that."

"Crap?" she asked.

I sighed. "Wise things like that."

She gave me a bit of a smile and a small nod and a few pieces fell into place. I had never seen Emma take a drink. I had never seen any sign of alcohol around her house.

"You're in recovery," I said.

She smiled widely, but only for a moment before her eyes darkened and the smile fled. "Six years," she said.

"Crikey, Emma," I said. "That's amazin'. Does... does it get any easier?"

"I wouldn't use the word 'easy,'" she said. "It does get more normal though. Your strategies get better developed and I guess you might say that makes it easier."

"But you wouldn't say that," I said, the case forgotten for the moment.

"No," she said with a thin-lipped smile. "I would not."

I nodded and stared into the depths of my nearly empty coffee cup.

"But you know, Conner," she said, her tone suddenly lighter. "Life was never meant to be easy."

"Amen to that," I said, raising my coffee mug to her.

Emma Shapiro is significantly smarter than me in most of the ways the world seems to care about. She's a good leader, can assimilate technology with ease, knows how to manage her money, and always seems to have the upper hand in life.

The only way I have her beat is in the school of hard knocks, the metaphorical kind and the physical kind.

On the physical side, I have been beaten down by both men and bulls.

On the metaphorical side, the day my best friend died at my

hand, my world was ripped apart. It was a party out in the desert near Globe, Arizona. We were teenagers and fighting over—you guessed it—a girl. I was in my truck trying to leave, Tommy was standing in front of the truck banging on the hood. We were both shouting at each other.

The truck was old with a manual transmission and a clutch. I was revving the engine, screaming at Tommy to get out of the way when my foot slipped off the clutch, the truck lurched forward, and that was the end of his life and the end of my life as I knew it.

It was big news for Arizona, and national news too. I was a poster child for the terrible things that happen when teenagers drink. I had reporters stalking me more than a year later.

This is why I became Conner Bright. Legally. Why I hide in plain sight by being this crazy detective with alligator skin boots on my feet, a bowie knife on my belt, and an Australian bush hat on my head.

But back to Emma Shapiro being smarter than me, back in her lovely but comfortable home. She put a gentle hand on my shoulder and said, "I know who you are."

I didn't say a thing. I didn't breathe. I just stared into the depths of my coffee mug, at the dark dregs that were left.

In truth, being Conner Bright started as my way of hiding from those that remembered my past, but it was, at this point, mainly about hiding my past from my present, from myself.

Her voice was calm and quiet. Her hand warm and gentle but not invasive. "And if you don't want to talk about it, I will never mention it again. But if you do need to talk... about anything. I'm here."

I didn't look up and I was quite sure she must have been able to hear my heart galloping along in my chest.

"What gave it away?" I asked.

"Scatterwood, Australia," she said. "It doesn't exist. I'm sure you picked it before the internet was what it is now. I can help you with that."

I still didn't look at her but asked, "Why?"

She sighed, removed her hand, and sank back into the couch. "You may not understand this, but it's lonely being the boss. Not knowing if people are being nice to you because they like you or because they are trying to get ahead or need something from you.

"You are making a good go at being sober, Conner, but you need someone that knows who you really are, that you can really talk to."

"I talk at meetin's," I said, still not daring to look at her.

"But you are anonymous then," she said. "It would be good to have someone with whom you are not."

"Are you offerin' to be my sponsor?" I asked.

To her credit Emma didn't hesitate. Not even for a moment. "I am."

Being a sponsor is part of recovery. To truly learn something, you need to teach it, but it was one hell of a commitment and I hadn't found a sponsor, not one that worked out for more than a few weeks, not one I could tell the whole truth to.

When I go to meetings I drop the accent and use my real name. I say, "Hello, my name is Evan and I'm an alcoholic," but I haven't gone any further. Even going that far was terrifying. It still is.

Not having a sponsor, not talking about all of it, this was a huge risk to my sobriety. I needed exactly what Emma was offering, but it scared the hell out of me. I'd rather, quite frankly, face down an angry bull with only my wits and my speed between me and a downed cowboy that needed to be protected.

I finally looked at her and her face was strained, like she was in pain, her years showing, but she looked absolutely sincere.

"It's a mighty fine offer, Emma," I said, still using the

Australian accent. "Aces, really. And I appreciate the hell out of it. But I gotta think on it, ya know?"

What I didn't say was that I was a lot for anyone to take on and that I didn't want to be a burden.

She nodded and, bless her heart, eased the tension when she asked, "More coffee?"

TEN

Part of the problem with having done what I have done, having my foot slip off the clutch when I was young and very drunk, is that I figure I deserve every bad thing that happens to me.

I took a life.

My best friend's life.

It is a debt I can never repay. I can't make it right for his parents or his sister. I can't do anything for the children that were never born because of that terrible moment. The only thing I can do is to try to help as many people as I can while staying under the radar.

After her offer, Emma was all business. I don't know how she did it, but the offer felt completely genuine, but then she refilled our coffees and made a sharp turn towards what I had come for.

"It's called sound beaming," Emma said. I was still on the couch and she was sitting in a chair across the hardwood coffee table from me, somehow knowing I needed some physical space to stand in for the psychological space I desperately needed after her revelation and offer.

I nodded for her to continue, the words sounding right but not making any particular sense.

"The military application I remembered is from a couple of decades ago," she said. "I found mentions of it. No idea where it went. But companies are working on this now with a couple of applications. The consumer application is for shared spaces, it's basically a headphones experience without headphones. Someone even a few feet away from you wouldn't hear it. The commercial application is for concert venues where each seat gets the same high-end audio experience."

"Can you buy it?" I asked.

She shook her head. "Not yet. There are some prototypes, some companies getting ready to launch, but nothing you can buy off the shelf."

"What would it take to do it?" I asked. She got a squint-eyed look on her face and I knew she was trying to figure out how much tech I could take, so I added, "Could you put somethin' like that together? How long would it take and what would it look like?"

She nodded. "Yes. I'd need a little help but yes, I could pull it off. In a few days if I was focused. It wouldn't be commercial grade, of course, probably wouldn't sound great, but it would do the trick."

"How about to cobble together a proof of concept?" I asked. "Wouldn't need to be pretty or small, just work."

She sat back, crossed her arms, and stared at me. "You want something to show your client," she said.

Like I said, Emma is smart. Maybe it's all the years as a manager, maybe it's her fights with her own demons and her fight with cancer, but she knows people. Well, she knows me, for sure.

I nodded and held her steady gaze but didn't say anything.

"Why?" she asked.

I took a deep breath and it came out as a noisy sigh. "I need time," I said. "If there was money here, I'd follow it, but there really doesn't seem to be. This is the kinda thing that..." I shrugged, trying to find the words. "The kinda thing that can make you believe in bad things, that can make ya twitchy and afraid. If ya could demo the tech, that just may break the hold superstition has on her."

Emma didn't say anything right away, but just stared at me. I met her gaze. Emma knew who I was, so for the first time in a very long time I didn't have anything to hide.

She finally nodded, just a small bob of her head. "You like her," she said.

"I do," I said without thinking about it, and as I heard my words I could feel that they were true. Her toughness, the bond over fathers lost too soon, and, of course, her beauty. I did like her in a way that wasn't safe, but there it was.

"Okay," she said, getting up and rubbing her hands together. "I better get to work. Bring her by at noon tomorrow. It'll be ugly, but I should have something and I'll text you if I don't."

ELEVEN

After my time with Emma Shapiro, I have rarely been more eager to get into my El Camino and drive. It's not just that I love this car, it's not just that it was my father's before it was mine, something we restored together, it was my need for something entirely mundane and normal.

I am not used to being known. I don't want to be known. My whole life is structured so that I am not truly known.

Conner Bright from Scatterwood, Australia is not some piece of performance art, it is necessary insulation against that terrible moment when I was a drunk teenager fighting with my best friend over a girl and my foot slipped off the clutch.

Emma had offered to be my sponsor, had offered to help me with my Scatterwood problem so I can keep my insulation of lies going.

As the tires hummed on the highway, as the other cars jockeyed around me while I kept just under the speed limit, something about that began to gnaw at me.

Shouldn't my sponsor be encouraging me to discard the façade and embrace my past, be who I really am?

And who am I really?

Except for the accent, the bowie knife, and the made-up past, Conner Bright *is* who I am. I'm something of a cowboy trying to make a living in the big city haunted by his past.

There are plenty of people that fit that description.

And at this point in my recovery, I would expect my sponsor, Emma in this case as my prospective sponsor, to discourage me from working for a woman I am clearly attracted to that owns a bar.

Red flags all over the place there.

And my continued association with bars was one of the reasons that I had had trouble finding and keeping a sponsor. On paper, quitting my job as a bouncer sounds good, but it's steady income compared to the investigative work I do and I was barely holding on to my home.

And why not go get a "real" job? Besides the fact that I lack the skills and the temperament for most real jobs, my name may have changed but my social security number hasn't. Might not make a difference in most cases, but I wasn't willing to take the chance.

I was too tired to think clearly but I resolved to keep my mind open.

To Emma's offer to be my sponsor.

To Emma's reasons for doing what she was doing.

To the facts of this case as I find them.

To the fact that Ann McGee who dresses up like the devil professionally was more than a little dangerous to me.

I didn't know what was going on, and that, in and of itself, was not a big deal at this point in a case, but what was very worrisome is that I was starting to feel like this was all about me.

Either I was just tired and paranoid or this was one hell of an elaborate setup.

To sort that out, I needed help.

So I headed downtown to the Major Crimes Division of the Maricopa County Sheriff's Office.

TWELVE

"Wʜᴀᴛ ᴅᴏ ʏᴏᴜ ᴡᴀɴᴛ, Bʀɪɢʜᴛ?" Dᴇᴛᴇᴄᴛɪᴠᴇ Tʀɪꜱʜᴀ Sanchez asked from behind her reflective sunglasses, a smile pulling at her lean face.

Her black hair was pulled back into its eternal ponytail. She was a few years younger than me, in her late thirties, short and wiry, all coiled energy, and even though I was over a foot taller than her and about sixty pounds heavier, I wouldn't give me the edge in a fight. She always seemed like she was wound just a tad too tight and if you set her off there would be hell to pay and plenty of pain.

"G'day, Detective," I said with a tip of my hat.

We were out in the parking lot in front of Major Crimes, which isn't much to look at. It's one of a series of one-story buildings in an industrial area of town, west of the flashy sheriff's headquarters in downtown Phoenix.

Sanchez had her usual reflective sunglasses on so I couldn't see her eyes. She was dressed in her usual dark pantsuit, her arms crossed.

"Out with it," she said.

"Remember the Metrocenter case?" I asked. It was only last Christmas so I know she did. This was a case she pointed me at that turned out to be a trap. I was hoping she felt just a little bit bad about it.

"What about it?" she asked, her tone at least a bit curious.

"Maybe just bein' paranoid," I said, "but this one reminds me of that one. It's not feelin' right."

I didn't point out that just like the Metrocenter case she was the one that pointed me at this case.

"What are you asking for, Bright?" she asked.

"I need to know how the case came to ya," I said. Mill Avenue is in Tempe and out of the jurisdiction of the sheriff's office, so the how might illuminate something.

She nodded, once and quickly. "What else?" she asked. She knew me pretty well too.

"I need a background check done on an associate of mine," I said.

She cocked her head a little bit and even with the sunglasses, I could tell that she was staring intently at me. "Why?" she asked.

"Somethin' doesn't smell right," I said.

"How long since you took a shower, Bright?" she asked, a wicked grin showing off her perfect teeth.

I can't say that Sanchez and I have ever been friends, but we used to be colleagues that respected each other. I trashed my end of that, but I still respected her. She was smart and tough. She had the kind of job that chewed people up and spit them out and she just seemed to thrive in it all.

But I was getting tired of the attitude she had adopted concerning me. I had made a mistake, a stupid one, the kind of mistake addicts make if they aren't dealing with their problem in the right way. Since then I had taken every bizarre case she had gleefully sent my way, and almost died several times for my troubles.

There had been moments when the old relationship shined through, usually right after I had avoided death and gotten pretty banged up, but I was tired of this.

"A charmer as always," I said, tipping my hat again and turning sharply around. "Thanks for your time, Detective."

This was the problem with my Conner Bright persona with the insulation that I had created around my past. It made it hard to create deep relationships. Intimacy requires the truth which was probably why Helen and I could never hold it together for long, even before I got sober.

But I was making strides. I was battling my demons every day and was seven months and six days sober. I deserved some respect.

I was to the El Camino when Sanchez caught up to me.

"Sorry," she said. "We just found some..." She shook her head either trying to clear it or to cut the words off. "Some bodies. I'm not feeling warm and fuzzy about anyone right now. And you do need a shower."

I just stared at her, my arms crossed like hers had been as I leaned on the car.

She sighed and said, "Give me the name and I'll do a quick search. And as to how this came to me..." She looked around and it was just us amongst the cars with the buzzing of the nearby street.

"Look," she said. "It's a long story but I know the McGees. I went to high school with one of Ann's cousins. My father was obsessed with her father during his glory days, he still loves that bar. He bought me my first drink there when I turned twenty-one. He's the one that told me that they hit hard times."

I took a deep breath and nodded, letting it sink in. I had been longing for her respect but it turned out she had been giving it to me with the cases she was entrusting me with.

Sure they all had weird phenomena, but some of them were important to her.

"What else," I said, because I knew her pretty well too and there was definitely more.

She shifted her weight back and forth and kicked at the pavement. "I know Ann McGee," she said quietly. "Been going to that bar my entire drinking life, so of course I know her. But the thing you're digging for is that she's the woman my husband left me for."

I KNEW THAT DETECTIVE TRISHA SANCHEZ HAD BEEN married. What kind of a private investigator would I be if I didn't know that? I knew that her husband had cheated on her, and while I felt bad for Sanchez, I felt, frankly, sorry for the bastard. I can't imagine that she was gentle with him. Not her style. Not at all.

But I had no idea that my new case was with the woman Sanchez's husband left her for.

This, obviously, puts her motives in question and left me completely out to sea on this case. Could I trust her? Add that on to not being able to trust myself with Ann McGee and having doubts about Emma Shapiro, that left me feeling very much alone.

Despite the temperature being in the low seventies, I started sweating, the sound of traffic suddenly feeling very loud.

All that "open mind" stuff I have rattled on about before, this was the moment I should have been practicing it and utterly failed. But I got lucky, Sanchez didn't leave me out to dry.

"Oh, relax," Sanchez said. "They didn't last long. By the

time the divorce was complete, they were long over and I went and had a talk with Ann."

"Had a talk" here could easily be a euphemism for "put her in the hospital."

"Just a talk," Sanchez said, clearly reading my face like a book. "We had kind of been friends before, you know, casually. I was a customer. My father was one of her regulars. But after that…" She shrugged like what she was describing was no big deal. "We bonded over that bastard and how he treated us. When my father told me what was going on, I called her. And then I called you."

I nodded as I let it sink in. This was important to her and she had entrusted it to me. That just added weight to my confusion.

"Don't screw this up, Bright," she said. "And text me the name of the person you want me to look into, and an address if you have it. Even though a background check sounds like a job for a private investigator, I'll take a look."

She gave me one of her patent-pending predatorial smiles, and after this conversation I had no idea if I was on her good side or her bad side, whether this case was an act of trust or more punishment for my mistake, or both.

"I'll do that," I said.

"What am I looking for?" she asked.

"A connection to me," I said. "I handled a situation for her a few years back, but I'm wonderin' if there is more. If this isn't some kind of long…"

I couldn't say "long con." I didn't want to believe it, but like I said, Emma Shapiro is very smart and very patient.

"How far back am I going?" she asked, her voice quite a bit quieter and her head cocked to the side a bit making it clear that the question was loaded.

Sanchez and I have never talked about my past, and I have always been grateful for that, but she had to know all about it.

She must have done a background check on me before the first time she hired me.

"As far back as you need to go," I said.

Her brow furrowed for a moment, and for the thousandth time I really wished she didn't wear those reflective sunglasses so I could see her eyes and have some idea what the hell goes on in that head of hers. But, then again, that's probably the reason she wears them.

"No promises, Bright," she said. "But I'll take a look if I get a chance." She turned on her heel and left me alone with my confusion.

THIRTEEN

When Ann McGee unlocked the door to The Devil You Know at 2:00 p.m. she was not, thankfully, dressed as the devil.

Not that it mattered much. Jeans and a T-shirt with only a little eyeliner and her blond hair pulled back into a loose ponytail was quite enough, thank you very much. And that is despite her looking just about as tired as I felt.

"G'day," I said, tipping my hat.

She gave me a wan smile that said without saying it, "Is it, really?"

"Can I get you something to drink?" she asked.

"I'm in recovery," I said as I followed her in and couldn't help but notice just how well those jeans fit. "So it'll always be club for me."

She moved behind the bar and I perched myself on a stool feeling a little awkward about the confession, but maybe I needed at least a little truth to counterbalance the risk here. And, at this point, this was an essential truth.

Ann didn't say anything but got a tall drink glass out, scooped some ice in, used the soda gun to fill it up, and added a wedge of lime.

"I respect that," she said as she put the glass in front of me. "Thanks for letting me know."

I nodded, took a sip, and couldn't help but think of the many alcoholic drinks that were in this glass before in a sadly wistful way.

An awkward silence descended with Ann standing there shifting from foot to foot like she didn't know what to do, like we were a couple of teenagers who had forgotten how to talk.

"Any updates?" she finally asked, her voice quiet but sounding loud with the bar empty except for us.

"I have an explanation for the voice," I said, and then did my best to explain "sound beaming" and what Emma Shapiro had told me. I don't think I did that great of a job because Ann looked more than a little dubious.

"Why would someone do that?" she asked, and it seemed like the superstition was, at least, penetrable.

"That's the question, ain't it?" I said. "It might take me some time to figure that out. My tech person should be able to demo this for us tomorrow. We need to be in Sun City at noon."

"Sun City?" she asked with a quizzical smile. Sun City was the polar opposite of Tempe and her curiosity was to be expected.

"Didn't ya hear about all the tech wizzes in Sun City?" I asked.

She laughed. It was short lived but the sound of it woke me up more than the morning coffee and I wanted nothing more than to hear her laugh some again. "Okay, Conner," she said. "I trust you."

I kept the smile on my face, but my stomach took a tumble

when she said that. I wanted her to trust me, very badly, but I couldn't trust her, or at least I couldn't trust myself around her. Or something like that. The attraction I was feeling was truly messing with my mind.

FOURTEEN

The owner of the building that housed The Devil You Know was short, mid-forties, a bit pudgy around the middle, with short brown hair that had retreated to a fringe around his head. His dress of choice seemed to be dark slacks and a white button-down shirt open at the collar.

He looked like so many other middle-aged dads that had jobs that weren't quite formal enough to require a tie. The kind of guy that could just fade into a crowd, unless that crowd was late-night Tempe when it's mostly a sea of young looking for booze and a companion.

I had seen him the first night I worked the door. There was something about his manner, his intent as his eyes found Ann. I had just waved him through but kept an eye on him.

He and Ann had had a short conversation and then he had left.

Ann didn't mention him and I didn't ask. I had ideas as to who he was but it didn't seem important yet.

That second night working there, I set my stool up outside the bar, thinking maybe I could get a few more folks to come in.

And, if I'm being honest, the door between me and the alcohol was not much of a safeguard, but it was something.

The second time this guy walked by, peering in the windows but not going in, I said, "You the owner, ain't ya?"

"Excuse me?" he asked, looking me up and down, like he was seeing me and my outfit for the first time.

"The buildin'," I said pointing at the red brick structure I was camped out in front of. "Don't ya own this buildin'?"

And then he really looked at me. His eyes were brown and as bland as the rest of him but there was an intensity there that I hadn't expected.

"And who are you?" he asked.

I stood up and extended my hand. Even though I am skinny, my height often intimidates people and I wanted to see how he would react. "Name's Conner Bright," I said. "And you are?"

He took my hand and shook it, his grip quite strong and he didn't seem at all intimidated. "Alan Trent," he said. "And I am the owner of this building."

"You checkin' in on her," I asked, nodding at Ann who was visible behind the bar dressed as the devil complete with horns and a tail.

"You seem rather observant for a bouncer," he said.

I shrugged, letting it go that he had ignored my question. He was clearly used to being in charge, and while I couldn't identify the fancy watch on his wrist, I'd wager it was very expensive. "Bouncers need to be observant," I said with a smile. "But I'm a private investigator, too. Ya need anythin' investigated?"

He blinked twice and looked me up and down again and I'm quite sure he was reevaluating me, yet again, and surprised that he had to.

This wasn't a problem for me, it happens often enough, but this guy could easily have motive to kill the bar if he had a more lucrative renter on the line or a buyer for the property with deep pockets.

"I might," he said with a small nod once his reevaluation of me was over. "You take care of this for Ann and we'll talk, okay?"

"Aces," I said with a tip of my hat. "Nice meetin' ya, Mr. Trent."

He gave me a thin-lipped, barely there smile, another small nod, and then walked off.

I resolved to keep my mind open regarding him. What he said really didn't mean anything. It's actions that counted.

FIFTEEN

I felt it before I heard it.

I don't know any other way to describe it.

It was right around midnight and Mill Avenue was pretty quiet, most of those that were out late already having found their chosen watering hole. The night was cloudy so the yellow light of the city was reflecting back down on the street casting everything in a sepia glow.

The red brick buildings stood quietly, only a trickle of traffic on the four lanes of Mill Avenue. No bikers on the bike lanes. No pedestrians in view. The hum of the 202 not too far off sounding like distant, angry bees.

There was a slight breeze ruffling the leaves of some of the trees planted on the edge of the sidewalk which was edged with red pavers.

There were about eight customers in the bar including Amber Black and her flock of goths waiting to hear the voice. The bar wasn't silent, but it wasn't the wash of white noise that a bar should be.

It was a strange and rare moment of peace. I was just sitting there, perched on the stool, enjoying the cool of the winter's evening when the hairs on the back of my neck stood up.

Suddenly it wasn't peaceful at all. It was creepy, the things that had seemed nice now seeming dangerous. This wasn't right. Something was very, very wrong. I almost looked up, like the thin cloud layer high above were actually some big thunderheads getting ready to hurl thunderbolts down on me.

It was entirely uncomfortable in a way that is so hard to describe. I felt like running, but I just sat there placidly like nothing at all was happening.

All of this happened in seconds and my mind hadn't figured out what was going on, but I suspected that whatever it was it wasn't going to be good and that I was being watched.

And then I heard it.

Laughter.

Terrible laughter.

The sound of it wasn't clear, it was mangled and distorted making it sound entirely malevolent. It was clearly a male voice and it was the kind of laughter that only belonged in a truly terrifying horror movie.

And then he spoke and I had no trouble, at all, believing it was the devil himself speaking to me. "I am the devil you know," he said. "You will die tonight, Conner Bright."

The first thing the rational part of my brain grabbed onto, the part of me that was resisting running away like a terrified child, was that the voice had used my name. And somehow, that made it just a little better because the last sentence rhymed and you just don't picture the devil rhyming, and worse because the devil knew my name.

The laughter continued after that, both manic and malevolent.

I could totally see how Vince Rogers hearing this voice had bolted out into the street and gotten hit by a car. I was doing my best to look calm, but my heart was pounding so hard in my chest it seemed like it was going to break out soon.

Given what Emma had told me, I stood up, as casually as I could, the voice still doing its villainous laugh, stretched, and walked a few paces down the street.

This was something I had done many times. Sitting for a long time isn't good for my battered frame. Neither is standing for a long time, so I tend to alternate the two.

And sure enough, as I moved, the voice faded quickly and then was gone.

Rarely have I been so relieved, but once it faded, I turned around and moved back towards the stool and the voice came back and repeated its prophecy about my impending death with the odd little rhythm at the end, "You will die tonight, Conner Bright."

I had just experienced the "sound beaming" Emma Shapiro had told me about.

And that rational explanation helped, but only a little.

I still wanted to run away as fast and as far as I could.

Which meant I wasn't gonna budge. Not a goddamn inch. Because whoever was behind this had turned their high-tech toy on me and that meant that they were worried. That meant that I was getting close. That meant they were getting desperate.

I reached into my back pocket, found the volume button on my phone and pressed it until the phone briefly vibrated.

This was as casual a gesture as I could make it. I didn't pull the phone out. I didn't make a show of it. But now, because of the little app I had running on it, my phone was recording audio.

"I know you can hear me," the voice said, the tone of it a sneering malevolence. "You will die tonight."

This personalization just ramped up my anger. Whoever was doing this was watching. Which meant they were likely across the street above one of the shops there. A bridal shop or a bookstore, both closed.

What was their game? Why turn their sound beam on me?

And then it clicked. If they managed to chase me away, if they then did it to someone else in the bar, then Ann would be truly desperate.

Something else clicked and I turned around and looked at the bar. The front of it was all windows and Amber Black was sitting there with her dark cohorts looking listlessly out onto the quiet street. Can sound beaming work through glass? If so, that wasn't enough since there were reports of people hearing "the voice" in the bathrooms and that meant the tech had to be installed inside the bar.

I wanted to smack myself. I should have searched the bar earlier, but a bar has plenty of speakers, how would I know if one had been altered?

"I am the devil you know," the voice that seemed like it was in my head said again, but I ignored it. I didn't care.

I stood up and pulled my phone out, tapped on it, and put it to my ear like I had just gotten a phone call.

"You got Bright," I said, standing up and moving a few feet towards the street.

"Right," I said to my phone that was recording. I needed to see if the phone could pick up the sound. My body, despite my efforts, was responding to it in such a visceral way that I needed proof it was a real sound. For me and for Ann.

"Sorry, mate," I said. "Not available tonight. I'm on a case, but I got a few minutes."

The voice continued which, in retrospect, was strange. If it was an actual sound, then my phone could pick it up and then whoever was on the line would hear it too and that would shatter the illusion.

"Stop pretending, Conner Bright," the voice said. "I am the

devil you know. I know your every thought, your every fear, and I know what you did. You will die tonight."

I pretended to hang up the phone and then I really did dial someone, but I did it in an exaggerated way that would, hopefully, make it look like I was still pretending.

The phone rang. For a long time. And when it finally picked up a sleepy Detective Trisha Sanchez said, "This better be good, Bright, or I'll arrest you for disturbing my peace."

SIXTEEN

For some reason, it seems that the human default is to believe. We, as a species, believe the strangest damn things, the flimsiest conspiracies, the weirdest stories.

It's in our very fiber. Religion runs off belief, quite out in the open, actually. I don't say this to comment on religion but on our need to believe things, to think we know what is going on, to feel like we understand the brief madness on this chaotic planet that is our lives.

Because of all of this, I have come to distrust my desire to believe in things.

I guess I should unpack that a bit or it won't make sense. To believe is to accept something as true without proof. I prefer to find the proof and avoid the leap of faith as much as possible.

All of this is to say that I am not prone to superstition. I don't put much weight in conspiracy theories. I actively question my beliefs when I become aware of them.

And even with all of that, the voice that sounded like it was in my head saying, "I know your every thought, your every fear, and I know what you did. You will die tonight," felt like it was real.

The "I know what you did" part was particularly chilling, even though I know the psychology of it. I'm a private investigator who works as a bouncer. Use that phrase on anyone that fits my description and the recipient will remember something terrible.

Maybe not as bad as running over your friend while drunk and screaming at him, but something.

That's why I called Sanchez.

The voice had found my weak spot, and even though I knew there was a perfectly rational explanation for the voice, part of me wanted to believe. Even if it was believing that the devil had found me and was coming for me.

"Bright?" Sanchez asked. "You there?"

As soon as Sanchez picked up, the voice stopped its haranguing. Which meant either the voice was real, as in some real malevolent force, or those behind it could also hear what I was hearing.

"Right," I said. "Sorry 'bout that. I've gotta situation here and I need some backup."

There was a moment of silence and not the quip I expected, along the lines, "Well then call 911."

When Sanchez spoke again, she sounded wide awake. "What is it?"

"I'm about to break into a couple of buildin's on Mill Avenue across from Ann's Bar," I said, part of me rather surprised that I couldn't say the name of the bar. "I have good reason to believe that the perpetrators of this are there. And also I have good reason to believe that they are listenin' right now."

"Shit," Sanchez said and I could hear the rustling of clothing. "Don't do it. I'll be there in twenty."

I blinked and stared up at the buildings across the street. I was one man, I couldn't cover all the exits, twenty minutes was a lifetime, more than enough time for whoever was doing this to get away.

I opened my mouth to speak, to tell Sanchez that I couldn't wait, when I turned around and looked in the bar and saw Amber Black, the ASU journalism student, staring back at me.

I smiled at her and her youthful brow furrowed and she cocked her head in question.

"Better make it fifteen," I said. "Don't ya got a siren on your car or somethin'?"

I didn't wait for her reply. I hung up and walked into the bar.

SEVENTEEN

The truth is out there.

Catchy saying, right? You probably know what TV show used that as their motto.

And it's fine as far as it goes, but what is more appropriate is, "The truth is out there and it's a messy bugger and you'll be lucky to understand even a little piece of it."

But for some of us, truth is more of a siren song than belief. Even messy, partial truths. And if you are a journalist, or a journalism student, then you might even look at truth as something of a calling.

"I've got a story for ya," I said to Amber Black after I walked into the too quiet bar and up to her table. She was all gothed out again in black tights, a short black skirt, and a lacy black top. All of which is fine by me. All-black outfits have a good past, hell, that was the way Johnny Cash used to dress. It's the black lipstick and the black nail polish that gets me and makes it goth.

I just don't understand it.

"What story?" she asked, her eyes getting a bit wide.

"The story of the voice, of course," I said.

"What's going on?" Ann asked. No idea how she can be quiet on those heels, but I hadn't heard her come up and I barely kept myself from jumping. The voice had gotten to me.

Her maroon devil outfit was even brighter and more intoxicating next to the goth squad.

"Look all," I said. "There's no time. I heard the voice and I'm quite sure it's coming from one of those buildin's."

I pointed across the street and three people, including Ann, asked me something at the same time.

"I need eyes and cameras on the buildin's," I said. "But ya gotta stay in here. I'm goin' around back and waitin' for reinforcements."

It wasn't just Ann and the goth kids, most of the bar was crowded around now except for a couple of serious drunks still sitting at the bar nursing their drinks, foolishly waiting for the alcohol to take away their pain.

I looked directly at Ann. "This could get dangerous, keep everyone in here."

"I'll call the cops," she said, turning towards the bar.

I grabbed her arm and wished that I hadn't. Her skin was soft, her arms strong and toned. She was temptation, pure and simple, and I wanted nothing more than to dive into it.

"They won't understand," I said. "Sanchez is on her way, let us handle this."

Her blue eyes got a little wide. She had already talked to the police about this and it hadn't gone well, which is why I was here. "Be safe," she said, and it sounded like she meant it.

This was an odd thing to experience before heading out into the unknown. The devil herself wanted me to stay safe.

Clearly Ann didn't know me very well yet.

Even the back alleys of these Mill Avenue shops are nice. Red brick buildings, adequate space between them, extra parking in some cases, a few trees, a street light or two, and dumpsters mostly hidden behind fenced enclosures.

You couldn't mask the faint smell of garbage, but as alleys go this was upscale. The back doors even had the name of the establishments on them so it wasn't as disorienting as some and I knew I was in the right place. I was behind the bridal shop and the bookstore with a good view of the back entrance of both.

I was out of breath and my feet hurt. Cowboy boots are great for keeping you in the saddle but they are terrible for running.

I moved behind the fence that hid the dumpster and settled in to watch.

This was all too strange. Who goes through this kind of effort with bleeding edge technology to put a small Tempe bar out of business? These people had the tech to beam sound at me but they also had the tech to hear me clearly enough to know when I was faking a phone call or having a real one.

That last part is not hard, all you need is a parabolic microphone, and as I thought about it, it made sense. They needed to be able to monitor the reactions of their victims, to determine if what they were doing was working. This wasn't mature tech, so some need to tweak it made sense.

It wasn't just the setup that was odd but this night. They knew I had called for reinforcements. They could see into the bar where at least half a dozen phones were pointed their way while everyone stared out.

What they had done with me was so brazen it didn't really make sense. Did they think I would be that easily spooked?

And here I was alone with only a flimsy wooden fence for cover when they had to know that I was back here and that the longer they waited the harder escape was going to be.

I wasn't looking for a confrontation, just a clue, but my gut was telling me I wasn't going to even get that, that I had missed something essential, that I was being manipulated and doing exactly what they wanted.

Keeping an eye on those back doors, I pulled my phone out and called Ann. "Conner," she said, the fear in her voice palpable and I could hear shouts in the background. "I hear it. I hear the voice. It says that... that I'm going to die tonight."

NINETEEN

I HAD BEEN PLAYED.

That was clear.

The "voice" talking to me was about getting me out from in front of The Devil You Know.

Hearing Ann's fear made me want to run to her, but maybe that's what they wanted too and I had forgotten something entirely basic. There were two cars parked back here, and while you hope the bad guys aren't this lazy, you should never discount human nature.

"Is your phone recordin'?" I asked, flipping the phone to speaker and stepping out from behind the fence surrounding the dumpster.

I kept the call going and opened my phone's camera app, the fancy night version, and started taking pictures of the back of the shop and the cars parked there.

"What?" she asked. "Why?"

"Put it on record," I said. "The voice ain't just in your head. The recordin' of it is evidence."

It was good advice, but I hadn't had the time to review my

own recording to see if it captured anything, and I couldn't hear the voice on the call with Ann.

"Done," she said. "But..."

"What?" I asked.

"The Voice," she said, her tone making the "v" in "voice" capitalized. "It stopped when you called. It knows."

"Just keep the recordin' goin'," I said. It was taking everything I had to not run to her. "Keep the line open. I'm textin' Sanchez now to hurry up and to come direct to ya."

And that's what I did as I walked back behind the fence into position not having any idea if I was doing the right thing.

That's the problem with being manipulated. Once you realize it is happening you have no way to know if it's still happening or not, if your choices are your own of if the groundwork for them was laid long before you knew anything was going on.

This case, from the start, had made me good and paranoid and seemed custom designed to push me off my tenuous path of sobriety.

But maybe I am just being paranoid.

Or maybe someone is out to get me.

"Conner," Ann said, her voice quiet.

"I'm right here," I said. "Anyone else there hearin' it?"

"No," she said. "And I'm still not."

"Good," I said.

"Thank you," she said, her voice even quieter. "Thank you for believing me."

"My pleasure," I said. "This is nothin'. When we get clear of this, remind me to tell you of the time I hunted down a chupacabra."

"It's a date," she said, her voice just a tad husky or maybe I was hearing something that wasn't there, but she had definitely said "date."

There was psychology at play here. I was the rough Aussie that swooped in to help her when no one else would. But you sure as hell couldn't tell that to my hormones right then and there.

I was holding my phone with my left hand, shooting video of the back of the buildings, but I fished my six-month chip out of my pocket wishing it was a twelve-month chip and dating someone who owned a bar wasn't colossally and epically stupid.

I could only comfort myself with the fact that I do colossally and epically stupid things for a living, so why not in my personal life?

"If ya like that story," I said, "I got more. A purple unicorn, a haunted mall, and an alien abduction."

She chuckled, it was strained and thin but she was laughing so it felt like my day was officially made. "Who the hell are you?" she asked.

"That's a damn fine question," I said, fighting with my nearly hardwired Australian accent from putting a "love" at the end of that sentence.

TWENTY

Waiting with the adrenaline flowing is damn hard. Waiting for someone to leave one of these buildings. Waiting for Sanchez to arrive. Waiting to be twelve months sober so I could entertain dating.

Ann and I kept chatting now and then, the call between us remaining open. Not about much at all but somehow it felt like the most intimate thing we had done. It was almost like we were a couple in a romcom that had just had their "meet cute" and were in their respective beds having a sleepy conversation about nothing important that was very telling about each of them.

I liked Ann. Even without her distracting physical presence, I liked her. A lot. And it seemed like she liked me.

Tough times can bond people, and fast, but that doesn't mean the bond will hold during the regular times.

But who the hell was I kidding. "Regular times" fled my life years ago when my foot slipped off the clutch and my pickup lurched forward.

"Anything happening there?" Ann asked after a particularly long pause.

"Nah," I said. "If they're in there, they know I'm out here."

"What are they waiting for?" she asked.

"Ya got me," I said, and the subtext of that statement made my heart beat faster. "Anythin' happenin' over there?"

"No," she said. "Half the folks are back to their spots. The goth kids are still nose to the glass, though, phones out."

"The alpha-girl's name is Amber," I said.

"Good to know," she said.

The conversation was nice, really nice, but something wasn't right. When a puzzle doesn't fit together there are two possibilities. A piece is missing or a piece is in the wrong spot.

I certainly had missing pieces but I was really thinking I had misinterpreted something.

I was opening my mouth to speak to Ann when I felt it again. The hair on the back of my neck stood up and I knew that "The Voice" was about to return.

"Oh, shit," I said, the words slipping out before I could stop them.

"What is it?" Ann asked.

"I can feel it," I said. I had opened my mouth and I wasn't going to lie to her about it. "The voice is comin'."

"I'm here," she said. "Keep the line open. I got you, Conner."

What was I missing? What had I gotten wrong?

The hair on the back of my neck was still standing and I felt the creepy feeling and worried again that the clouds were more than they were and I was about to get hit by lightning, but the voice hadn't made its appearance.

And then I smiled.

"You're not gonna like this," I said to Ann. "But I gotta hang up for sec. I'll call ya back shortly."

She was replying, but I hung up. I put my phone in my pocket even though it was still recording video. I took a deep breath and the manic, horror-movie laughter started.

"I am the devil you know," the voice said. "And you will die tonight, Conner Bright."

"I rather doubt that," I said.

"I am the devil you know and—"

"Right, right," I said. "And I'm gonna die tonight. Sorry, but your routine is gettin' a little old, mate. I've almost died plenty a times. It don't scare me no more."

"You will die tonight," the voice hissed.

Before I had pretended that I couldn't hear it, this time I was talking to it because I had figured something out. The tech for this wasn't in the building I was watching—there was no one in there to come out.

My first instinct had been correct before I heard the voice the first time, worried that the clouds were going to rain down lightning on me. The voice was coming from above me.

I took my hat off and slowly tilted my head up. My neck doesn't like this position, at all. Too many jolts from a bucking bull, too many rolls in the dirt of a rodeo arena with a furious two-ton animal after me. And I really didn't expect to see anything, but I was as sure as I could be that there was a drone or two up above me doing the "sonic beaming" and pointing a parabolic mic at me.

Now drones are noisy so I wasn't sure how the mic would work, but I'm pretty sure Emma would.

This gave me a how, but not a who or a why.

"I am the devil—" the voice began.

"Will ya just shut the hell up," I said as I walked back to the bar.

TWENTY-ONE

Detective Trisha Sanchez pulled up in front of The
Devil You Know just as I was getting back. She hopped out of
her car and said, "Did you do it?"

She looked rather rumpled, an unusual look for her, dressed
in jeans and a maroon and gold Sun Devils sweatshirt. For once
her brown eyes were not hidden behind mirror shades.

"Hello to you too," I said with a grin.

She crossed her arms and cocked her hip, a clear sign of her
utter and total lack of amusement. Sanchez worked normal
hours, so she slept normal hours, and I had woken her up which
easily explained the grumpiness.

"Nah," I said, pointing up. "No need to. It's drones. They're
listenin' to us right now. Say hi, Detective."

I saw Amber Black staring at us inside the bar and waved at
her to come out. She did the look around "are you waving at
me?" routine and I waved again and nodded.

Amber walked out, her arms folded and she looked as nearly
put out as Sanchez did.

"Alrighty," I said. "My tech person told me about this up-

and-coming technology called 'sound beamin'.' With it, you know, you beam sound at a target so only they and those very close to them can hear it. That's what's been happenin' here. Happened to me tonight. A couple a times. And I'm pretty sure they are using drones." I pointed my thumb up for emphasis.

"They are also listenin'," I added. "No idea why they are targeting this bar but it seems like a case worthy of police investigations," I said looking at Sanchez.

She nodded.

"And worthy of journalistic investigation," I said to Amber.

She nodded like Sanchez had but she was wide-eyed. Maybe with fear, maybe with the lust that comes along with finding a good story, maybe at the bizarreness of it all.

I just grinned. This was far from over but at least I had a "how" and at least I had some partners in it, even if both of them didn't seem to like me, at all.

"And my tech person will be givin' a demonstration of it at noon tomorrow. You all in?"

TWENTY-TWO

I stayed until The Devil You Know was closed and it was just me and Ann. I wiped down tables and put the stools on them, and swept while Ann closed up the bar and dealt with the money. I know what the end of night looks like at a bar. And things were weird enough that I didn't want Ann to be alone.

And I wanted to be with Ann, even if it wasn't time to consider dating, even if it was more temptation than I should be exposing myself to without enough sleep.

I had briefed Ann about what I knew and what the plan was. In fact, most of the bar listened in, which was fine. Anything to dispel the superstition. Amber Black and I had exchanged phone numbers and I had texted Emma Shapiro telling her to expect a crowd in the morning.

We didn't have a perpetrator or motive, but the teeth of this thing were about to be pulled. The recording of "The Voice" I had attempted had, unfortunately, failed, the app glitching and not recording at all when the voice was speaking to me, but once Emma showed them how it was done, the magic trick wouldn't be magic anymore.

"Thanks for staying," Ann said as we walked out and she locked up.

"I'm a full-service PI," I said with a smile that was probably a little silly. "I investigate. I sweep. I work the door."

The street was silent, cast in yellow by the streetlights and it all felt just a touch apocalyptic. Even the buzz of the 202 to the north was restrained this early in the morning.

"Does that extend to walking me home?" she asked with a shy smile.

"Of course," I said despite the clear and present danger.

Ann had a long, dark jacket on against the morning chill and had taken her horns off but at this point she'd still be attractive as hell to me dressed in a trash bag.

She slipped her arm in mine and we strolled down Mill Avenue, just the two of us.

It was...

Well, it's been a while since I felt like a teenager, but it was that kind of feeling. We didn't talk and the relative silence felt enveloping, like we were really out camping, sitting by a fire sharing a blanket that was pulling us close.

"Are you this kind to all your clients?" she asked after a while. We had just turned off Mill onto 5th.

"I should tell ya somethin'," I said, my voice, much to my embarrassment, coming out rough and a little froggy.

"It's okay," she said. "You have someone. I understand."

I was trying to gently highlight the subtext but she leapfrogged that and just ripped the band-aid off.

"It's complicated," I said, my stomach doing somersaults.

"I understand," she said.

"I doubt ya do, but I'd like ya to," I said.

She stopped and disengaged her arm and I missed her closeness.

"I'd like to, too," she said, her green eyes washed out in the sodium glow of a nearby streetlight but still so lovely I almost forgot what I was talking about.

I dug my six-month chip out of my pocket and handed it to her. "I'm seven months and six days sober," I said.

"Okay..." she said, clearly not getting it and that made me happy for her. If she didn't know the details of AA, that probably meant she hadn't had an alcoholic close in her life.

"I should have my year chip before I..." I couldn't finish the sentence and my cheeks burned hot. I was over forty and I was acting like a teenager. It had been so long that I didn't even think I was capable of feeling this way.

"Okay," she said with a nod and a quirky little smile. She put the chip back in my hand, grabbed my arm and we started walking again.

I was so stunned it took me half a block to find my voice. "Ummm... Do ya mind elaboratin' a little? Whattya mean by 'okay'?"

She smiled and by God it was a sight to see, my knees wholeheartedly agreeing and turning to mush. My stomach joining the party doing an Olympic-level tumbling routine.

"I like you, Conner," she said. "Clearly you like me. So what's five months and twenty-five days in the scheme of things?"

My jaw worked but I could find no words.

She saw my face and laughed, the joyful sound bouncing off the two-story apartment buildings near us. "You do like me, don't you?" she asked.

"Very much," I said.

"Then 'okay,'" she said with a shrug. "Let's be friends for now. Let's see where we are in five months and twenty-five days."

I nodded and noticed I was sweating quite profusely despite the cool of the early morning. My "open mind" of a few days ago was gone. I was sunk. And those five months and twenty-five days could not pass quickly enough.

Ann laughed again when she saw my face and I felt so much like a teenager.

TWENTY-THREE

Emma Shapiro was ever the gracious host.

In her elegant and spare dining room with southwest touches were homemade muffins still warm from the oven, sliced cantaloupe, homemade croissant and egg sandwiches, and plenty of coffee.

It was just past noon and everyone seemed a little nervous. Ann was sticking close to me, which my newly minted middle-aged teenage self didn't mind one little bit.

Detective Trisha Sanchez stood leaning against a wall watching me like a hawk. Gone was the sweatshirt and she was back to wearing her seemingly ubiquitous dark pantsuit with her black hair pulled back into a neat ponytail. We were inside so the reflective sunglasses were hooked on her blouse.

She was watching Ann and me, and the teenager in me found the attention a touch parental.

Amber Black was only partially dressed in black this time with jeans and a zipped up black sweat jacket, sitting in a chair eating like she hadn't seen real food in weeks.

Which might be true. She was a college student, after all.

I had spent much of the morning driving. After walking Ann home, I had taken the time to drive across town to my single-wide on the outskirts of this metropolis, grabbed a few hours of sleep and a shower, drove back to Ann's place, picked her up, and then drove to Sun City.

That's the problem with the sprawl of the Valley of the Sun. It's not hard to spend most of your day driving.

"Okay," Emma said, rubbing her hands together, her lean face forming a bright smile. "It's a little fiddly, but I think I got it."

No one said a thing. I, frankly, was afraid I would say something stupid, the unusual hormones running through my system. I'm not sure what was going on with everyone else. Maybe the general lack of sleep.

"Who's first?" Emma asked.

"First?" Amber asked, putting down her second sandwich.

"Yes, first," Emma said. "Sound beaming is all about producing isolated sounds so you have to be in the foci of the wave pattern the two speakers produce, where the sound waves interact and create something you can hear."

Amber nodded, picked up her phone, her fingers flying over the virtual keyboard in a way that I could never do as she took notes.

"I'll go first," I said. "I already heard the damn voice."

Emma nodded and stepped into the hallway. I moved to follow and everyone else started to move. It was like Emma was the mother duck and we her chicks.

"One at a time," she said with an indulgent smile. "It's fiddly. Everyone will get their turn."

I followed her back into what must be a spare bedroom, a large one at that, but there was no bed or dresser in there. Most of the walls were lined with either metal shelves full of bins

marked with neat labels, or bookshelves stuffed with thick refer-
ence books, the kind you usually only see in a library.

There was a wooden desk on one wall and in the middle of
the room a large folding table was set up with a bunch of electronics stuff on it.

And, yes, "electronics stuff" is an accurate description if you
grew up in Globe, Arizona riding horses and ditching school as
much as you could get away with.

Some of the "electronics stuff" looked old with tubes and I
think the thing with a glowing round green screen was an oscilloscope. There were wires and speakers and a laptop computer
and lots of other things I couldn't identify.

"Stand there," she said, pointing at two pieces of duct tape
on the elegant tiled floor that formed a little "X."

I nodded and stood at the appointed spot.

"Tell me what you hear," she said.

"I hear a journalism student skulkin' around the hallway and
not stayin' put as requested," I said loud enough for my voice to
carry where Amber was hiding.

"Sorry," she said, and I heard her retreating footsteps.

Emma didn't do anything that would qualify as "mad scien-
tist," she just poked at the keyboard and then I saw a wave pattern
on the round screen of the oscilloscope and then I heard it.

The sound wasn't clear but it wasn't staticky either. The
sound didn't seem close, but it didn't seem far away. It's hard to
describe but it was like it was just out of focus.

I heard this resonant there-but-not-there man's voice say, "To
be or not to be, that is the question."

"Shakespeare," I said with a nod. "Hamlet."

She poked at the keyboard again and the voice stopped mid-
sentence. "Sir Laurence Olivier," she said. "From the 1948
movie."

"Ya did it, Emma," I said. "It's slightly different, the voice at the bar was more... in focus, I guess. But ya did it." I looked back and added, "Did ya get that, Amber?"

The girl had faked her retreat but I hadn't seen any harm, so I let it be.

"Yes," she said, her voice a touch defiant.

"Did ya hear the voice?" I asked.

"No," she said. There was a small pause and in a much quieter voice she asked, "Can I go next?"

TWENTY-FOUR

Everyone had their turn with everyone else crowded in the hallway proving that while the person standing on the duct tape X could hear it, no one else could.

I have to say that the superstitious vibe around "the voice" did not fall right away even with incontrovertible evidence.

For example, after Amber was done, Ann asked her, "You really heard something?"

Amber, wide-eyed, nodded. "That was so bizarre."

After Ann had her turn, she asked me, "You really didn't hear it?"

"Not a peep," I said.

I got it. This was something new. This didn't conform to how we thought the world worked, thus the stickiness of superstition. Fact is stranger than fiction and all of that.

Back in the living room, all of us but Amber standing around with coffee mugs in our hands—Amber was sitting down and eating more—the silence was a bit thick.

Life hits you with things that cause you to reevaluate your view of the world. No one likes to do that.

"Well, I'm still screwed," Ann said after the silence had gotten uncomfortable. "I can tell this to my old customers all day long and they won't believe it. I barely believe it."

"And we don't know who is doing this to you or why," Sanchez said. She had been almost silent during her turn on the "X" only saying "I hear it" when Emma did her thing.

"But we know how," I said. "And that's somethin'." I gave Ann a reassuring nod but she didn't seem reassured at all.

"I've got one week," she said, "maybe two before I have to give it up. My reserves are seriously low."

"Give it up" had a lot of weight for her. It was the bar her father had built and was a tribute to him. Me, I had a Christmas cookie tin with my father's ashes in it next to the TV and I talked to him every day. That was my way of keeping the connection alive. Ann McGee had a bar full of memorabilia that was also her livelihood that she used to keep her father's memory alive.

What would I do if someone was trying to take my dad's ashes away from me? How would I feel if I was about to lose them and there was nothing that I could do to stop it?

"There's gotta be a way," I said.

Amber stopped eating for a moment and said, "Too bad you can't bring all your customers here to experience it for themselves."

Everyone was silent, but my brain suddenly woke up and an idea hit me hard, like a furious rodeo bull. "That's brilliant!" I said, a huge smile on my face.

"What?" Amber asked. "You can't bring them all here."

"But what if we took the equipment to the bar," I said looking at Emma. "Can ya do it? Can we set this up there?"

"Wait, what?" Ann asked. "You want to..." And then her eyes got big as she got it. "Oh..."

"That's right," I said. "Everyone who stands on the X in The

Devil You Know gets to hear the voice while those standin' a few feet away won't hear a thing."

"That is…" Amber began. "Word will spread. People will come in just to experience it. You can claim the voice was a feature of the bar all along."

There was some excited chatter but then Sanchez said, "What about Vince Rogers?"

Vince Rogers was one of the first ones to hear the voice and had ended up getting hit by a car in front of the bar after hearing it.

"Shit," Ann said. "I'd be opening myself to a lawsuit from the family."

Silence descended again, but it was heavier this time. The new reality was being accepted but it didn't do Ann and her bar one bit of good.

And then Sanchez turned to Amber. "What about you?" she said. "Can't you write about all of this, tell the truth? About how someone was using this technology to harass Ann. How a technical genius that just so happens to be older than your typical technical genius figured out how to replicate it. How The Devil You Know will be showcasing the technology so everyone understands."

Amber sat there blinking, a half-eaten muffin clutched in her hand.

Sanchez turned to Emma, "Can you make this work in the bar?"

Emma got a look on her face. It's hard to describe but her eyes scrunched and her lips pursed like she might be getting angry but it was just a look of concentration for her. But there was something else there, a slight turning up of the lips, a glimmer in her eyes.

"I need a day, maybe two," Emma said with a small shrug.

"And it'll take some time to set up at the bar. But, yes, I can do it."

Sanchez turned to Amber. "And can you have an article ready and out by then?"

Amber nodded. "Sure." She glanced at Emma. "I'd like to shadow the process a bit. For the article, you know."

Emma chuckled. "Sure, kid. I could use an extra set of hands, and I'll feed you."

Amber still had a muffin in her hand clearly illustrating the need.

Emma turned to Ann and asked, "What do you want the voice to say?"

A shy smile lit up her beautiful face. She cleared her throat and said, "How about, 'I am the devil you know and you will have a good time tonight.'"

TWENTY-FIVE

Three nights later, I had my stool set up in front of
The Devil You Know. Emma Shapiro's sound beaming rig was
set up just inside the door and I was not only checking IDs and
putting on wristbands, but explaining the process to a throng of
excited college students.

Amber Black's article had done its job and the place was
packed. There was a line of people waiting to go in and experience "the voice" and it was quite clear that the bar was going to
be okay, but I was not happy. Not at all.

We hadn't solved the mystery, just pulled the teeth out of
whoever had done this.

I don't know about you, but an unsolved mystery rubs me the
wrong way. Granted, there hadn't been enough time to solve this
one yet. It's the kind of job that takes a lot of research, footwork,
and patience. And, frankly, it was going to be hard to solve this
one if I was working the door every night, but Ann had asked me
to keep doing it for a while and I just couldn't say no to her.

Just before midnight, Detective Trisha Sanchez showed up

dressed in her normal dark blue pantsuit that the sodium glow of the streetlights made look black.

She nodded at the crowded bar and the line of about ten people waiting to get it. "Ann's a hit," she said.

"Was there any doubt?" I asked, the grin on my face I'm quite sure qualifying as silly.

Thankfully she ignored my boyish reaction to the mention of Ann and said, "There's still work to do."

I nodded. "I know," I said. "I'm worried that whoever did this will come at it from another angle."

Sanchez bit her lower lip and nodded. She turned and looked through the windows into the crowded bar. There was a young man standing on the duct taped X, and while I couldn't hear what he was saying, I am quite sure he was asking his friends if they had heard the voice he just had.

But that's not what Sanchez was looking at. She was looking past the crowd at Ann who was behind the bar.

I know because I had done it many times that night myself.

"She seems happy," Sanchez said, her voice low almost like she was talking to herself.

"She's relieved," I said. "But still worried like the rest of us."

Sanchez turned to me and crossed her arms. "We have to talk. But not here. Come by Major Crimes tomorrow. Eleven sharp."

I nodded and watched Sanchez walk away, her shoulders back, her spine erect, and for some reason I was even more worried than I had been before she showed up.

TWENTY-SIX

Detective Trisha Sanchez's office was small and cramped, a box of a room with an old metal desk, one extra chair on the other side of that desk, a bookshelf that had binders and thick bound books, and a flat-grey metal cabinet that was closed.

The fluorescent lights were too bright and the buzz of them set my teeth on edge. Or, maybe it was that it seemed like every time in the last few years I appeared before Sanchez in her office I ended up wishing that I hadn't.

Sanchez wasn't there. I had been escorted in and told to wait with no details on why Sanchez was late. I wasn't offered coffee, just the usual stares as I walked past the other officers of the Maricopa County Sheriff's Office who weren't lucky enough to have a cramped office with buzzing fluorescent lights.

Oh, they all got the stupid buzzing lights, though, with no privacy.

Sanchez's office was neat. I mean, really neat. As in a bit OCD neat. Everything clearly had its place and it damn well better be there or there would be hell to pay.

There was a closed laptop on the desk, perfectly centered, a small desk lamp, and a larger torch lamp in the corner so it was clear that the damn fluorescents could be turned off.

The place stunk of old stale coffee with a chaser of gun oil. Not a terrible smell, but it just put me more on edge.

It had been almost half an hour and I was just about ready to go when Sanchez walked in, her stride so quick I could feel a slight breeze from it. "Sorry about that," she said without further explanation.

She closed the door and my stomach clenched up. After sitting down across the desk from me, she said, "We have to talk about Ann McGee."

"Alrighty," I said. This wasn't any different than I expected, but it sounded rather dire and my youthful emotions really didn't want to be examined.

"But first an update on that background search you asked," she said, and I felt like the Ann thing had been a feint and now I was really in for it.

"What did you find out about Emma?" I asked.

She shrugged, it was a casual gesture, but like most of her movements showed that she was wound a little tighter than most people, the motion quicker and more precise than was warranted. "Not much," she said. "Clean record. Likes to give to charities, mostly at-risk youth, was a glass ceiling breaker in her career, been married more than usual. You know."

And I did. I knew all of this about Emma except for the lack of a record. I had never looked into that.

"But..." I said, prompting her to continue.

"But I'm busy as hell and haven't gotten very far," she said, her brown eyes intense as she stared at me.

"You like her," I said with a nod.

She nodded back. "What's not to like?" she asked. "Brilliant, driven, successful, and she bakes a mean muffin. She seems like the kind of person you'd want on your side."

Her stare intensified and I stared right back. She wasn't saying everything that needed to be said and I was pretty damn sure this was a test. Sanchez wanted to see if I had my wits about me, if I was listening, if I was on the ball.

"Ask your question," I said. It was obvious that she had one.

"Are you sure you want me to continue?" she asked.

"No," I said. "Not sure at all. I am very fond of Emma. If there is something there, I am not at all sure that I wanna know, but if there is I suspect that I need to know."

Sanchez finally broke eye contact, pursed her lips, and nodded. "I'll keep going. Do you think she's involved in what's going on at The Devil You Know?"

I found it odd that Sanchez used the name of the bar not the name of my client, but I let it go.

I shook my head and sighed. "I hope to hell not, but it's pretty miraculous that Emma could put that sound beamin' demo together that quickly. Could be somethin'. Could be nothin'. I sure as hell don't know."

Sanchez nodded her head absently for a moment and I almost thought we were done, but then her patent-pending predatorial smile lit up her lean face and she said, "Ann likes you. Can't say I understand why, but she likes you."

And there it was. Starting the conversation with Ann's name, quickly detouring to Emma to make sure I was awake, and now we were down to it, and I felt like I had emotional whiplash.

Not that that mattered to the teenage boy in me—he was over the moon. All the signals were there, she had said as much, but doubt about these things is inevitable. But I did my best to not let any of that show. I dug my six-month AA chip out and put it on the desk and said, "I like her too. But I shouldn't date until I have a year chip."

Sanchez leaned back, the chair protesting with a noisy squeak. "She told me," she said. "You really mean that?"

"Absolutely," I said.

She eyed me for a few seconds and then said, "You think you have that kind of will power?"

It was a valid question but another part of me besides the smitten teenager responded and I had to work hard to not let the anger out. This conversation was a test and I didn't have the time for it.

"I haven't had a drink in seven months and six days," I said, slowly and evenly. "I regularly work in bars and I have found out a few things about managing my will power. Would you care for me to elaborate?"

The sharklike smile came back and she nodded. "Please."

"Number one," I said, holding up my index finger. "Do it for yourself. I can't see Irene if I'm not sober and spending time with that girl makes me happy and gives me a damn good reason to stay sober."

Sanchez nodded but didn't comment.

"Number two," I said, holding up my middle finger next to my index finger. "Embracin' the fact that I have limited will power so planning as best I can so that I have it when I need it."

She nodded again, the shark-smile still in place, and for some reason I had had enough of this. Who was she to mess with me like this, to question my commitment to my sobriety? Who was she to act like Ann's parent, questioning my intentions?

"And three," I said, folding my index finger back down so only the middle finger was standing.

Sanchez didn't say a thing, her smile getting a little more predatorial.

It was a little bit of a standoff. Me flipping her the bird, her smiling at me like a predator about to pounce.

Finally Sanchez sighed and rocked forward in her chair so our faces were much closer. As she did this, I lowered my hand.

"I know this is weird," she said. "I get it. But Ann is important to me. She's my sister and..."

She looked away, but before she did there was something in those dark eyes of hers, something that caused my guts to twist up.

"What is it?" I asked.

I could see her lips purse but she didn't look at me.

"I deserve to know," I said, my guts twisting even tighter. I had feelings for Ann. I can't say that I quite understood them, but they were strong.

She nodded and when she looked at me there was such sadness there in her deep brown eyes that I wanted to run. "I will tell no secrets," she said. "She's a strong woman, but we all have our breaking point. To tell you the truth, Bright, I worry about both of you with this thing."

I just sat there blinking. I couldn't find any words. And then Sachez's phone rang and she swept out of the office stirring up another breeze with the swiftness of her passage.

TWENTY-SEVEN

I had longed for the day when Detective Trisha Sanchez started treating me like a human being again. We were never exactly friends, but we were colleagues, people with mutual respect that could rely on each other.

When I walked out of Major Crimes into a warm winter's day in the Valley of the Sun, I was kind of wishing that things hadn't changed. That Sanchez was a gleeful imp torturing me with the weirdest cases, not worried about me. And Ann.

I stood right outside the door to Major Crimes staring at my phone and without thinking about it called Emma Shapiro.

"Yeah?" she said in answer.

"I... I need a meetin'," I said.

I was running on autopilot here. I wasn't thinking just acting, and at least that acting didn't involve heading to the nearest Circle-K and grabbing a case of cheap beer.

"Am I your sponsor?" she asked, her voice calm and steady which I really appreciated. There hadn't been enough time in the last few days to consider her offer, much less accept it.

"Please," I said, again running on instinct.

"Where are you?" she asked.

"Phoenix," I said. "Was just talkin' to Detective Sanchez."

"Can you drive?" she asked, and I heard the clack of a keyboard in the background.

"Sure," I said, but I didn't sound very sure.

"Okay," she said. "There's a meeting in Glendale in forty minutes. It's at a church about halfway between us. I'll text you the address and meet you there."

"Good," I said, my voice sounding anything but good. "Meet ya there."

"No stops, Conner," she said. "Drive there. Stay in your car until I come get you. Got it?"

"Got it," I said.

"Just drive. Don't stop. Stay in your car," she said, her tone gaining a little urgency as she repeated instructions like I was a six-year-old.

"Just drive," I said.

"Just drive," Emma repeated. "Wait for me. I'm coming."

Emma hung up and I got in my car and just drove.

HERE'S THE THING ABOUT BEING AN ALCOHOLIC. You never know what it is that's going to punch through your defenses. It's a day at a time, sometimes one hour at a time, and way too often, one breath at a time.

I realize that this level of uncertainty isn't restricted to addicts, that each of us never knows when the fates will take notice of us and piss all over our lives. The difference with addicts is there is more fragility there and a known destructive path we'll go down. And, the biggest difference is we know we're fragile, we know we have to follow the steps, take care of ourselves, or something totally normal can take us out.

We can't walk through our lives thinking we are indestructible—that's a quick ticket back to the bottle (or whatever your addiction is).

I knew I was in trouble, I could feel it at a visceral level, but it wasn't logical or in focus yet, thus all that "acting on instinct," which is really not a good way to put it. I was acting on the training I had gotten as part of AA.

As I walked to my car, what my mind latched on to was Sanchez's worry about me. But I was still fighting, my mind cushioning the real blow and that there was something going on with Ann.

Sanchez had said, "She's a strong woman, but we all have our breaking point." What did she mean by that? What had broken Ann?

Don't get me wrong. There's no shame in the world breaking you. It's what the world does to us all from time to time, especially if you are living a life worth living, out there trying to make your way and do a little bit of good now and then.

The world will break you, but what broke Ann? And for Sanchez to be concerned, that thing still had to be lingering. And was Sanchez worried that our relationship would break Ann further? Was Sanchez worried that *I* would break Ann?

Driving can be good medicine and there was time so I took back streets, cruising the El Camino along with the throng of newer vehicles. I didn't turn the radio on but I had the window down in case the cool air was able to help me stay present.

And I mean it about there not being shame about the world breaking you. It broke me. Badly. The day my foot slipped off the clutch and I killed my best friend in the entire world. I was shattered.

That break is reflected in nearly every aspect of my life.

What could it be for Ann?

"Her father," I said aloud. He was murdered behind the bar

she is so desperately trying to keep open. The course of her life was altered that day. I don't know her history, but it's easy to imagine that she had other ambitions besides running a college bar in Tempe, Arizona.

There's no shame in that job, or any job done well, but one would imagine an intelligent, ambitious young woman having different plans.

It didn't bother me that she was broken. What bothered me was how much I wanted to get that year chip and be with her. From what Sanchez said, it seems like she's worried we won't be good for each other, that we'll break each other further.

In a good relationship, on average, you heal over time, become more whole, and in a bad one, on average, you become more broken.

Was Sanchez worried we would be the latter?

As I drove, as the sameness of the Phoenix sprawl slid by with islands of retail shops huddled together amidst the endless housing subdivisions, I realized that that was why I called Emma without thinking about it. That's why I needed a meeting.

I had begun to hope for a less lonely life, a life with someone to walk through it with, and Sanchez had pretty much burst that bubble with her strange warning and worry.

I had hoped for a future with Ann, a stunning woman of strength and beauty, and Sanchez's warning made me realize that it was, honestly, long odds and my mostly lonely life was likely to continue, and if things went bad with Ann, I would be, to be sure, more broken.

Not that I wouldn't fight. I would fight like hell. To find whoever was trying to put Ann out of business. To stay sober and get my one-year chip and keep going. To be a man that is worth a woman like Ann's time and affection.

TWENTY-EIGHT

EMMA SHAPIRO WAS THERE WHEN I ARRIVED AT THE church, a rather bland Lutheran church made of pale brick with a nearly empty parking lot. She got in the El Camino with me and said, "There is no meeting here. I lied to get you moving and to get you to me."

Emma was put together as always in her usual pedal push-ers, this time her sweater was blue. Her grey hair was pulled back into a nub of a ponytail and her lipstick appeared to be freshly applied. She looked rather rushed and a bit tired, but I was impressed that she had shown up for me.

I opened my mouth to speak before my brain had digested what she said, but she didn't give me a chance to speak and said, "So we are going to have a meeting. Here in your car. Right now. Hello, my name is Emma and I'm an alcoholic."

I blinked, trying to get my brain to catch up, still rather distracted by my revelations driving over.

"Umm... Hello, Emma," I said. It felt strange to not have at least a few other people saying it with me. People who I knew nothing about except their first name and that they were alcoholics like me.

Emma gave me a small smile and nodded. It was my turn.

I shook my head, not yet able to articulate my hesitation. Part of me knew what Emma wanted. She wanted me to drop the Conner Bright façade and be who I am, who I used to be.

Sitting in my car, with a bowie knife on my hip, an alligator claw hanging at my neck, and my alligator skin boots on, that didn't feel right.

I discard the trappings of Conner Bright before I go into a meeting. I use my real name. I use my real voice. As awkward as both of those things feel at this point. I tend to move about with the meetings I go to and haven't gotten too close to anyone, thus my lack of a long-term sponsor.

"You need a meeting," Emma said gently. "I'm here."

But this wasn't even the way the ritual went. At this point, Emma should be sharing, there should be coffee and sweets, and it wouldn't be my turn until I was ready to go, if I was ready to go.

"What is this, Emma?" I asked, finally able to get a few words out.

Emma's deeply wrinkled forehead furrowed into an impressive show. Her tan from all the time in the garden was earned, the Arizona sun having contributed to her wrinkles. "You called me saying you needed a meeting," she said, her words precise like she had chosen them and was saying them very carefully. "This seemed like the best way."

Early in the case, I had dedicated myself to keeping an open mind, to learning the lesson from the Metro Center case when it had been all about me, and to keep my eyes open during a case, to not interpret things but to just follow the facts.

But Ann had changed that, or, rather, my growing feelings

for Ann had, but in my car in front of that bland church all of that came back into play.

I hardly knew Ann and I didn't know Emma very well either. We had a congenial working relationship and we were friendly, but that was something different than being a friend.

I did know Detective Sanchez, not that we were really friends, but I had faced danger with her multiple times and I knew what kind of person she was. A bit vengeful with all the crazy cases she seemed to be punishing me with, but she hadn't cut me off after my alcohol-fueled mistake, she hadn't cut me out of her life. She was hard on me, to be sure, but she was still there.

"And I appreciate it," I said with a tentative smile. "But I think I'm too new to the program for somethin' this... this is too intimate to feel right. I think I still need the second 'A.'"

"Anonymous," she said with a tight smile and a small nod.

I nodded back.

"But I already know, Conner," she said.

"I know," I said, but in my clearer view of things, I realized that I didn't know how much she knew, only that she knew the whole "from a little town called Scatterwood deep in the Outback" was bunk. And as she pointed out, that wasn't that hard to figure out in this day and age.

At this point, it was noticeable that she hadn't used my real first name. Well, to be specific since I legally changed my name, she hadn't used the name I was born with.

Maybe this was Emma being a bit bored and I was her vehicle to spice her life up a bit. All good, but not here, not now, not this.

"Look," she said, crossing her arms. "Am I your sponsor or not? Do you trust me or not?"

Looking into her sharp blue eyes, I wanted to trust her and I figured she was trustworthy. Her actions thus far had proven her trustworthy in certain areas. Hell, I'd probably be better off trusting her, but I couldn't.

"Emma," I said, "you're one of the smartest people I know. When it comes to tech, I trust ya with my life. But with my past? I don't even trust myself."

A wave of emotion passed over Emma's face. Was it surprise or compassion? Maybe a touch of anger. Maybe all three. But it didn't last long and she swallowed and nodded. "Fair enough," she said. "We both know we are alcoholics. Do you want to tell me what's going on?"

And I did. It was strange that her slightly different tact removed the pressure, but it did and I told her about my meeting with Sanchez and it really helped to talk about it.

TWENTY-NINE

Conner Bright is my armor against the past.

Because I can't live with what I did. I can't forgive myself that moment where my foot slipped off the clutch and my old pickup lurched forward and I ended the life of my best friend.

I understand that I was drunk, very drunk, and under the influence of teenage hormones. I understand that it was not my intent to harm him even though you might not have known that by the things we were shouting at each other. I even understand that I am human and I make mistakes, especially when I'm drunk.

All of those are nice thoughts and it changes nothing about what I feel. Time has, to some extent, blunted things a bit. My years putting myself in harm's way for others lets me sleep at night, occasionally.

But I took the life of someone I loved in a moment of drunken anger. I can't undo that. Being Conner Bright lets me function in the world.

After Emma left, as I was still sitting in the El Camino

staring at the bland brick Lutheran church, I realized I wasn't ready to take off the armor of Conner Bright.

Not with Emma.

Not with Sanchez, although she had to know.

Not with Ann.

Not even with myself.

And only occasionally at an AA meeting where I was actually anonymous.

I can't tell you what was causing Sanchez's worry about Ann and me, but after that realization I can tell you what was worrying me.

At this point it's hard to say that Conner Bright is all a lie. This is who I have been legally and otherwise for decades. A part-time PI, part-time bouncer, part-time handyman struggling to get by and to do a bit of good now and then.

But I can say clearly that Conner Bright is armor that I am unwilling to take off, and armored up like I am is no way to be in a relationship. Walling off my past like that makes it hard to be intimate.

I knew this, of course, but I knew it intellectually. The little crisis Sanchez threw me into made me feel it on a gut level.

Ann McGee deserved someone that could be open with her, that could be truly intimate, and I wasn't capable of that with anyone right now.

Maybe someday. Maybe even by the time I got my year sobriety chip, but I shook that thought off. I needed to see clearly. This case. My self. My future. I couldn't put Ann out there as a prize for staying sober and coming to grips with my past. That wasn't fair to her or to me.

And I couldn't put a clock on trying to come to terms with my past—something I was fairly sure wasn't possible. I needed to stay on the road I was on. Taking the weird cases. Doing good when I can. Trying to atone for something that couldn't be atoned for.

———

"WHAT'S WRONG, CONNER?" ANN ASKED THAT MORNING AS I walked her home after the bar closed. The city was relatively quiet like it was taking a breath before morning came.

We were off Mill Avenue and had just left the businesses behind, two- and three-story apartment buildings rising up on either side, cars densely parked along the street.

I had worked the door again and I thought I had done a good job of hiding my disappointment from the day's revelations but apparently not.

I am proud to say that I didn't say something stupid like "Nothing's wrong, why do you ask?" or try to evade the question. "I have a past," I said slowly, carefully choosing my words.

"We all do," she said, holding my arm tighter and pulling me closer as we walked.

There was genuine affection between us. It was easy and it felt natural, and although some people seem to find this kind of thing easily, I do not, which made it valuable.

"Not like I do," I said.

"So tell me about it," she said. We had just walked into the focal point of a streetlight, the sodium-yellow light seeming too bright, making me long for a darker corner.

I wanted to break contact with her, say what I needed to say without that bond of genuine affection, but I didn't, because of that affection. Ann would probably think it was about her when this is, really, all about me.

"I did somethin'," I said, again speaking slowly as if there was somehow a way to find the right words. "Somethin' terrible.

Somethin' unforgivable. Somethin' that caused me to... to change who I am. Somethin' I can never make right."

Ann stopped and I was glad we were in the relative dim between pools of yellow light. She maneuvered slowly so she never lost contact with me until she was holding my hands and staring up into my eyes.

"I want you to hear this, Conner Bright," she said slowly, the serious look on her face compounded by the relative dimness. "Are you listening?"

My heart leapt into a gallop as sweat broke out on the back of my neck and my stomach knotted up. I nodded; it was all I could do.

"I do not care what you did," she said. "Do you want to know why?"

"Yes," I said, but it came out as a croak.

"Because I know who you are, Conner," she said. "I can see the pain in your eyes, the pain you try to hide. I can see it because I see the same thing in my own eyes. I know how one terrible thing can completely change a life, change who you are at a fundamental level."

I nodded and fought back the tears that wanted to escape. To use the language of my recent revelation, Ann was telling me that she saw my armor, understood why someone might change so drastically because of trauma, and that she did not care.

"I think that is one of the reasons we clicked," she said. "You and I, we really have a past."

"Your father," I said.

She nodded. "I am not the same person I was before he was murdered."

"I am very sorry for your loss," I said.

"Thank you," she said, but I saw that saying it had caused her pain and wished I hadn't. She took a deep breath, like she was trying to get herself back on track and said, "No matter what you did in the past, you are a good man today. And the world doesn't have nearly enough good men."

With that she took my arm again and we started walking. I was glad she couldn't see those tears finally escape my eyes.

THIRTY

Three Weeks Later

Ann wanted to be my friend, and more, even with my armor on.

Ann was willing to wait for physical intimacy even though I was more emotionally intimate with her than I had been with anyone since my father died.

All of this after I made it clear that I had armor on, that I had a past that haunted me, that I wasn't exactly whole.

I thought she would be better off without me. She made it clear that that was not what she wanted.

I couldn't walk away.

That easy affection, that emotional intimacy, it hurt in ways that are hard for me to explain, but it felt good too. And beyond that it felt necessary. Like I had been starving and the first bites of food were hard for my starved body to take in but exactly what it needed.

So as the mild Phoenix winter slipped past, my life fell into a comfortable rhythm. Whenever my caseload allowed, I worked at The Devil You Know five nights a week, the same nights Ann worked. I would walk her home in the wee hours of the morning.

Whether we talked much or not, it was always comfortable, always easy and hard at the same time, because while my armor was still on there were gaps in it that she was able to see through, and that wasn't comfortable yet.

I was having a hard time being seen at this level by another human being.

I treasure those walks and always will. Ann was so easy to be with, but it was so hard to not do more. To not kiss her at her apartment door before she went in. Before we walked, she always took the horns out of her hair and put some kind of jacket on over that form hugging red dress, but I knew what was underneath and wanted to do much more than kiss her. So much more.

I had to manage my reserve of willpower to make sure I had enough to say no to that temptation. I owed it to myself and I owed it to her to wait the full year. At least.

"I'm gonna be gone for a few days," I said. "I've got someone trustworthy that can cover the door for me."

This was three weeks after Emma had installed the sound beaming setup and the bar was doing great.

"Oh?" she asked, but I caught the slight note of fear in her voice and she held my arm just a little tighter as we walked.

I could feel it too. Our bond had continued to grow. I didn't want to be away from her.

"Picked up a case in Tucson," I said. "Doesn't even involve unicorns or hauntin's or anything like that."

"That's great," she said, but I could hear the effort she was putting into being supportive.

We were, frankly, headed towards codependence, not uncommon early in a relationship, but one of the reasons I said yes to the case was because I thought a little distance would be good.

"Nothing excitin', I said, "just an old-fashioned tail and stakeout, but the pay's good."

I let her pay me for working at the bar, but since I hadn't really solved the mystery of the voice, I didn't feel right being paid for that.

Well... to be specific, I didn't feel right letting Ann pay me for that. For most clients it's a per-hour charge plus expenses.

"I'll miss you," she said, finally giving voice to what I knew she was feeling.

"Likewise," I said. "Every damn moment. But stakeouts are borin'. Call me on your walk home. I'll pick up if I can. We'll chat like we always do."

She nodded but didn't say anything.

My gut twisted up and I almost said that I would turn the case down, but I didn't.

Much of me wanted to, but Ann had become so precious to me that I could not trust myself. Besides, I was behind on the payments for my place and I really needed the money.

THIRTY-ONE

The mystery of the haunting of The Devil You Know was ameliorated but it wasn't solved. And even worse, I had expected another attack on the bar, but it had not come, and it seemed inevitable there would be another attempt to drive Ann out of business.

Leaving Ann was hard, but as I got on the I-10 and headed towards Tucson, this is what stuck with me.

Truth is that my waking hours had been filled with work and my mind had been preoccupied with Ann so I hadn't spent much time thinking about it.

And I really should have been thinking about it more.

In my rented Camry—a blue 1976 El Camino is not a good car for tailing people—as Phoenix thinned out and the Sonoran Desert took over, my mind finally went back to the case.

It appeared to be a haunting where people heard a terrible voice that only they could hear saying, "I am the devil you know and you will die tonight."

Enough people heard it that most of the patrons stopped

coming and one person stepped out in front of a moving car and was killed. When I was brought in by Detective Trisha Sanchez, my client, Ann McGee, was close to losing the place.

(And yes, in my mental review I am trying to distance myself from the Ann I walk home in the early morning hours by using her full name or referring to her as "my client.")

But it was no haunting but an early incarnation of sound beaming technology as aptly demonstrated by Emma Shapiro. I even experienced it and the theory is that drones were used to execute this.

Among all the ways you could drive someone out of business, using cutting edge technology that wasn't even being used commercially yet was a strange one.

It didn't feel right. At all. But nothing about this case felt right, especially my suspect list.

At this point in a case, there should be a long list of them, but I only had two and they were both weak as can be.

The first was Emma Shapiro, my tech person, my friend, and my AA sponsor. I felt guilty for being paranoid enough to even have her on my list but, I was still wary of how quickly she was able to cobble together the sound beaming tech.

She was brilliant and it was in her capacity to do something like that and I had no other reason to suspect her, but there was doubt. Doubt that I really hated. Doubt that was affecting my relationship with her.

We had talked since our impromptu AA meeting in the parking lot of the Lutheran church, but not that much and that felt a little strange.

The second suspect was the owner of the building that housed The Devil You Know, Alan Trent. I had been investigating him here and there but hadn't come up with anything. I was pretty sure he was cheating on his wife and cheated on his taxes, but I could find no motive for him to drive Ann out of business.

That meant that I was missing a piece of the puzzle, a big piece, and that never felt good. But worse than that, I worried it put Ann in harm's way.

This couldn't be over. It just couldn't be.

THIRTY-TWO

"I just want to apologize," Ann said on my cell phone. It was the next day, early afternoon, and I was camped out in the rented Camry in a seedy part of Tucson.

"What for?" I asked.

This case so far had been quite boring. And boring is better than dangerous, but I, frankly, am not wired for boring. I have a lot of experience with stakeouts and find them to be exhausting on so many levels. I was just glad to hear Ann's voice.

"When you told me you were leaving," she said. "I was... well, I acted a bit needy and I feel the need to explain."

The person I was tailing, Mathew Caige, had walked into a strip club about an hour ago. I had gone in early, disguised in a baseball cap and tennis shoes—believe me, that is a disguise for me—and confirmed he was just watching the girls dance.

Caige was a scumbag to be sure, rich and privileged, but nothing exciting had happened at all.

"You noticed," Ann said when I didn't reply right away. "I know you did."

"I did," I said. "But it's not a bother. I rather like it that the person you need is me."

"Me too," she said. "But I want you to understand." She was quiet for a moment and then she sighed. "It's my father. The anniversary of his death is tomorrow. I was hoping to feel a little less alone this year."

I felt a rush of emotion. Embarrassed that I hadn't put it together. Touched that she thought I could somehow help make the day easier for her. Curious that she used the word "death" instead of "murder."

I thought back to Detective Sanchez's words when she was expressing her worry about Ann and my relationship. "I will tell no secrets. She's a strong woman, but we all have our breaking point."

I had suspected it was about her father and this seemed to confirm that.

But I got it. We both lost our fathers traumatically.

Her father was murdered and my father died way too young of cancer.

Cancer is what I tell everyone and, to some degree, it is the truth, but it's a hell of a lot more complicated than that.

My father got cancer young, in his late twenties when I was a boy, lung cancer to be specific. And he kicked it. But when it came back in his forties and when they found it everywhere, he decided not to treat. He had been through the hell of chemo and radiation and wasn't going to do it again.

My mother was already gone by then and I was off working as a rodeo clown, kind of trying to get myself killed in some halfway noble way to atone for the death of my best friend.

There's more to the story, but I'm not ready to tell it yet. Let's just say my father took the quick way out.

I don't blame him, not a bit, but it was a hell of a thing to deal with.

Much to my surprise, I had told Ann all of this. Our bond wasn't just that we both lost our fathers relatively young but that it was quick and traumatic and messy as hell.

"I'm so sorry, Ann," I said. "I should have put that together."

"It's okay," she said. "Really it is. I need to learn how to speak my needs."

"Do you need me to be there tomorrow?" I asked.

"No," she said, but it was a very weak "no." "You've got work, good work, you should do it."

"Tell ya what," I said. "Mr. Borin' here was in bed by midnight last night. If that pattern holds, I can slip away tomorrow night, drive back to Phoenix, and be there to walk ya home."

She was silent for a moment and I was afraid the connection had dropped. I checked my smartphone—it had plenty of juice and the call was still open. And then I heard her sniff. "That would be great, but I don't want you to risk your job."

"No worries, love," I said. "I gotta tracker on his car. Emma hooked me up with it so ya know it's good. I'll know if he goes anywhere."

"Thank you, Conner," she said. "That... that really means a lot."

There in a rented Camry outside a strip club in Tucson, I felt an emotion I hadn't felt very often since the accident. I felt my heart swell with pride. I truly cared for Ann and I knew she cared for me and I had found a way to make a very bad day a little better for her.

If only it had been that simple.

THIRTY-THREE

We all have weaknesses. Ones that can be exploited. This is basic human nature and it is dangerous to think that this rule does not apply to you, that you, of all humans, understand yourself well enough to avoid such things as exploitable weaknesses.

I wasn't delusional. I knew that I had such weaknesses that could be exploited. I also knew that some of my strengths could be exploited and turned against me, another inevitable fact of being human.

Knowing I had weaknesses and knowing they could be exploited was a world away from knowing when such exploitation was happening.

I had had my doubts during this case, all along, but it wasn't just a case anymore, was it? This was now my life. Ann was someone I cared deeply about. And such caring makes you vulnerable.

Mathew Caige had stayed up till almost 1:00 a.m. the next night and I was driving back to Phoenix as fast as I dared.

I was tired and strung out, having survived with too little

sleep and too much coffee for far too long. I was anxious. It seemed very important that I get back to The Devil You Know before Ann finished closing up for the night. And I felt a little flutter in my belly thinking about seeing Ann, that feeling I hadn't experienced much since I was a teenager before my foot slipped off the clutch.

I was approaching the outskirts of Phoenix when my phone rang.

One nice thing about a modern car was all the lovely tech. I could see it was Sanchez and hit the button on the steering wheel to pick it up.

"You got Bright," I said. "What's up, Detective?"

"Where are you?" she asked, the tension in her voice obvious.

"I'm on the I-10 headin' into town," I said. "Almost to the 202."

"Okay," she said, taking a breath. "You are headed to Ann, right?"

"Right," I said. "What's goin' on?"

"I was at the bar earlier," she said. "Ann is not in a great place. But that's not unusual for today. The bar, in particular, is a hard place for her to be. I tried to talk her into taking the day off, but you know how stubborn she can be. I think she would feel like she was betraying her father if she wasn't there on the anniversary of his death."

I didn't reply. Clearly Sanchez had something to say and was winding up to it.

"I got a call and had to leave," she said. "I ended up back at the office and started poking around on her case. There's something not right here."

"I'm with ya there," I said. "Someone goes through great lengths to drive her outta business and then just stops when we figure it out. Makes no sense at all."

"None," she said. "So I started digging again."

"Find anythin'?" I asked, my mouth suddenly dry and my stomach tightening up.

"Not quite," she said. "That guy you talked to outside the bar the second night you worked there. Remember him?"

I nodded, although she couldn't see it. "Yeah. Alan Trent, the owner of the place."

"That's just it," she said. "He's not the owner."

My stomach tightened up some more. "He claimed to be," I said. And I had believed him. He's who I had been looking into. Without really thinking about it, I started going faster, the 202 now behind me as I drove into the southern edge of Phoenix.

"He's not," she said. "He's the manager. A guy named Mathew Caige is the owner. He lives in Tucson."

Cold sweat popped out on my forehead and under my arms, my foot pressing harder on the accelerator. I needed to speak, but I couldn't find any words.

"Bright?" Sanchez asked. "Are you there? Did you hear what I said? A guy named Mathew Caige is the owner of Ann's building."

My hands were white knuckled on the steering wheel. I was now going fast enough that I was changing lanes pretty often despite how light traffic was at that hour.

"I heard ya," I said, my throat tight and my voice rough. "That's who I've been tailin' in Tucson."

My heart was a loud whoosh in my ear and I regretted my last cup of coffee only an hour ago.

"Can ya hear me?" I asked when Sanchez didn't reply, because what I had said was worth a reply, one that contained numerous curse words.

I glanced down at the LCD display in the center of the dash, the one that is basically my smartphone, but it was back to the home screen. I glanced at my phone and it was dark.

"What the hell," I said.

I poked the phone but it seemed to be dead.

How could my phone be dead? It had been plugged into the car and charging.

That nervous sweat prickled along the back of my neck and my arms. Something wasn't right. Something was very, very wrong.

I leaned on the accelerator even more, hoping, praying, there were no cops out and that my phone had just died and nothing terrible was going on at The Devil You Know.

THIRTY-FOUR

My phone was still dead. No matter how many times I poked at it or held a button down, it was very, very dead.

I remember the world before cell phones, where you couldn't call anyone at any time, and I often remember it fondly. You could more readily focus, couldn't always distract yourself, could really think.

In many ways, the world seemed better off before cell phones, especially before "smart" phones, except for one thing. Emergencies. Being able to readily reach people was crucial in emergencies.

I was out in front of The Devil You Know standing in the sodium glow of the streetlights on Mill Avenue knocking on the door.

The place was locked up and quiet as a tomb.

It shouldn't be.

Ann knew I was going to be late. Ann should have been waiting for me.

I looked around the street, my eyes restless and I realized I was looking for a payphone, that long ago feature of cities before cell phones changed everything.

I needed to be able to call Ann, to know that she was all right.

This was a bad day for Ann, the anniversary of her father's death. He was shot in the alley behind The Devil You Know. His murder was never solved.

That nervous sweat prickled up on my forehead and the back of my neck again despite the cool of the night. Something was roiling in my brain, something terrifying.

It wasn't so much a thought as a bad feeling—a knowing that something was very, very wrong. A knowing that I had missed so very, very much. That my weaknesses and my strengths had been used against me. That I had been manipulated this whole time.

I didn't think, I started running, my dead phone in my hand.

My body was in the lead and I was a few steps down the sidewalk, my cowboy boots slapping loudly against the concrete, before I realized I was running around the building, to where Jack McGee was murdered eight years ago.

When I realized where my instincts were taking me, I ran faster.

But I wasn't fast enough.

The person that had been manipulating me made sure of that.

Just as I turned the corner, the sound of a gunshot shattered the quiet night.

THIRTY-FIVE

The maroon color of Ann's dress made it hard to tell she was bleeding at first.

She was lying on the asphalt behind The Devil You Know, her green eyes too wide, her mouth moving but no words coming out, her face pale even in the yellowish glow of the sodium streetlights.

Her horns were still on which were a sharp contrast to her painful repose and her hands clasping her belly, blood staining them. Despite the outfit and the tail on the asphalt, she no longer looked like a she-devil. She looked like someone I loved, someone in need.

There were too many things I needed to do at once. I needed to go to Ann, to let her know I was here, to try to stop the bleeding. I needed to call for help. And I needed to find whoever had shot her and beat them senseless with my fists.

But, I knew who had shot her.

I knew who had been manipulating me.

I knew who had bricked my phone before I could tell Sanchez who I had been sent to Tucson to tail.

The terrible fact of the matter is I had been doubting this person, suspecting them since the beginning of this case, but not trusting my gut.

What I wanted to do most was to go to Ann, but what I needed to do was to defend her, give her a fighting chance to live. Someone had heard that gunshot and had hopefully called the cops.

I could tell which direction Ann fell so I could tell what direction the shooter had been in so I stood in front of her.

"Come on out, Emma," I said. "I know it's you." I turned towards Ann and said, "Put as much pressure on the wound as you can. Help is on the way. You're gonna be okay."

I was lying of course, but it was a hopeful lie. I don't carry a gun. I had a bowie knife on my belt and a can of pepper spray in my back pocket and that was it.

Emma sighed and stepped out from behind a dumpster and pointed a gun at me. "You know, Evan," she said, using the name I was born with. "You are not a very good detective." She nodded past me towards Ann. "At least not when you are distracted by that pretty little thing."

Emma wasn't dressed in her usual pedal pushers and sweater. She was dressed in black, head to toe, but designer black something that wouldn't stand out if you stopped by a bar but would make it hard to see you in a dark alley.

"So what, exactly, do you know?" she asked, giving me a smirking smile. She was about twenty-five feet away, close enough to hit what she was aiming at, too far for me to do anything.

"I know that you are goin' to jail," I said. "Sanchez will be here any minute."

"Maybe," she said with a shrug. "But doubtful. She'll probably chalk up what happened to bad cell reception."

"How long have you been listenin' to my calls?" I asked.

"Since the first time you gave me your phone," she said.

I did my best to try to hide my reaction. That was over four years ago and that meant this manipulation went back much further than I had thought.

I used to face down angry bulls for a living, I know what it is to look into the face of danger, the face of death or serious injury, but this was something different. Those bulls were angry, justifiably so given that we were using them for sport, but this was on a different level.

This was more than premeditated, this had been schemed and planned, worked patiently over time.

"Tell me what you know, Evan," she said. "All of it. Or I put another bullet into your pretty little platonic girlfriend there."

I swallowed and nodded, trying to factor in this new information, trying not to freak out about the scope of this thing, trying to hatch a plan to stop Emma and save Ann.

I didn't just want to save Ann, I *needed* to. My very being depended on it. I knew that if Ann died here tonight, the same way her father had, I knew it would be on me, it would be as much my fault as when I ran over my best friend.

And what I knew beyond a shadow of a doubt was that I wouldn't survive it. Well... maybe for a year or two until I had drunk enough to kill myself, but if Ann died tonight, I was as good as dead too.

I, quite literally, had nothing to lose. I just had to hope that Emma didn't realize that.

And I knew I had to figure out what I had been missing—I had to see the big picture—if either Ann or I were going to survive.

THIRTY-SIX

I met Emma Shapiro just after noon on a scalding hot August day in Sun City about four and a half years ago.

She was tending to her garden, dressed in her much-loved pedal pushers and a bright blue T-shirt from the Phoenix Marathon.

She had called me that morning, told me she had heard good things about my work, and had given me precise instructions on when and where to meet her.

"G'day, Miss Shapiro," I said with a tip of my hat. I was, of course, decked in my full Crocodile Dundee regalia. "How might I help ya?"

This was long before AA and while I wasn't still drunk from the beer I had drunk the night before so I could sleep, I wasn't as sharp as I could have been, a pounding pain developing behind my left eye speaking of the hangover to come.

Emma was still in her mid-sixties then, her hair a bit less grey, her face a bit less lined, her wiry form making me think she earned the marathon shirt she was wearing. She was kneeling on a pad in front of a raised garden bed with a pergola built over it with a mesh covering it that blunted the sun.

"Thank you for coming, Mr. Bright," she said.

She got up quickly, but I could tell it hurt her some, probably her knees. I knew the look because my knees protested when I got up from that position.

We shook hands, and while her hands were small, they were strong. I caught a whiff of expensive perfume underneath the smell of loamy soil.

"Happy to help," I said. "And call me Conner."

The fact was that I was more than happy to help. I needed to help. I needed the money.

Emma was just staring at me, looking me up and down, a quizzical look on her face.

I was used to being looked at, it was part of my "hiding in plain sight" routine, but this made me just a little bit uncomfortable. I, honestly, couldn't tell if the look was sexual or not, but I felt a bit like an object.

When she was done and my cheeks were flushed red, she took a deep breath, crossed her arms, sighed, and said, "You'll do."

"Excuse me?" I said.

She smiled and it really changed her face. The lines deepened, of course, but she looked much younger, and for a moment I felt a flash of familiarity. I couldn't place it, but it felt like I knew her.

"I apologize," she said, "if I made you feel uncomfortable. The little problem I have is a man who is having a hard time hearing the word 'no.' I had heard of you, this rugged Australian PI, but I just had to see you."

"Ma'am?" I asked, still not following.

"Oh," she said with a wave of her hand. "I'm an old lady who is not making sense. My apologies. Reed, the man I need help with, he is a big guy, a bit younger than me. Long ago he played football. But I don't think you'll have any trouble with him."

"Perhaps you should start from the beginnin'," I said, still not clear and feeling a bit dizzy. Perhaps it was from the August heat. Perhaps it was from how this meeting had gone so far.

Whatever it was, two things were clear. I liked Emma. She had an unexpected toughness to her, especially for a Sun City retiree. And I felt a bit off balance from that first moment, from the way she looked at me.

"That's a fine idea, Conner," she said, wiping sweat from her brow. "Please call me Emma because I think we are going to be great friends. Let's go in. I made lemonade."

<h1 style="text-align:center">THIRTY-SEVEN</h1>

Back in the alley behind The Devil You Know, I took a deep breath. I smelled garbage and the darker scent of blood. Even though it's all I wanted to do, I didn't dare turn around and look at Ann and draw Emma's attention to her.

"I'm done waiting," Emma said with a wave of her gun. "Tell me what you know. Now."

"Alrighty," I said, still gathering my thoughts, considering which guesses might be real. "That job, that first one, dealing with that man that wouldn't take no for an answer. That was as much a setup as the job I just had in Tucson."

Emma smiled and it was decidedly predatorial. I know that I describe Detective Sanchez's smile that way, but this was on another level completely and I suddenly felt very cold. Not just because my guess had been right, but because it was clear that Emma wanted me to know exactly how badly she had duped me before I died.

"Good," she said. "So you aren't brain dead. What else?"

My phone was still in my hand, which was sweating way too

much. "Ya did this," I said. "Before Sanchez could hear the truth, ya bricked my phone."

"That I did," she said, and my stomach twisted up like some carnival contortionist. This was much worse than I imagined.

"You were my tech person," I said, still thinking over what had happened to the phone. "You installed spyware on it the first time I let you have my phone."

"Yes and yes," she said with a bored wave of her gun. "But this is all surface stuff. Do you know why, Evan? Why I hired that actor to pretend to be my clingy ex-boyfriend? Why I projected voices into pretty-girl's bar knowing she would tell Sanchez and knowing Sanchez would call you? Do you know why?"

Her voice was loud at the end, too loud for this time of the morning, too loud for Emma in general. There was a feral edge to her voice, an urgency I didn't understand.

It was clear that she didn't want to tell me the why, that she wanted me to figure it out, that it would be that much more devastating if I did.

"I got ideas," I said. "Believe me I do. Happy to share them, but I want somethin' first."

Her brow furrowed and she got this look of surprised disgust on her face like a mother might give their little boy when they saw them playing with a spider.

I took a small step forward and her aim steadied, the gun pointing at the middle of my chest. Emma knew how to shoot, she had talked about how she liked to go to the shooting range and outshoot the boys.

"No," she said. "Keep talking or I start shooting."

"No," I said back, taking another small step forward. We were about twenty feet apart now and she could easily kill me if she wanted to. But I was pretty sure she didn't want that. She wanted me to suffer. She had called me by my given name, Evan. And that meant the "why" she was so desperate for me to understand had to do with Tommy Wilkins, my best friend that I ran over.

She wanted me to suffer and a quick death was not good enough, obviously, considering she had been manipulating me for years.

"I'm not kidding, Conner," she said, slipping and calling me by the name she'd called me by all these years.

I stopped and held my hands halfway up, still holding my dead phone, and said, "All I want from you, Emma, is to understand why now. You're not gettin' away with this, we both know that." I nodded at a security camera behind the back door of The Devil You Know. "Even if you disabled that one, there are three more in this alley. Even if we both die tonight, you won't get away with this."

I took another small step forward. "Why now, Emma? Why are you in such a rush?"

She let out a weak snort and shook her head. It was hard to tell in the light of the streetlamps but it looked like she might be tearing up a little. "You missed all those signs too, Evan," she said. "The little white bags from the pharmacy, how pale I've been lately." She shook her head some more, the gun coming down just a little bit. "I'm dying, of course," she said. "It doesn't matter if I get caught. I have nothing to—"

Her words entered my brain but I wasn't processing them, not really, not yet. I was watching her like I used to watch mad bulls when I was a rodeo clown, waiting for my moment.

When it came, I threw my dead phone at her. It was the only weapon I had ready, but my aim was true and it hit her in the head, cutting off her little speech.

But Emma wasn't a dummy. She fired the gun and I felt a searing pain in my left leg, but I didn't care. I rushed forward and plowed into her, driving her back into the dumpster with a loud clang.

Part of me couldn't believe I was doing it, smashing into a woman in her seventies, into my long-time friend and collaborator, into my AA sponsor.

But the person I plowed into wasn't that Emma anymore. That Emma had been an illusion, one that I hadn't seen through in four and a half years.

Emma cried out in pain, the gun clattering to the asphalt. She was slumped against the dumpster and I was still upright, the pain in my leg throbbing with every heartbeat.

I didn't dare look at it yet. It hurt like hell but I could still stand so I grabbed the gun and pointed it at Emma.

"Phone," I said. "Give me your phone, now."

"No," she said with a high-pitched giggling laugh that chilled my blood. Not only was Emma not the person I thought she was, she was not mentally well.

I guess we all have our own personal levels of mental unwellness, but let's just say that she was far more gone than I had thought.

"I'm not kiddin', Emma," I said through gritted teeth. "Give me your goddamn phone."

"No," she said with another high-pitched giggle.

I tossed the gun down behind me and went over to Emma.

"What do you know, Evan?" she said, her voice a breathy whisper as I leaned close. She was sitting on the asphalt at this point and there didn't seem to be much energy in her.

I was patting her pockets, looking for her phone. "Who were ya to Tommy Wilkins?" I asked. "Not his mother, not one of his aunts, I know all of 'em."

It was the only thing it could be. Emma had been playing a long game, a very long game, to exact revenge on me for the death of Tommy. Part of me didn't blame her. I could not atone for what I had done, but Ann didn't deserve this.

"We met, you know," she said. "You were a kid, maybe six. I was married to my second husband then and I went by my middle name. Does Janis Thompson ring any bells?"

I had found her phone stashed in a back pocket. I activated it but it was demanding a code. She hadn't even set up the fingerprint recognition.

"What's the code?" I asked.

"Do you remember Janis Thompson?" she asked.

"What's the goddamn code, Emma?" I asked.

"You're bleeding," she said, chuckling.

I was starting to feel weak and took a moment to look at my leg. Emma had shot me in the thigh and it was bleeding freely. She might have gotten an artery and I didn't know how much time I had.

I sat back, pulled off my belt, and cinched it around my thigh above the wound. I needed to slow the bleeding and buy more time.

"The code," I growled.

I felt like I was missing something, something important.

"Do you remember me?" she asked. "Tell me who I was and I'll tell you the code."

I did remember Janis Thompson. She had longer hair back then, very dark, but those intense blue eyes are what stuck in my brain.

"You were Tommy's godmother," I said.

"Bingo!" she said.

"What's the code?" I asked.

She just laughed in answer.

I was tired. I was losing blood. I was overwhelmed by the illusion that had just been shattered. But I knew I was missing something, something important.

I finally let myself glance back at Ann and saw that she was unconscious. Shit.

I tried to unlock the phone, putting in random codes when I saw it. The "Emergency" button. How could I be so stupid? How could I miss something so obvious for so long?

I stabbed the button. It took a few seconds but the 911 operator picked up.

"There's been a shootin'," I said.

THIRTY-EIGHT

"She wants to talk to you," Detective Trisha Sanchez said to me, her jaw clenched, her face grim.

The hospital waiting room I had been in for the last few hours was all bland colors and bland furniture, filled with nervous people like me praying for good news but bracing for bad.

I swallowed hard and nodded.

It was late afternoon and I had spent most of the day in the hospital. First getting my leg patched up. The bullet went clean through and had just missed the femoral artery so I got lucky there. They had wanted to admit me for the night but I had refused, so they sewed me up, bandaged me, and gave me some pain meds—which I refused to take—and some crutches.

To say I was tired was ridiculously underplaying it. What I needed was to sleep for a week or two, but it wasn't time yet.

I struggled up, got the crutches underneath me, and followed Sanchez down the hospital hallway.

"Any word on Ann?" I asked.

"She's still in surgery," Sanchez said. "I take no news as good news at this point."

The antiseptic smell of the hospital was stuck in my nose and I was afraid it would never get out, but I guess it was better than the blood I couldn't help but smell behind The Devil You Know.

Sanchez stopped and looked at me. "You don't have to do this," she said.

"She agreed to the terms?" I asked.

Sanchez nodded. "Camera's already set up. She has agreed to confess, with details, but only to you, and only if you are alone."

I hadn't counted on many people in the last few years, much of the time I couldn't even count on myself, but I had counted on Emma Shapiro, and the betrayal I felt was so fundamental I had to wonder how I could ever trust anyone else like that again.

"You don't have to do this," Sanchez said again.

"Kind of ya, Detective," I said. "But I do."

Sanchez nodded and led me deeper into the hospital to where Emma Shapiro was.

———

SEEING EMMA SHAPIRO'S THIN FORM IN A HOSPITAL BED snugged under some white sheets made it clear that she was sick. She was thinner than usual, her color off, her eyes not quite as bright as they used to be.

Her right arm was in a sling. That was my doing. I had broken her arm when I rammed her into the dumpster. Her other arm was handcuffed to the rail of the bed.

After checking the camera, Sanchez had closed the door and left us alone.

The room was dominated by the hospital bed. There was a

TV hanging on the wall opposite it, an IV on one side, and the usual heart monitor on the other. There was a single upholstered beige chair and a window overlooking the parking lot.

"Sit down before you fall down, Evan," Emma said. She wasn't doing the terrifying cackling she had been doing behind the bar, but I could still hear the undertones of it.

"My name is Conner," I said, and as I did I felt something shift in me. I wasn't just saying that, I believed it, and more than that, I felt it. There was more there, things that needed reflection, but the realization itself was rather surprising. "Either you call me Conner or I'm leavin'."

Emma pursed her lips and nodded. "Very well, Conner. Please sit. I'm not exactly in good enough shape to help you if you fall down."

I made my way over to the chair. I wasn't very fast or graceful in the crutches, but there was just enough room. I sat and leaned the crutches against the wall.

"Why am I here, Emma?" I said. "What ya did is clear. You inserted yourself into my life four and a half years ago so you could make sure I was properly punished for killin' your godson."

Emma gave me a patronizing smile and shook her head. "Oh, Conner," she said. "There is so much more to it than that, and I want to make sure you understand everything I did."

"Why?" I asked. "What's it matter now?"

She smiled and it was the kind of predatorial smile that Detective Sanchez only aspired to. It was cruel and heartless. It was calculating and a bit gleeful. "Why, I want you to spend the rest of your miserable life at the bottom of a bottle, of course. Why else?"

I almost left. Sanchez didn't really need any more confessions from Emma. She didn't have long to live and she was going to be in custody for the rest of her days as it was. But I didn't leave, I really couldn't.

I've thought long and hard about why I didn't and the only answer I can come up with is that in some ways I agreed with her. I cannot atone for the death of Tommy Wilkins and part of me believes I deserve, as she put it, "to spend the rest of my miserable life at the bottom of a bottle."

Part of me thought the betrayal I felt couldn't get any deeper, but I was wrong.

"Alrighty," I said. "Lay it on me Emma. Exactly how long have ya been messin' with my life?"

Emma smiled and a cold chill ran down my spine.

THIRTY-NINE

It took an hour, and in that time Emma Shapiro laid out in startling detail how she had monitored and interfered with my life.

I won't document it all here, suffice it to say the breadth of it was vast and it started the moment I got out of juvie and my records were sealed. There wasn't a moment in my adult life when Emma Shapiro hadn't been at least monitoring me and many, many incidents where she injected chaos and difficulty in my life.

It was terrifying, but I had to admire her thoroughness and commitment to the effort. It finally made sense why her home in Sun City was just a nice home and did not properly reflect the millions she had made as a tech CTO. Most of that money had been spent trying to make sure I spent my life "at the bottom of a bottle."

"It was all going so well," she said with that bone chilling smile of hers. "That is until you met adorable Irene Campos on the purple unicorn case and you suddenly had a reason to stay sober. We had already met, I had already inserted myself in your life, and you were too unobservant to figure it out, so fortunately I had options."

At the mention of Irene I felt my blood pressure rise and I sat up straight in the chair.

Emma gave me a weak wave. "Calm down, big boy," she said. "The girl is fine. I wouldn't think of doing a thing to her."

"You'll forgive, Emma," I said. "But I find that hard to believe."

She shrugged weakly, her face clenching in pain from the movement and said, "What I will say is that I could have easily sent you back into the bottle by harming the girl and I clearly did not. Believe it, don't believe it. Frankly, I don't care."

"Were you involved in the Chupacabra case?" I asked. Irene had been threatened in that case.

"Only as a spectator," she said. "I was rooting for you Conner, glad you survived."

"Wait," I said. "Ya wanted me to survive?"

"Of course," she said with that damn unnerving smile. "A noble death is not what I have planned for you."

Not what I have planned for you.

Those words broke through my fatigue and my pain better than a pot of coffee and some good pain killers.

I think Emma realized she had slipped because she got silent after talking almost nonstop for an hour. But this being my betrayer, that could have been done intentionally to get under my skin, to make me paranoid.

I let the silence stretch out as I thought about it. Emma Shapiro had spent the last several decades focused on me, focused on making sure I was properly punished. She was brilliant and resourceful, she had had some warning of her death with the cancer coming back.

I needed to confront her on this, but I needed more time.

"So it's because of Irene that you targeted Ann and The Devil You know," I said.

"Yes," she said. "With my time limited, I needed to see you drunk again before I died."

"And how was this supposed to send me back into the bottle?" I asked.

"That's easy," she said. "She was supposed to die, after you had fallen for her, of course. She still might."

I felt my face flush hot and it was all I could do to not clench my fists.

"Bullshit," I said. "I'll grant ya that my falling for Ann was pretty obvious, but the other way around." I shook my head. "Not so much."

Emma gave me an eye roll fitting of a teenager. "Very well. Let's just say that the situation was fraught enough that there were multiple opportunities for you to slip up. The one that is playing out now, just one of many."

"Enough," I said. I wanted to storm out but with my leg that was quite impossible so an awkward exit on unfamiliar crutches was all I could manage.

FORTY

"You want to talk about it?" Sanchez asked, sitting down next to me in the waiting room. It had been long enough since I left Emma and Sanchez had had enough time to review the footage so I assumed she had and knew just how bad it was.

I was slumped over in the worn padded chair, staring at my alligator skin cowboy boots.

"She had hired people to get me drunk when I was on the rodeo circuit," I said, my voice just above a whisper.

"I know, Conner," she said, and that told me just how bad it was. She almost never uses my first name unless the news was terrible or I had just almost died.

"She told Fred Arlington where to find me and funded that mess at Metro Center last Christmas Eve," I said.

"If you were anyone else," she said, "I'd be offering you a stiff drink right now."

I looked at her and her face was grim, her lips pursed.

"Ya know what I told her?" I asked, which was a silly question, because she had watched the tape and knew exactly what I told her.

"What?" she asked.

"I told her I deserved everything she did to me," I said. "And none of it could balance the scales because nothing could bring my friend and her godson back."

Sanchez took a deep breath and said, "Listen to me, Conner, because I am only going to say this once. You're wrong. What happened when you were only a kid was a tragedy, a terrible mistake. It broke her and it broke you.

"But there's a big difference between the two of you. You are trying, Conner. You are trying to help people, every day. Trying to atone for something you didn't mean to do. You did not mean to harm Tommy.

"Her, though? She broke and hasn't fought her way up from the darkness. She justifies hurting other people to exact her revenge against you.

"You do not deserve what she's done to you."

I took a deep breath and nodded. "Kind of ya, but..."

I trailed off because I realized I had been obsessed with myself and Sanchez may have come in for another reason. "Ann?" I asked. "Is she...?"

Sanchez smiled. It was a small, tentative smile, but genuine. "She's out of surgery and in recovery. Things went well but she's still in critical condition. The next twenty-four hours are crucial."

I smiled back and rubbed away the tears trying to escape my eyes.

"There's one more thing, Conner," Sanchez said.

"What?" I asked, worry smothering the brief moment of hope.

"It's not about Ann," she said. "It's Emma. She says she has more to confess."

"I'm not interested," I said.

"She says it involves a murder and will clear up a cold case," she said.

Sanchez wasn't directly asking me to subject myself to more time with my torturer, but it was clear this was important to her, so she was indirectly asking.

I was exhausted, in a lot of pain, and wrung out, my life suddenly not what I thought it was. How did I have the fortitude to subject myself to more abuse from Emma designed to "send me to the bottom of a bottle"?

What I needed was sleep, but that was impossible with Ann's life still hanging in the balance.

"One condition," I said with a nod.

"Anything," she said.

"You wait right outside the door and listen in," I said.

Her brow furrowed. "Why?"

I shrugged. "Just afraid of what I might do to her."

Sanchez blinked and stared at me, her brown eyes intense. Maybe she was trying to figure out if I was joking or serious, if I was capable of really doing something, but she didn't hesitate long. "Done," she said.

FORTY-ONE

"You should really sit, Conner," Emma said from her hospital bed. "You are pale, I think you might pass out."

I was awkwardly balanced on my crutches in front of her hospital bed, only able to put weight on one leg, and Emma was probably right. I was a bit lightheaded, but I wasn't going to give her the satisfaction.

I gave her a smile that I am sure was twisted. "Well, that'd be better than this. Say what you need to say. I got better things to do."

"Very well," she said. "I'll rip the band-aid off then." She took a deep breath and swallowed. "I murdered Jack McGee."

She stared at me and I'm sure she was looking for some kind of reaction but I was having trouble processing it.

Emma Shapiro had murdered Ann's father, former Sun Devil football star Jack McGee and the man who started The Devil You Know bar.

That put this thing with Ann on a whole different level. It hinted that involving me with Ann had been a "two birds, one stone" kind of thing for her. It also expanded the scope of

Emma's wrongdoing, and even though her revelation was horrifying, it was a tiny relief knowing I wasn't the only person she had been obsessed with.

"Aren't you going to say something?" she asked.

"Let me guess," I said. "You and Jack McGee had an affair. You were attracted to the charismatic former football star. He made promises to ya. Told ya you were the one and that he would leave Ann's mother. Maybe he meant it, maybe he didn't, but being the psycho that you are, at some point ya broke. You confronted him in the alley behind the bar. When you didn't get the answers you wanted, you shot him and left him to die."

Emma blinked, taking deep breaths through her nose so they flared like some angry bull. "It... it was more complicated than that," she said, almost spitting the words out.

"Oh, I betcha," I said. "Your jealousy is so special, so different than everyone else's. And this means this latest scheme of yours wasn't just to send me to the bottom of a bottle. You always planned for Ann to die in the end to punish me and to punish her mother."

"It's. More. Complicated. Than. That," she spit out between gritted teeth.

"Sorry, mate, but I don't think so," I said, moving to leave the room.

"Ask about it," she said, her voice low and fierce, almost a growl. "I know you caught my slip earlier. Ask about it."

I had. Earlier she had said, "A noble death is not what I have planned for you," which caught my attention since Emma was dying, presumably much sooner than I was, and that statement implied that she had plans for me that extended beyond her existence on this planet.

But I didn't need to ask her about it. I had Emma's number now. I knew she had plans made and her money poised and ready to mess with my life long after she's dead, in creative ways

I couldn't possibly see coming. In ways that would cause me to "spend the rest of my miserable life at the bottom of a bottle."

She wanted to see me squirm. She wanted to gloat. I wasn't going to give her the satisfaction. I didn't curse her or say anything, I didn't even look at her again. I just left.

Her curses followed me out of the hospital room, but I didn't care. I was done with Emma Shapiro.

FORTY-TWO

Later—I can't tell you how much later, I was so strung out and exhausted that I had no real sense of time—I was in Ann's hospital room sitting next to her and holding her hand.

Ann looked very pale and nothing at all like the she-devil she looked like when I met her. She looked somehow small in the bed, smaller than Emma even though she was bigger. The bed seemed to swallow her up. And the intubation tube and the hissing machine beside the bed that was helping her breathe looked like some ancient torture device.

"You should sleep," Sanchez said. She had just brought me in and helped me get into the chair. "She probably won't wake up for hours."

"She's gonna be all right?" I asked.

She had already told me, I had already heard it, but I needed to hear it again.

"The doctors are optimistic," Sanchez said. "But she will be closely monitored for the next few days."

"And her mother is all right?" I asked. It was probable that Emma had something planned for Ann's mother before she died.

"She's in Spain," Sanchez said. "She's been living there for a few years, but, yes, she's fine and arranging to get back here."

I nodded but didn't say anything. It was hard seeing Ann this way, but it wasn't as hard as seeing her in her horns and red dress behind the bar bleeding.

"We have more to talk about, but not right now," Sanchez said, putting a warm hand on my shoulder. "Just let yourself rest. I got this."

I knew she meant a lot by "I got this." There were other law enforcement agencies to talk to. Emma needed more questioning. And her conspiracy against Ann and me needed to be unraveled, but that would take time.

"Thanks, Sanchez," I said as she walked out. "Much appreciated."

She paused and looked at me. She was a bit haggard, dark hair escaping her normally perfect ponytail and framing her tired face. Her navy-blue pantsuit was rumpled and she wasn't standing ramrod straight like she usually did.

She smiled and it wasn't sharklike or predatorial at all. "Any time, Bright. Any time."

FORTY-THREE

Let me cut to the chase since some of what happened in the hospital doesn't really fit with my image as a big, tough, former rodeo clown turned private investigator and bouncer who hails from Scatterwood, Australia deep in the Outback.

Suffice it to say that Ann woke up, that it was all rather emotional for me, and that while she was in the hospital for a while, she recovered, and I was there.

I was with her when she woke up panicked because of the intubation tube. I was with her when they transferred her out of the ICU into a regular room. I was with her when she was able to speak and started asking questions.

And I answered them all. Honestly. I didn't hold back, and I ended up telling her about Evan, the person I used to be.

The sad thing about all of this is that Emma's aim was true. If Ann had died it would have broken me again in a way that nearly ensured that I would have gone back to drinking in a big way.

So the first thing I did after leaving Ann at the hospital—her mother was there by then and she insisted—and getting some sleep, was to go to an AA meeting.

As I mentioned before, when I had been going to AA meetings, jumping around town so I truly felt anonymous, I would use my given name of Evan.

But something had changed since I met Ann at the door to The Devil You Know looking like a she-devil and she offered me a drink.

This was what I liked to call a "podium" meeting, where you didn't just speak from your chair but you had to walk up to a podium so everyone could get a good look at you.

This meeting was held in the "everything room" of a small church, so the walls were covered with cartoony Sunday School art work and there were bins full of toys. There were lots of windows and the sun was streaming in over the assembled alcoholics, about twenty of us.

I clumped up to the podium on my crutches. The doctors told me I was going to need them for a while and then some rehab afterward.

While I had left the bowie knife in the El Camino, I was dressed in my full Crocodile Dundee regalia, another thing I hadn't done for one of these meetings before.

"Alrighty, then," I said as I got behind the podium. The faces looking back at me were all sizes and shapes but all their eyes were on me and for once I didn't think it was mostly about the outfit. No, it was because my presence here was a declaration that I was one of them, that I belonged.

"My name is Conner," I said. "And I'm an alcoholic."

"Hello, Conner," they all intoned.

I felt this wave of emotion hit me, hard. I had been through a lot in the last month and to feel unconditional support from a group of strangers was amazing.

"I just been through somethin'," I said, swallowing hard.

"Someone close to me, someone I trusted, had been betrayin' me for years. Workin' against me. Trying to drive me back to drinkin'."

I took a deep breath and sighed. I felt the support, it was the only reason I could speak at all, but this was hard.

"I won't bore ya with the gory details—and they are gory, I assure ya," I said, nodding at my wounded leg. "And I can't say that the person that did this didn't have good reason to cause me pain—I've done some terrible things while drinkin'—but after it was over I decided somethin'. I decided that I was gonna stay sober for the rest of my life just to spite this person.

"I decided to dedicate my sobriety to provin' 'em wrong."

I shook my head slowly and I could see some wide eyes in the audience and a few people shaking their heads too.

"Before that," I said. "I met an orphaned girl that needed me and I stayed sober for her. And recently I met an amazin' woman that gives me a really good reason to stay sober, so I started doin' it for her too.

"Those second and third reasons are a hell of a lot better than the first, but what I have finally come to really understand is that there is only one person I can stay sober for. Me."

There was nodding in the audience. This was a core principle of AA; your motivation has to be internal, but I finally understood it at a visceral level.

I said more, but what was important was that I said it as Conner Bright. When I was talking to Emma in the hospital and insisted that she call me Conner instead of Evan, it wasn't because Conner was my legal name now, it was because I am Conner Bright now.

I created the persona to escape my past but now it has become my future. It is no longer a tool to hide who I am, armor if you will, it is who I am.

I am Conner Bright. A private investigator, a bouncer, and

sometimes handyman. I am an alcoholic working every day to stay sober. I am a flawed human being who has made terrible mistakes trying to do just a little bit of good every day.

My name used to be Evan and I am still the same person that accidentally ran over their best friend Tommy Wilkins and killed him. I don't expect the nightmares to go away or the lingering guilt. I do expect to keep trying to help other people even if it costs me a lot.

Because that is who I am.

I am Conner Bright.

EPILOGUE

Two Weeks Later

"I'm asking too much of you," Ann said.

We were sitting on the couch in her apartment where we had met less than two months ago, but it felt like so much longer.

Ann was diminished from her ten days in the hospital, she had lost weight and even her freckles looked rather pale, but her green eyes were bright and fierce.

Her mother was rattling around in her bedroom giving us a few minutes of privacy.

"Not at all," I said, gently squeezing her hand. "Happy to do it."

She shook her head slowly back and forth as if she did it fast she might get dizzy. She was still very weak. "But you are an alcoholic. It's not reasonable to ask you to run a bar."

I shrugged. "I've been workin' in bars for years. It ain't no big thing."

"But you'll be behind the bar," she said. "You'll be dealing with alcohol for hours at a time."

We had had this discussion. Several times. Ann's mother was going to take her back to Spain to recover while Sanchez and I worked on unraveling whatever Emma Shapiro had arranged for us. None of us wanted to see The Devil You Know close permanently, so we had come up with this plan.

I would manage and work at the bar while Sanchez would handle the finances and the ordering and we would keep the employees Ann had.

It was better this way. I would miss Ann, like hell, but I'd rather know that she was far far away and safe than worry about her every day. It was clear that while Emma wanted me to have a long and miserable life, she'd be happy with Ann being dead in service of that.

And there was a lot for Sanchez and me to do. Sanchez was working the case through Maricopa County Major Crimes and we had a lawsuit started against Emma—that hour of her detailing how she had manipulated my life over the years gave us plenty of material. But even so, it was not going to be easy to unravel and it wouldn't be quick or safe.

"And if it gets to be too much," I said, getting lost in those green eyes of hers, "if I don't think I can handle it, I'll close the bar and walk away. Besides, I won't be there every night. Juniper will handle it three nights a week. We got this, Ann."

I didn't mention Ann's father, Jack McGee, and how this was his legacy, how the place was decorated with memorabilia from his time as an ASU Sun Devil. Learning that Emma had murdered him had brought that grief back to the forefront for Ann. There were more reasons than getting away from Emma for Ann to leave for a while.

"I am asking too much of you," she said, the discussion coming back to the beginning again.

"Listen to me," I said, scooting closer to her. "It means a lot to me that ya trust me with the bar. It means even more to me that you will be a long way away from here. I won't lie, it's gonna be hard, both being at the bar and being away from you, but I'm happy to do it for you, Ann. I want to do it. And it's not too much. Not for you."

I was close enough that I could smell her soapy scent. She was diminished and pale, still healing from her wound, but to me she was the most beautiful woman I had ever seen. Even knowing that a crazy woman had brought us together to harm me couldn't blunt the attraction.

Ann felt it too. I know she did. Her eyes kept flicking from my eyes to my lips and back.

"I need to kiss you," she said, her voice low and husky.

I swallowed hard. "I haven't been sober a year yet," I said.

"Jesus, Conner," she said. "We are clearly in a relationship. I'm leaving the country in the morning and my mother is in the next room. This can't go any further than that right now, even if I was well enough. Can you please just kiss me?"

We spent a lot of time talking in the hospital, and at this point Ann knew everything. She knew about my past when I used to be Evan and ran over my best friend. She knew about my struggles with alcohol. She knew how Conner Bright had been my way to escape, my armor, until it became who I am. And she knew how Emma's dark obsession with me had caused us to be where we were.

And she was still here and she still wanted to be with me.

I leaned in, closing the distance between us, and smelled coffee on her breath. "Are you sure?" I whispered.

In answer, she put her hand on the back of my head and pulled me the rest of the way to her lips and we kissed.

And it was amazing.

I won't describe the kiss, not in any tangible ways, that feels too personal, but I will say that I felt something deep in me stir. All the madness of the last few weeks, the close calls we had both had, the revelation of Emma's betrayal and reframing of my adult life, all of that energy seemed to feed into this kiss.

I didn't realize it right then what I was feeling, the moment was too powerful for that, but later I did.

That feeling was love. Deep love.

And when I did figure out what it was, I realized I would do almost anything to protect that love.

When we parted—I couldn't tell you how long the kiss was, but it felt like a long time—Ann leaned back, a big smile on her face.

"Better?" I asked, the same silly grin on my face.

"Much better," she said. "I just had to be sure."

"Sure of what?" I asked, a look of feigned indignation on my face.

"Sure that this is something," she said.

"And is it?" I asked

In answer she kissed me again.

***

One Month Later

"Welcome to The Devil You Know," I said from behind the polished wooden bar with alcohol all around me, an alcoholic amidst a sea of booze. "What can I getcha?"

I was not dressed in any kind of devil outfit, just my usual bush hat, leather vest, and crocodile claw around my neck. It was early evening on a Tuesday and things were slow. I had been polishing some glasses and hadn't really looked at the woman with dark hair that had approached the bar.

When I looked up, I said, "Well if it ain't the future Pulitzer Prize winner, Amber Black. What can I getcha, love?"

Amber still looked young enough to need to be carded and was dressed head-to-toe in black, jeans this time and a black sweater with heavy eyeliner and purple lipstick so dark it was almost black.

"A quote," she said, pointing her phone at me which I had to guess was on record. "What happened here on the night of March the twentieth when police scanners said there was a shooting behind this establishment? Where is Ann McGee, the owner of this bar? What happened to Emma Shapiro and why is her sound beaming gear not here anymore? And why are you the bartender now and not the bouncer?"

"Oh," I said with a smile. "I'm still the bouncer." I was done with the crutches but I still had a bit of a limp but something like that wasn't going to stop me from rousting someone who got too rowdy.

I really liked Amber, the young lady had what my father would have called "spunk" and I was, honestly, glad to see her, but this wasn't a tale I could tell.

"Well?" she asked

"Sorry, mate," I said. "On advice of law enforcement and my lawyer, I cannot comment. But I can getcha a drink. First one's on the house, what will ya have?"

Amber sighed, pulled up a bar stool, and put her phone down, but I noticed she didn't stop it from recording. Clever girl, she definitely had potential.

"Beer," she said. "Dark."

"Of course," I said, going over to the tap and decanting a pint of Guinness and putting it in front of her.

I was used to working in bars, smelling alcohol all night long, but I have to admit it was more intense behind the bar.

"Seriously," she said. "What happened to Emma? We had an interview scheduled and she didn't show. She's not answering her phone or texts."

"Turn your phone off," I said, nodding at it.

"What?" she asked.

I smiled. "It's still recordin' there, Amber. Let me see you turn it off and I'll tell ya what I can, off the record."

She sighed, and I watched as she turned it off, but I was pretty convinced she had another recording device on her. She had an admirable level of ambition.

"So," she said after taking a sip of beer, a small mustache of foam lingering on her upper lip. "Where is Emma?"

"Emma is not well," I said, which was the truth on multiple levels. "I don't think you'll be gettin' an interview."

"And Ann?" she asked.

"Out of the country visitin' her mother," I said, which was also true.

Amber shook her head and sighed. "You're not going to give me anything are you?"

"Not a thing, love," I said. "You are the kind of enterprising young lady that I expect has another recordin' device on her."

"Two," she said with a smile that seemed to be one of approval. "I warn you, I'm not giving up."

"I would expect nothin' less," I said.

Another customer came up to the bar and I left the journalism student alone, wondering if she might be a useful ally in the future.

Long after Amber Black left and even after the bar was closed and I was back in my single-wide unable to sleep, I wondered about the future.

Would Sanchez and I be able to unravel Emma's plans against me enough to make it safe for Ann to come back? Would our relationship be able to survive if we got the chance to pursue it? And, most importantly, would I be able to stay sober long enough to give any of this a chance?

While I had embraced my adopted identity, that didn't erase my past and that terrible, terrible mistake I made, something I would live with every day for the rest of my life, something I could never truly atone for but would never stop trying.

But something had changed with this case, something that gave me hope, and that is Ann McGee. God knows she could do better than me, but nevertheless she had chosen me even though she knew exactly who I was and what I had done.

My father liked to say that the love of another is what we all need to be our best, that we all do better walking the rocky road of life hand-in-hand with a partner. And he knew, he and my mother had been the real deal, but she had died way too young so he had experienced it both ways.

I knew that I needed to stay sober for myself, but knowing that a woman as spectacular as Ann McGee cared for me sure helped.

Maybe the thing that has truly changed is that it wasn't just worry that was keeping me awake, or guilt, but wondering what the future held and being eager to actually find out.

I am Conner Bright, and I think, I hope, this is just the beginning of my story.

If you want more Conner Bright, your best bet is to sign up for my newsletter at RobertJMcCarter.com/newsletter. You'll get some free ebooks and you'll find out when the next case is available. Or go to RobertJMcCarter.com/ConnerBright for a complete list of books.

If you want more mystery, I've got a two other series you might want to check out:

Carterville

Carterville, AZ

Population: 286. People with powers: 198

Just a sleepy former mining town turned tourist haven in the mountains of Northern Arizona until the "incident." The meteor that gave everyone in the town powers, but only while near Carterville.

There are two books out in the series with another novel

coming in 2021. Find out more at CartervilleAZ.com.

Walter Anchor, Ghost Detective

Walter Anchor: He's a ghost trying to solve his own murder. A ghost with plenty of unfinished business.

Emily: She died at the age of four and still looks it but she's been dead for eighty years. She has a nose for murder.

Together: They solve murders.

There are six cases so far. Be sure to check out the omnibus edition, *Unfinished Business*, which has all six cases in one volume. Find out more at RobertJMcCarter.com/WalterAnchor.

AFTERWORD

Conner Bright is a really fun character to write (and I sure hope to read). In many ways he's my "classic" private investigator. He's a loner, has a troubled past, and is an alcoholic. Pretty standard for a character like him, but what sets him apart is the whole "hiding in plain sight by pretending to be from Australia" thing.

You might be wondering how such a character comes about. Well, I had just taken a class on creating characters with Dean Wesley Smith and was invited to write for an anthology featuring stories about purple unicorns.

One thing I have learned about landing stories in anthologies is it's usually best to come at them sidewise. I knew that a purple unicorn anthology would be full of fantasy stories, so I was determined to write a contemporary story where a purple unicorn actually made sense.

Combine the anthology call with the class on creating characters and out popped Conner Bright!

There's one more ingredient in this creative stew. In 2014 when I wrote the first story, my wife and I were really enjoying the TV series *Castle*. That show occasionally had a story that veered into paranormal territory but never was enough to move the show out of the real world. There would be something that looked paranormal but either wasn't or could go either way. Being playful with these kinds of things fed into these stories.

I don't know about you, but I'm sure glad Conner Bright is around. I've really enjoyed writing these stories.

This collection of four stories, despite each being stand-alone, really does have a larger story arc and that is the story of Conner's journey to sobriety while battling his demons. Honestly, this arc wasn't planned, at all. When I started *The Devil You Know* I had no idea I was heading for a nice conclusion for Conner, but here we are.

If you want more Conner, be sure to sign up for my newsletter at RobertJMcCarter.com/newsletter. I have a story that predates all of these and shows a rougher Conner that will appear in a holiday story collection scheduled for late 2025. I've also got a couple of other unfinished Conner Bright stories I'd love to get back to one of these days.

If you love Conner, do let me know. Write a review, tell a friend, or reach out to me directly at RobertJMcCarter.com/contact.

ACKNOWLEDGMENTS

Big thanks to Dean Wesley Smith for the great class that was germane to the creation of this character. And, also, a big thank you to Kevin J. Anderson and Lisa Magnum for the purple unicorn story prompt and for publishing the first story in *One Horn to Rule Them All: A Purple Unicorn Anthology*. That book was published in 2014 and being a part of it along with some great writers like Peter S. Beagle and Todd McCaffrey was a real boost to my confidence.

As always, a big shout-out to my ever supportive wife and first listener, Aleia. I can't do this with you!

Thanks to the team that helps find my mistakes, my beta readers Roni Hornstein, Peter Klein, and Eliot Schipper, and my amazing proofreader Diana Cox.

And an extra big thanks to you for reading!

ABOUT THE AUTHOR

Robert J. McCarter is the author of more than fifteen novels and over one hundred and fifty short stories. He is a regular contributor to *Pulphouse Fiction Magazine* and his short fiction has also appeared in *The Saturday Evening Post, Andromeda Spaceways Inflight Magazine, Everyday Fiction,* and numerous anthologies.

Robert writes in a variety of genres from contemporary fantasy to science fiction and just about everything in between. His diverse background–including a career in software engineering, growing up on a ranch riding horses, and acting–colors the stories he tells.

He lives in the mountains of Arizona with his amazing wife and his ridiculously adorable dogs.

Find out more at:
RobertJMcCarter.com

BOOKS BY ROBERT J. MCCARTER

Conner Bright Mysteries

- **The Case of the Purple Unicorn**
- **Chupacabra**
- **Haunted by the Past**
- **The Devil You Know**
- **I Am Conner Bright (a collection of all four Conner Bright Mysteries)**

For a complete list go to RobertJMcCarter.com/ConnerBright

Carterville Mysteries

- **Out of a Christmas Sky**
- **Destroyer of Carterville**
- **The Blood of Carterville**
- **Faces of Carterville**
- **Return to Carterville**

For a complete list go to CartervilleAZ.com

Walter Anchor, Ghost Detective Stories

- **Case 1: Detecting Haley**
- **Case 2: The Ghost Bride's Gift**
- **Case 3: A Long Hard Fall**
- **Case 4: Death of a Dentist**
- **Case 5: A Hollywood Kind of a Murder**
- **Case 6: The Red Arrow Murders**

- **Unfinished Business: The Cases of Walter Anchor Ghost Detective**

For a complete list of Walter Anchor stories, go to RobertJMcCarter.com/WalterAnchor

Short Stores Collections

- Life After: Stories of Life, Death, and the Places in Between
- Anomalous Readings: Thirteen Curious and Confounding Tales
- Creatures Featured: Thirteen Stories of Monsters and Other Creatures
- Contemporary Musings: Sixteen Contemporary Stories from a Sci-Fi Writer
- Gg

Novels in the "Ghost's Memoir" world:

Find out more at ShuffledOff.com

The Woody and June versus the Apocalypse Series

Find out more at WoodyAndJune.com

The Neutrinoman and Lightningirl Series

Find out more at Neutrinoman.com

Other Novels:

- Seeing Forever

- Where the Past Belongs: An Angelica and Ash Time
Travel Adventure

For a more information, go to RobertJMcCarter.com